Fae Guardian

Book Two: Soulstealer Trilogy

NICOLETTE REED

This is a work of fiction. Names, places, businesses,
characters and incidents are either the product of the
author's imagination or are used in a fictitious manner. Any
resemblance to actual persons living or dead, actual events or
locales is purely coincidental.

EPub Edition December 2012 ISBN: 978-0-9856401-3-2
Print Edition ISBN: 978-0-9856401-4-9

PRAISE FOR FAE HUNTER

"Once you start reading Fae Hunter, you won't be able to put it down. The action starts on the first page and never lets up for the entire book. Just when you think you can take a deep breath and maybe even put the book down for the evening, a new twist erupts that makes you keep reading for one more chapter and one more chapter and one more chapter…"

-Romance and Mystery Author and Editor Sally Berneathy

"This book has so many surprises, twists, and turns, I couldn't put it down."

-Paranormal Romance Guild Reviews

"I think it's this love triangle that made the book for me."

-Fantasy and Romance Author J.F. Jenkins

"Great world-building, engaging characters that quickly draw you into the story, and enough twists and turns to keep you flipping the pages."

-Fantasy and Romance Author Crista McHugh

"…if you want a kick-ass heroine who struggles to do her best and save her world then you should definitely check this book – and series – out."

-The Flutterby Room Reviews

TITLES BY NICOLETTE REED

Fae Hunter (The Soulstealer Trilogy, Book #1)
Mane Attraction (A Soulstealer Novella, Book #1.5)
Fae Guardian (The Soulstealer Trilogy, Book #2)

"Every person is a new door to a different world."
- Six Degrees of Separation, 1993

ACKNOWLEDGMENTS

To my dear husband who always makes sure that I continue to eat even when I am in the midst of my creative frenzy.

To my son who, at age six, asks me rather poignant questions about my plot and storylines in an effort to understand why his mother spends so much time at the computer.

To my family who has enthusiastically supported me. From my second cousins who aren't old enough to read these books to my grandmother who informed me that she didn't get to be her age without knowing a thing or two about sex.

To my co-workers and my boss who politely ignore the fact that I kind of write about some crazy shit even though my day job is quite conservative.

To the wonderfully supportive writers I have met, namely Crista McHugh, who have encouraged me to become what I am today. The camaraderie we have shared has meant a lot to me.

I love you all and I wouldn't be able to pursue my dreams without you. Thank you!

CHAPTER ONE

The scene crept slowly into my consciousness. The Peixes, once a majestic airship, now lay battered, its bow bent at an unnatural angle and its wings ripped and torn to shreds. It wasn't until a bright purple fish swam across my field of vision that I realized the scene was underwater. My eyes followed the fish as it found a knothole in the side of the ship and floated towards a body that lay on the ground covered in heavy chains. The swirling water obscured the image and I couldn't quite make out who it was. Before the eddies cleared something caught my eye, a copper chain hanging from the neck of the figure. As I approached the stone flared, casting a reddish glow into the surrounding water. The figure sat bolt upright despite the weight of the chains.

"Valora!"

My eyes snapped open and I choked on the sweet air that forced its way into my lungs. A heavy weight crushed my breast and I looked down to see a tan muscled arm covered in bold swaths of black tattoos. I sat up, pushing Dooley's arm off me and causing him to stir. His lids were heavy as he peered out at me through his thick lashes.

"Is everything okay? You seem like you're out of breath."

"I'm fine. I think I just had a nightmare induced by your bear hug." I focused on the mural painted on the ceiling above the bed. It was a depiction of the Goddess Varuna. She hovered like an angel far above any of the cloud cities of the Overworld. The winged fae of all of the cloud cities were represented in the painting as her devoted followers. A reminder that even though we might not agree on everything, the Goddess brought us all together.

Dooley reached over and snatched me across the waist, pulling me down on top of him and out of my reverie. "I would say that I was sorry, but I think I'm really going to miss having you next to me tonight." Dooley reached up and tucked a lock of hair behind my ear. His words weren't the only thing that alerted me to his desire.

"It's only one night." I made the barest of efforts to wiggle off him, knowing I was just teasing him further.

"I've spent far too many of them away from you already."

"We've been together every night since you came through the portal." I shivered as Dooley reached up to stroke the sensitive spot at the base of my wings.

"I'm talking about every night before we met."

He grasped my hair and pulled me down towards him just as the door to our room flew open.

"Okay you two, save it for after the wedding." Kit was standing in the door, her brilliant blue hair shining in the morning light which poured through the windows along with the intoxicating scent of Winter Haven. A curious mixture of wet earth surrounded by a delightfully sweet but pungent cloud. An addicting scent that was difficult to pinpoint and seemed to permeate everything.

I rolled off Dooley and pulled the sheet around my naked body. "You certainly are eager to get the day started, Kit. Are the guests arriving already?" I told my father I didn't want a public ceremony, but he said that there was nothing I could do to stop it. All the fae of Dell'Aria wanted to be at the wedding of the fae who had brought the treachery of King Aric to light and saved Dell'Aria from being destroyed by his machine which not only stole the magic from their blood but had also stolen their sense of peace. Only a few months had passed since Aric had fled the city with Kali after his execution was ordered.

My friend's betrayal still made my heart ache. Kali gave up everything. She agreed to help Aric with his plan in exchange for him helping her to replace her broken wings. A bride typically had her best friends by her side on her wedding day, but with Franca dead and Kali gone there was no one left except Kit. Her mother had agreed to allow her to leave the selkie colony of Lake Mavrovo to attend the wedding on the condition that she and Ralph be allowed to attend as well.

"Not yet but they will be here soon," she said in response to my question about the arrival of the guests. "And I want us to have a bachelorette party tonight!" A wide grin crossed Kit's face.

Kit had lived most of her life on Earth with her father Ralph until I met her and realized that she was half-selkie. If she hadn't come through the portal back to the Realms she wouldn't have survived on Earth. The amulet of Queen Elemi, Kit's mother, hung around her neck. Its stone shone as brilliant blue as her hair and allowed her to walk around on two feet instead of the tail she had when she was swimming around in the waters of Lake Mavrovo with the rest of her selkie kin. At least that was what I knew of the amulet. Considering I knew very little about the one hanging around my neck I could be completely wrong.

"I still have to get used to all these strange customs, Kit. Exactly what is a bachelorette party?" I asked.

"Oh, you'll love it," said Dooley. He swung his legs to the side of the bed, a wisp of the sheet covering his lap. "Just don't take her to see any dwarf strip shows. I hear they aren't all they're advertised to be."

Kit and Dooley broke out in laughter. I still didn't get the joke, but I was glad to see them happy. Both of them were here because they had followed me from the suburbs of Seattle. A short trip through one of the many Portals from the Realms to Earth. Short, that is, if you knew what you were doing. I wasn't all that good at traveling through Portals.

Dooley had wanted to know how it was that he became half-fae and, although we now knew that he and King Aric were half-brothers, we weren't any closer to finding out what that meant. All I knew was that from the moment I saw Dooley his spirit had called to me, and when our lips first met the goddesses of Winter Haven had blessed our union. It was only natural that we were here now to celebrate their blessing under the stars of the most sacred of places to the fae. Winter Haven. The birthplace of the Goddess Varuna who watched over all of the winged fae. There had been many times in my life that I had wondered if the Goddess had cursed me. I was born with short wings, never able to truly take to the sky like my fae brethren. I was only beginning to learn to accept my shortcomings and to appreciate the good things that had come into my life.

"If we're going to get moving I'm going to need to get some clothes on. And hopefully a hot shower will erase this headache I can't seem to get rid of," said Dooley. He had started to complain of headaches not too long after we arrived in the Realms. I kept telling him he needed to talk to Pryn, but he insisted it was just him getting used to living at a higher altitude.

Dooley jumped out of bed and ran towards the bathroom, the taunt muscles of his backside putting me into a trance as I watched him slide into the dark room. Dooley stuck his head out of the door and gave a wink of his chocolate eyes. A loose curl of his shoulder length brown hair fell over his forehead. "Don't give her too much mead to drink. She isn't allowed to have a hangover tomorrow. I intend to make sure her first night as a married woman is something to remember."

He shut the door behind him. Kit's mouth hung agape. "Dang, that man has a nice behind. No disrespect of course, Valora."

"None taken, but weren't you like eight years old last time I checked?" I recalled with fondness the first time I met Kit and her father Ralph. She was such a delicate creature when we met, and now she was surrounded by the vicious selkies. Underwater vampires. But it was also only half of who she was.

Kit shook her head and stared down at her hands. Her long blue hair hung in her face as she talked to her toes. "I suppose, but after a few months in Lake Mavrovo I have come to maturity. That's what Mother tells me anyway. She says that time moves differently there. I am basically nineteen Earth years old now. And I have to tell you, I'm sure glad I missed those awkward teenage years."

The magic of the selkies was a mystery to me. I knew that now that Kit's father Ralph had wed the Queen he would likely be made immortal. I hadn't seen him since I left them both on the banks of Lake Mavrovo, but I had seen Kit many times since she liked to use the portals between Dell'Aria and Mavrovo and seemed to be free to do so. I had to admit to feeling a slight jealousy at her freedom when I had been brought up within the walls of the Court, my only escape being the large volumes of the history of the Realms that were contained within the Court's library.

Kit sat down on the bed next to me as the steam from Dooley's shower puffed out from under the bathroom door. "You seem to be in another world this morning. You aren't nervous, are you? If you are, that's okay. I hear it's perfectly normal."

I bit at my lip as my throat went dry. Kit had once given me her blood to save my life and she was my closest confidant. But it was more about admitting it to myself, not to Kit. "I had a dream of Aric."

"Was it a dream or a vision?" She stared back at me with gleaming blue eyes. Much brighter than the dark blue storms that swirled through the gaze of Aric, but no less intimidating. Kit's selkie powers were meant to enchant. Sitting close to me I could see the tips of her incisors just below her bright red lips. She was certainly growing into her powers. Goosebumps broke out across my skin.

"I—I…"

"Oh, I'm so sorry." Kit reached into the front of her skirt, which was really just made up of a magical rearranging of her iridescent scales, and pulled out a pair of red cat eye glasses. The lenses were darkened and there were sparkling rhinestones in the corners. As soon as she slipped them over her eyes the spell was broken. "I am still getting used to all this."

"Don't worry, we all have a lot of new things to get used to. Dooley especially, so I really would appreciate it if you wouldn't tell him that I had a dream about Aric."

There was a time when Aric was the only man in my dreams. I had grown up within the Court beside him. My father was the hand of his father, the King, and he was a prince. I had always admired him from afar. His white blond hair and the soft blue feathers of his wings attracted the attention of many of the fae women. But he was a King's son and was expected to take his father's place as King to the next Queen. The Queens of the fae battled for their position as Queen and ruled with absolute authority. The King merely held a place on the throne. It had always been that way until recently. When Aric's machine caused a Blight to descend on Dell'Aria the Queen had vanished and the fae all believed that she had abandoned us to die. Her Royal Guard ruled in her stead, confident that their Queen would return. In the end only her head had returned, tossed to the feet of Aric by Queen Elemi who revealed the extent of his treachery. After Aric's execution was ordered and he fled the city the Royal Guard had appointed my father King and agreed to let him keep the throne without a Queen until the time that I was ready to rule Dell'Aria.

I guess that made me a princess. I shuddered at the title.

I wasn't sure I would ever be ready to rule the city. I had been a Hunter, one charged with seeking out those that Aric called "Soulstealers." He was the only Soulstealer I had ever found and I had spent my life hunting down my own kind. The fae of Dell'Aria might have forgiven me but I hadn't forgiven myself. My father had decreed that all Hunters were now to be known as Guardians. Guardians of Dell'Aria and its inhabitants. I had taken the new title, but I wasn't sure what to do with it. I still grieved for my lost purpose.

Kit waited patiently as I reflected on my next words. I stared at her without allowing myself to focus. "It might not have been a dream."

"Did you speak to him?" Kit studied the amulet around my neck. The red stone lay dormant, as it had since the last time I was with Aric. We were connected by two matching amulets which he had forged to protect me from the effects of the machine he had created. While the life force of all the other fae, including my mother, were drained away until their death, this amulet kept me alive. Now I was unable to take off the amulet without my life force draining away. It was a powerful magic that not even the high priests of Dell'Aria had been able to undo. Just how Aric's amulet worked wasn't clear, but what was clear was that it connected us on a mental and physical level. Before Pryn taught me how to shield my mind Aric was able to come to me in thoughts and in other ways as well.

"I didn't speak to him. But he called out to me."

"It was probably just a dream. Wedding day jitters. I know how to solve that." Kit jumped up and took my hands in hers. She danced from one foot to the other.

"Please tell me it has nothing to do with naked dwarfs."

Kit fanned herself with her hand. "No naked dwarfs. But I can't guarantee no naked." She clapped her hands together, reminding me of the eight year old girl she had been only months before. Selkie magic was powerful, but physical changes didn't always mean mental changes. Kit tossed a pair of black leather pants at my face. "Get dressed and meet me downstairs. Make sure to pack an overnight bag."

"You do know I'm supposed to be married tomorrow, right?"

"I said overnight. I'll make sure to bring you home tomorrow with very few battle wounds. Master Pryn has already made me promise to bring you by his quarters so he

8

can give you a few lessons before we go."

"Why exactly would I need magic lessons before we go on this bachelorette party? Are we planning on engaging in battle?"

"A good girl scout is always prepared." Before I could prod her any more she gave me a wink and shot back out of the room as quickly as she had come in. Her shimmering scales swirled about her as if she was swimming across the surface of the cool marbled floors before the heavy wooden door shut behind her.

I fell back onto the bed and brought the leather of the pants to my face, inhaling deeply. The leather still held the faint scent of Aric. Kit didn't know he had ordered a dragon slain to create the leather these pants were made from, and I didn't know why I had kept them. I wanted to blame the amulet for my feelings which became convoluted wherever Dooley and his half-brother Aric were concerned, but there was something else that lay beneath the surface. An awareness that I tried to shove deep down into the recesses of my mind as my wedding day approached. My one chance at true happiness would not be ruined.

As if he was reading my mind, Dooley opened the door to the bathroom and came out holding a wet towel wrapped around his waist. His soggy locks fell down his back and beads of water cast a sheen upon the hard muscles of his chest. He stepped forward into a strip of light that fell from the window, his gaze holding mine with an even more powerful pull than Kit's had, no magic required. He gave me a smirk and let his towel drop to the floor.

"I can't let you leave without reminding you why you should come back."

৵৽

I slung my knapsack over my shoulder and padded down the hallway of the temple at Winter Haven leaving Dooley to take another nap after our morning workout. I should have had a smile on my face, but my stomach was in knots. I had slipped on the dragon leather after giving Dooley one final kiss and felt as if I had immediately betrayed him. The dream of Aric calling out to me bothered me more than I wanted to admit. *What if Aric really was in trouble?*

The high priests still weren't sure how the amulets worked, but I knew that they linked Aric and me together. If something were to happen to him then something might happen to me. Deep in my ruminations, I reached Pryn's door before I knew it. My mother's former mentor and teacher, Pryn. He had taught her all of the healing spells she knew which garnered her a position at Court where she had met my father. My mother had died in the first wave of the Blight, and I had shunned magic ever since. Her strength in magic was what had gotten her killed, and I wanted nothing to do with it. Both Dooley and Pryn were helping me to realize that hiding from my own magic was impossible and not necessary. It was better to know how to control the magic inside me rather than to deny it existed.

I brought up my hand to knock on Pryn's door, and it opened before I touched it. Pryn's golden eyes sparkled. He wore the same white priest's robes as when I first met him. When I had dragged him from the dragon's lair at Mount Elbrus. He had been an accused Soulstealer, but we all knew now that wasn't true.

"Good morning, child. I was hoping I wouldn't have to fetch you in person. Now I realize you have an exciting day ahead of you tomorrow, but we really need to get in another lesson before you go off and have your fun." Pryn reached out and slipped the strap of my knapsack off my shoulder, setting it down on a stool just inside the door.

He opened the door wider and gestured me inside. The priest's chambers at Winter Haven were packed full with every resource they could ever need. The walls were covered in dark wooden bookcases from floor to ceiling. Large volumes of every text known to the fae of the Realms were stored in this massive library. Spell books, history books, and everything important to our people. There were many faces that I didn't recognize, those who had journeyed here from other colonies of Overworld. This was one place that had always remained sacred. No matter how the fae had fought over the years Winter Haven was our neutral zone. One place we could all agree deserved to be worshiped and preserved at all costs.

"I've cleared a room for us where we can practice undisturbed." I followed Pryn past those who were deeply ensconced in their texts, some who sat in prayer and others who blatantly stared at me with confused looks on their faces. I was immediately self-conscious again. The fae of Dell'Aria had stopped staring at my short wings. After everything that happened at our colony I finally had achieved a level of acceptance, but outside of Dell'Aria I was still an anomaly.

As I entered the room behind Pryn the warmth of the sun cascaded through the windows casting a brilliant pattern of colored light onto the ground through the stained glass. The clouds moved fast past the sun creating a kaleidoscope of color that danced across the smooth marble floor. I was dizzy for a moment and reached out to steady myself against something. Pryn rushed to my side.

"What is wrong, Valora? Is it nerves? I can give you a remedy for that." He helped me to a wooden stool and set me down gently before making his way to a sideboard stacked tall with glass bottles containing all manner of potion making materials. Pryn expected me to know how to somehow manipulate those ingredients and become the healer my mother once was. I again felt dizzy.

Pryn's back was to me as he took a pinch of this and a dab of that and crushed them together using a small mortar and pestle, reminding me of Dooley. If anyone should learn magic it was Dooley. He already had a natural talent for it. That and other things.

Everything out the window took on a reddish glow. I thought it was the shadows from the stained glass until I realized it was reflected in everything I saw, much like the dream I had of Aric the night before. I checked my amulet and saw a faint pulsating light. I clasped my hand down around the stone and shoved it into my shirt. The amulet hadn't done more than be a weight around my neck since I last saw Aric fly away. If it was going to become active again, I didn't want anyone to know about it until after the wedding. Nothing was going to ruin this day for me.

Pryn handed me a cup of frothing brew. "Drink it quick before it bubbles over. It should take the edge off a little."

I downed the cup in one quick gulp. The warm liquid cascaded down my throat, burning as it went down. I choked a bit and wiped away a few tears. "What kind of medicine is that?"

"A medicine every good priest has in their stocks — homemade mead. Quite tasty."

"You're giving me alcohol before noon? Shouldn't I be focusing on my lesson?"

"Yes, but I won't get you to focus if you are off worrying about the wedding. That is all you are worried about, right?" Pryn's brows drew together, his face tightened.

I confirmed with a weak nod that told him I didn't want to talk about it. I knew Pryn could be trusted, but I didn't even know if there was anything I needed to tell him. I had a dream and my nerves caused me to see a red light. That was it. The sooner we finished this lesson the sooner I could get through with the torture that Kit had planned for me.

"Right, then we are going to work on a spell which I believe could save your life."

"Isn't that a little heavy? Wouldn't a glamour spell help me to keep myself hidden if I were in danger? I already have that down." I rose off the stool, and Pryn set me down gently with a hand at my shoulder.

"A glamour spell will not help you if you are tumbling through the sky, my dear Valora. I won't always be there to save you, and your new husband has no wings. How will you live in a cloud city if you have to worry about the two of you falling to your deaths?"

"You are going to teach me to fly without wings?"

"That's rather difficult. No, what I intend to do is teach you how to stop falling. It is a way of freezing yourself in time and space. It is the first step. Later we can move on to more difficult magic." Pryn moved to the sideboard and returned the potions to their places.

"I suppose that wouldn't be bad to know." I moved over to the table beside Pryn and let him take both of my hands in his.

"I will need you to concentrate, child. Concentrate hard. Know that if you ever intend to use this spell it will not be under these guarded circumstances. You will likely be under attack. Your focus will be the only thing that will allow you to properly cast the spell. Close your eyes and repeat after me, Congelar no Tempo."

I took a deep breath and let my mind wander inside

itself, focusing on only my heartbeat and the gentle thrum of Pryn's pulse beneath my thumbs as they pressed into his wrists. I muttered the enchantment over and over again under my breath.

"But Pryn, how will I know if it's working?" I opened my eyes and looked across at him.

"By practicing." Pryn released my hands and took two steps backwards. "Livre Como Passaro."

The floor suddenly disappeared beneath my feet and there was nothing for me to grab onto. My heart flew into my throat and I couldn't take a breath as the ground below me rushed into view. My wings tried to move, but the speed of my descent prevented them from slowing me down any. All they did was send me into a spin which took all my sense of direction from me. I tried to slow my racing thoughts and remember the enchantment. "Congelar no Tempo," I whispered in my mind, my voice having left my throat entirely.

"Valora!"

My chest was on fire. The amulet burned hot at my breast and even though I knew Pryn wouldn't let me die, I had a feeling that keeping secrets might be my undoing. Hands clasped around my middle before I jerked to a stop. Pryn gave out a groan as he hit the ground with me in his arms. I was briefly dazed at the sight of his brilliant white wings which were extended to the sides. Pryn's golden eyes became the sun and Winter Haven was only a small set of clouds far above in the sky.

Pryn pulled at the chain around my neck and the amulet beneath my bodice flared a brilliant red before becoming dead again.

"When did this start happening again?"

My voice returned to my throat. "Only today."

"You should have said something to me. I would never have asked you to practice such strong magic if I knew he was trying to contact you again." Pryn grabbed my shoulders and gave a few hard shakes.

"If you had warned me maybe I would have told you. Don't ever spring anything like that on me again." I knew Pryn had been my mother's teacher and meant well, but I didn't like magic anyway because it had killed my mother. And I feared it was going to get me killed as well. I much preferred a sword to fight my battles. "I figured I was dead until I heard you call out my name."

Beads of sweat broke out on Pryn's lip as he released his hold on me. "Valora, I never called out your name."

CHAPTER TWO

Pryn apologized, but I refused to tell him anything about what I heard. After hearing Aric's voice I was now convinced my dream had been a vision. The amulet had once worked to draw magic into itself for my benefit, but it was also a conduit between Aric and me. If he was in trouble, maybe he was trying to draw magic through me to save himself. I wouldn't put it past him to do such a thing. Pryn wouldn't be able to help me out with that problem. The priests kept me under observation for weeks after Aric fled Dell'Aria. The amulet was born from a dark magic that they had no knowledge of and wanted nothing to do with. I was lucky that they were the only ones who knew about it, otherwise the amulet would become another thing the people of Dell'Aria would shun me for.

After Pryn flew us back to Winter Haven I went directly to Kit's room. One torture for the day was over, it was time to get the other one done with.

The room Kit was staying in was one of the most modest I had seen in Winter Haven, but the room was chosen specifically for her. Outside the window a waterfall was within arm's reach. Perfect for a half-selkie from Lake Mavrovo. The sound of the rushing water immediately put my mind at ease.

Kit sat at the small vanity and was busily pinning her bright blue locks into an intricate pattern atop her head, her fingers moving deftly from side to side.

"How in the world do you do that?" I marveled at the designs she had woven with the small braids.

Kit cocked her head to the side, and I saw her smile in the mirror's reflection. "I can do yours if you want. Let me." She avoided my direct gaze as I sat in the chair in front of the mirror. The ache at my chest simmered down to a gentle throb. Kit ran her brush through my hair, and I pushed aside the top of my bodice to see if any damage had been done. When the stone flared to life it had felt as if my heart was being ripped out of my chest. Now the red stone lay dormant and a small red mark was left behind. I pressed at it absentmindedly.

"You'll get used to it," said Kit as she braided my hair. "The pain doesn't last long. At least that's the way it works with mine."

I noticed Kit's amulet with its bright blue stone. "It is?"

"Yes. It draws the power it needs, or you need, and then it leaves you alone for a while."

"But why exactly?"

She shrugged. "Mother isn't one for big explanations. Father assured me that it will never harm me. My mother has enchanted the amulet to recognize me as its master. Whatever pain it produces is because it needs to do so to save insure my safety."

"Have your mother and father arrived yet?" Kit's fingers pulled a little too hard on my hair and I winced.

"Sorry!" She pressed on my scalp to lessen the pain.

"They aren't due to arrive until tomorrow. I still have one last day of freedom."

I always wondered if Kit was happy since she came to the Realms. I knew she had no choice. It was either come home to the waters or die, but sometimes death was a welcome respite to those who were chronically ill and that was the condition she lived with on Earth. A lot had changed since then.

"Are you happy, Kit?"

She answered without pausing the fast work of her hands through my hair, her voice monotone. "You don't need to worry about me anymore. Whatever battles I have now are my own, and much better than death. That I assure you. The selkie aren't like the fae, Valora. Not like them at all." She hung her head and continued with my hair until she had finished.

"Now enough of this serious talk." Kit slid on her glasses and rubbed her hands together. "We are going to go out and have some good old fashioned fun. Are you ready?"

"Let me just say good-bye to Dooley and then I'm yours." I tucked the amulet into my bodice and tried to pull the top high enough to cover the red mark it had left on my chest.

"I'm pretty sure you had your good-byes this morning." Kit pressed her fists into her hips and gave a smirk.

"I keep forgetting you aren't a child anymore."

"Besides, Dooley has already gone with Pryn, Orris and your father for some manhood ceremony," said Kit.

I burst out laughing. "Are you joking? Dooley has more manhood than all of them put together."

"You would know," Kit taunted. "I don't get your silly fae customs."

I laughed again at the thought of Dooley being forced to

go on a ritual hunt when in his world he would be going to a bachelor party that included looking at nude women and drinking entirely too much. "I suppose if he can get through an imp hunt intact then he will truly be welcomed by the fae of Dell'Aria."

The hunt was a custom where you had to chase down and capture an imp. Imps are winged creatures whose claws contain a toxin which would likely make you throw up but not die, which as I understand it is the point of drinking too much at a bachelor party. Perhaps he wouldn't find it so foreign after all.

"Then let's go create our own custom, shall we?"

I took Kit's hand and let her lead me down the hall. As we got closer to the center of the temple the narrow passageway opened up into a vast circular room with a domed ceiling. A glimmering pool swirled with bright white light at the center. A portal. It was the only way Kit could travel here, and she intended to take me through it. My hand turned clammy in Kit's grip. I froze as she reached the edge.

"We could just take in some of the sights at Winter Haven." My voice sounded shrill even to myself.

A playful grin crossed Kit's face. The teeth of the selkie were all pointed and sharp, but being half-selkie, only Kit's canine teeth were pointed. "I know exactly where we're going. Don't worry, we'll be able to get back just fine."

My luck with portal travel hadn't exactly been great. The first time I traveled through one I became trapped on Earth, and the second time I descended into the depths of Mount Elbrus. And while that wasn't all bad, it certainly wouldn't have turned out the same if Franca hadn't been there. I reached into my pocket and stroked the braid I cut from her hair after the echidna killed her. Franca's ashes were returned to her family at Mount Elbrus, but I would always carry a

19

piece of her with me.

"Just know that if I'm not back tomorrow then your mother will kill you." I pulled my shoulders back and lifted my chin high. Even if I didn't feel confident inside, maybe I could fake it.

Kit winked and squeezed my hand tight as she hopped over the edge and plunged feet first into the snow white eddies of the portal.

The trip was remarkably calm. My last trip was like being pushed out of the birth canal, but this time for a moment I was surrounded by the same peace and tranquility that Winter Haven seemed to evoke. That feeling disappeared quickly as the smell of dense pine and fire surrounded me just before I landed on the ground with a thud. A groan escaped my lips as the wind was knocked out of me.

At Winter Haven there had been daylight, but now it was dark and I was in an unfamiliar forest. Panic gripped me. Memories of my trip through the portal to Earth made my stomach roll. I sincerely hoped that Kit hadn't been that stupid.

Kit lay huddled on the ground next to me. She put her finger to her lips then pointed towards the firelight that broke through the dense underbrush. The rhythmic sound of drums echoed against the clear night sky.

I scooted on my belly through the dirt towards Kit and whispered to her through clenched teeth. "If you have brought me to Earth I can do you a favor and put you out of your misery right now."

"Shhh." She gestured again through the brush and I dipped my head down to look through the break in the branches.

All the muscles in my body went rigid and I couldn't find my breath. I was glad to already be lying on the ground, but I was immediately aware of how exposed we were and the fact that I didn't bring a weapon with me. On the other side of the brush was a clearing. In the middle was a blazing fire surrounded by a cluster of elves who were partaking in what appeared to be another ritual of manhood. Their heads were shaved clean and their muscled bodies were surrounded with only a thin piece of loin cloth. They passed around a wineskin and drank deeply. In their free hands they each clenched a sharpened dagger flecked with crystalline scarlet that glistened in the firelight. Kit had brought me to a sacred ritual of the elves which I had only read about in books. And one that I understood they protected on penalty of death to any trespassers. If they discovered us here they would swiftly remove our heads and make sure that we were cleansed of all memory of their secrets.

Kit wiggled her eyebrows at me. She had no idea what she had gotten us into.

৯৯

My body was frozen in panic and my mind raced as I went over all the ways I could possibly get us out of this situation. The portal Kit brought us through dumped us in the middle of the thick forest of the Riparian. I could only hope that the blaze of the elves' fire had prevented their keen vision from seeing it activate.

"We're about to get a great show in a minute," Kit whispered.

I put my finger to my lips while raising my eyebrows to the back of my neck. Now I knew how my mother felt when she scolded me as a child. Kit might look like she was grown, but she was operating in a world with rules she hadn't yet grasped.

Our only hope was to wait them out. Once they were

done they would either leave or maybe pass out from all the wine they were drinking, hopefully giving us enough time to sneak away. In the darkness there was no telling how deep inside the forest we were.

The men began to chant. Each one growling out a note in a synchronous pattern that echoed against the trees that were tightly woven around the clearing. These men were the elven warriors, their bodies reflecting their hard work and their even harder muscles. The elves were a race older than the fae and shrouded in as much mystery as the selkies.

Their song rang out louder as they pounded their feet on the ground, the vibrations rattling through my belly and down deeper. Their movements became frenzied as each one followed the other in a dance around the blazing fire. Kit and I peered under the bushes, and their hardened muscles flexed mere feet away from us. As the roar of their deep voices came to a crescendo they each whipped off their loin clothes, tossing them into the fire one by one.

They all froze in place as another man stepped from the shadows behind them. His body, as nude as the others, was so impressive I had to forcibly close my mouth with my hand as my jaw dropped. His face was shrouded with a hood. He raised his arm, revealing one of the sharpened daggers. The words he spoke weren't of any language I had ever heard in the Realms.

The light of the fire bounced off the chiseled backsides of the elves as they each placed the sharpened stone daggers to the inside of their forearms. At the shrouded man's command I watched as they rubbed the edge of the blade against the soft flesh of their arms. Blood welled up from their wounds and dripped down, forming a ring around the periphery of the fire.

Although it would make sense that this act would cause

pain, it seemed to have the opposite effect as evidenced by the sight I had of many of their hard lengths. I felt a small hand at my chin. Kit stifled a giggle as she assisted me in closing my mouth again.

Kit rubbed her tongue against the sharpened points of her fangs. Clearly her animal instincts were kicking in. My mind started to return to normal. How in the hell were we going to get out of this again? I was pretty certain that if any of those elves caught us we would be dead.

Amid the groans of ecstasy the shrouded man stepped forward, adding his blood to the circle. The flames shot up higher and within them I saw the form of a man writhing in pain before the entire column of fire collapsed onto itself plunging the clearing into darkness.

I bit down into the back of my leather bracer stifling the scream of fear that threatened to expose our position. A small flame erupted from the palm of the shrouded man as he beckoned the others forth. The men all retreated from the deadened fire into the woods in the opposite direction of where Kit and I were hiding. As the last one passed out of the clearing the shrouded man made no movement to investigate where Kit and I lay hidden, and I watched his chiseled behind as he disappeared into the forest.

"You can thank me now." Kit eyes were wide and glowing.

"You still need to keep your voice down. Their hearing is second to none. Do you have any idea what danger you put us in?" Although they were gone, something still didn't feel right to me. My skin prickled with the remains of an unfamiliar magic that seemed to be growing closer.

Kit sat up and crossed her arms over her chest. "I know you still see me as a child, Valora, but please. I knew exactly what I was doing."

Kit gave a small scream as she was suddenly pulled into the air by a dark figure.

I shot my hand out and it closed down over a discarded tree limb which I tried to brandish as I would a sword. It hadn't done the tree much good and it wasn't going to do me much good either, but we were in the middle of a forest and weapons were difficult to come by.

"In the name of the Goddess Varuna I command you to let her go," I yelled out.

The hooded figure closed over Kit's neck, and she let out a groan. I picked up the largest rock I could find and hurled it at the figure's head. His hand shot out and grabbed the rock before it could strike him. He dropped the rock to the ground in front of him and produced a small flame from the palm of his hand.

"I believe that throwing rocks at your host is considered rude." The man released Kit and pulled back his hood to reveal a shaved head with slight points at his ears. The shrouded figure from the circle, except now he had a robe draped over his body as well. A flush crept across my cheeks as I remembered how particularly impressive the body was beneath his robe, and was I glad that the shadows mostly hid my reaction.

Kit giggled and threw her arms around the man's neck. "Mane, this is my friend, Valora, the one getting married tomorrow." She drew out her enunciation of his name with a flirtatious lilt. "Valora, this is my boyfriend, Mane Searing."

Mane pulled a small staff from his robe and set the end alight before handing it to Kit. He brought his hand up to his face, and his eyes seemed to glitter red before he pursed his lips together and blew away the flame from his palm. He extended it to me in greeting and as I shook his hand the stone at my chest began to pulse, but it was unlike when Aric called out to me. There was no heat, only light.

"You're marked." Mane gestured to the amulet at my neck which had come loose from my bodice.

"Isn't it rude to point out your guest's shortcomings?" I tucked the amulet into my bodice and fastened the clasps of my dragon leather coat up to my neckline even though the humid air didn't call for it.

He tilted his head slightly and raised an eyebrow which I noticed was pierced with a small band of silver. "I hope you enjoyed our wedding gift to you."

I pulled at the neckline of my jacket which now seemed to be making my neck impossibly hot. The picture of Mane's muscled and well-endowed body displayed naked before the fire was embedded in my mind. "That was a sacred ceremony to the elves, right? Why would you allow us to see it?"

"Kit has enchanted me." He paused, licking his lips as he took in a view of her from head to toe. "She explained the human custom of the 'bachelorette party,' and I thought perhaps this would be comparable." He reached down and clasped his arm around her waist. He stood at least a full foot taller than Kit.

"You would risk the elves knowing you betrayed their ritual by inviting us to watch just for Kit?"

Mane's face grew serious. "I risked nothing. Kit brought you to a spot where you were cloaked by powerful magic. Hers and mine. There was never a danger of you being seen. But I was able to see the both of you the entire time." He gave a wicked smirk that seemed to drill right into my mind, forcing the picture of him to rise to the forefront again. An awkward one note laugh fell from my mouth before I clamped my hand down over it.

"I would love to stay and visit, but I need to rejoin the

others." Mane stepped forward and bowed, placing a gentle kiss on my hand. "We shall see each other again soon. I wish you well tomorrow, Valora Delos."

He took Kit into his arms once more and gave her a powerful kiss, as he pulled her body into his own. I had a feeling this was not the first time these two had gotten together. He released her and disappeared into the forest.

"Isn't he dreamy?" Kit planted the torch into the ground and plopped down on the nearest boulder, her head tilted to the side as she stared into space.

"Dear Goddess, Kit, you're dating an elf? How did this happen?" I took her by the shoulders. Even in the darkness I could feel her influence weave its way around my better judgment.

She reached her hand onto the top of her head and pushed the dark lenses in front of her eyes. "I went to the surface one day to collect some asphodel fruit from the shores of Lake Mavrovo. He was alone and we talked," she said.

I pressed the base of my palm into the bridge of my nose, trying to push away the slight twinge of magic. Her glamour was undeniably strong. "Have you considered that perhaps your powers of enthrallment may be to blame for this?"

"I didn't use my powers on him." Even in the low light of the torch I could see the color rising in her cheeks. I definitely didn't mean to cause an argument, but sometimes thrill and danger feel a lot alike, and when you're young it's hard to know the difference.

"I know you don't mean to, Kit, but even this morning you accidentally—"

Kit stood before I finished my sentence and stalked off into the woods. The last thing I needed was to lose her in the forest. I chased after her, catching up with her quickly. I closed my hand over her wrist. "Wait!"

She hissed at me before quickly covering her mouth with her hands. Tears sprang to her eyes. "Oh, Valora, I'm so sorry, I didn't mean to do that."

The little girl seemed to appear before me once more and my frustration softened. "It's okay, Kit. I have to admit, that was a great show."

Her tears retreated. "It certainly was." She collected the torch and hooked her arm in mine. "Let's go back to Winter Haven."

Kit busied herself with activating the portal, and I stared into the woods of the Riparian. The breeze was still, but something out there was watching us. The same unfamiliar pulse of magic as before. I tried to reach out with my mind. As I did I seemed to hit a brick wall that bounced my energy back to me twofold. I reached out to brace myself against a branch. The amulet at my neck pulsed brightly once more and red light reflected off a pair of glowing orbs peering out from the trees.

"Are you ready to go?" Kit called to me as she finished activating the portal. The bright white light from it burst forth and blocked out any sign of my stalker.

I hesitated a moment before taking her hand. The stone of my amulet dimmed as the feeling of unease drew further away. "Sure."

As long as whatever was in the Riparian stayed where it was and didn't follow us to Winter Haven.

CHAPTER THREE

I was glad to find that night had descended at Winter Haven, and I wasted no time in passing out. When I awoke the next morning my head ached like I had too much to drink the night before even though I had nothing. Probably just too much portal travel. I could use a drink now. Today was my wedding day, and I had just witnessed a naked elven ritual hundreds of miles away in the Riparian Forest. But there was something else there, too, something much more sinister. Something I was pretty sure Mane knew more about.

I rolled over and realized that Dooley was in bed next to me.

"Are you awake?" I whispered.

"Yes, and ready to get this over with." Dooley stared up at the mural on the ceiling.

"What do you mean?" I clutched at my throat, rubbing at the mark it left behind after Aric called out to me the day before.

Dooley tapped his index finger against his lip. "I mean that I never wanted a large wedding. When a wedding gets too big it's more for the guests and less for the bride and groom." Dooley rolled onto his side, propping his hand under his cheek and reaching out to push a lock of hair behind my ear. "Then again, I hadn't ever expected to be marrying a fae princess in a cloud city in another world. So I'm going to let it slide."

I bit down on my lip as the ache in my skull pulsed once more. I agreed with Dooley, but there were a lot of other things on my mind.

Dooley cocked his head to the side. "I don't suppose you had as much fun as I did yesterday."

"The imp hunt! Did you catch one?" Dooley rubbed at his forehead, evidence that at least one of the imps had probably nicked him and caused a slight headache.

"Several. Your father and the others were quite impressed if I do say so myself." He leaned back on the bed and folded his arms behind him. My mouth went dry as I soaked in the view. He was perfect in every way. He treated me like a queen and was more than patient with me. He had adapted to living in the Realms and was willing to sacrifice everything he knew in order to be with me. *Then why can't you be honest with him?*

"Though I was home long before you were. Something in the forest spooked your little pikaki and the fuzzy orange fur ball wouldn't stop barking. Scared all the imps away."

"You were in the Riparian last night? Dooley, there's something I need to tell you."

A sharp knock sounded at the door before it swung open. Pryn entered, his formal robes billowing about his ankles as snowy white as his wings. "Your guests are arriving. I'm here to bring Dooley to prepare with the men while you are readied for the ceremony."

Dooley swung his legs out of bed and slipped on a pair

of his old jeans. The sight of him in those jeans and nothing else made my heart skip more than a few beats. "I'll see you at the altar, darling." Dooley bent down and kissed my forehead before following Pryn out of the room. Before the door could close Kit barged in.

"So have you recovered yet? I need to get you in your dress. The guests are here already." Her words rushed out all at the same time.

"What time is it?"

Kit clasped her hands together. "Well, the ceremony is in thirty minutes." She raised her hands palms up as I jumped out of bed. "And I know I was supposed to have you ready before now but I was not expecting the spell that Mane and I conjured up to have such a strong after effect. Is your head pounding, too, or is it just me?"

I sat down and tucked my legs under my vanity. "Forget your head and do my hair up like you did last night. I can't let anything ruin today."

❧

Between my training as Guardian and Dooley's spell casting with Pryn, he and I had spent very little time together in the last several months. I wasn't sure if any of that would change much after today, but then again, after today I wouldn't have much to worry about anything anymore. My path would be chosen and I would walk along it. That was what I kept telling myself anyway.

"Valora, are you ready?" My father offered his arm to me as we stood at the closed doors to the main temple. They were awe-inspiring, reaching up high enough to touch the edges of the domed ceiling.

My hands involuntarily tugged at the multi-colored ribbons that adorned my skirt. I stared down at the amulet that sat dormant at the cleavage of the plunging neckline of my tight white bodice. Air seemed to be in short supply, and the room tipped a second before righting itself.

My father tapped a soothing beat into the back of my hand as I eyed the exits. That same unease that had settled deep within my gut in the Riparian revealed itself again, making my shoulders tense. Kit had reassured me that nothing could have followed us here from the Riparian. I wasn't so sure.

Then the doors cracked open and the joyous sound of the music behind them broke free and flooded over us. I shuffled back a step or two as the temple full of fae gave me their full attention. Those that couldn't find seats were hovering in the air off to the sides. The fae of Dell'Aria had come in droves, and they all threw flowers at my feet as I passed them. They shouted well wishes to my father and me. I greatly wished my mother could be here to see everything.

A woman near the aisle on my right grabbed my hand as I passed by, her golden eyes soft and filled with an inner glow. "You will save us all."

"Are you okay?" my father, leaning over, whispered into my ear. I gave my father a quick nod, but when I returned my gaze to the woman who had stopped me she was no longer there. My nerves were definitely playing tricks on me.

Dooley stood at the front with Orris and Ralph, Kit's father. My heartbeat quickened and my fears melted away. Dooley was wearing a robe similar to Pryn's. His tan skin was even darker against the white of the robe. I watched the muscles in his arms flex as he clasped his hands in front of him, the black swaths of tattoos standing out on his bare arms.

Ralph was so dapper in his dress robes though nothing had changed about his rotund figure and balding head except that he looked as though he was filled with happiness. Kit gave a small wave at me from the left of Pryn who stood front and center holding the sacred book of the Goddess Varuna.

My father leaned in and whispered to me, "Dear daughter, I am so proud of what you have become."

Tears welled up, making my vision foggy. "Thank you."

Dooley stepped forward, giving a slight bow in respect for his new father-in-law and King, as was the custom. My father gave my hand a quick squeeze before placing it into Dooley's hand.

Pryn motioned us forward. Kit gave a squeal of delight as she arranged the ribbons flowing down the train of my dress so that I wouldn't trip on them.

Dooley took my hands in his as we stood before all of Overworld. Pryn's words faded into the background as Dooley said his vow to me. "I will cherish our union and love you more each day than I did the day before. I will trust you and respect you, laugh with you and cry with you, loving you faithfully through good times and bad, regardless of the obstacles we may face together."

I tried to repeat his words but was stopped. My breathing became labored and a viselike grip pressed down on the wellspring of magic within me.

Dooley's eyes reflected the blast of red light that burst forth from my amulet before he let go of my hands and shielded his face.

Voices around me became faint. I heard shouts and screams but they sounded as though they were all coming from underwater. The burning at my chest returned, but it was a cold burn. Ice cold. And then he appeared before me. Aric. His white blond hair soaked and slicked to the sides of his face. His wings drooping to the sides of his body. His wrists and ankles bloodied from heavy chains that surrounded him. I saw him clearer than anything. He reached a hand out to me. "Help me."

"Valora!"

I sank into someone's arms and looked up to see Kit cradling my head. The nave was empty. Queen Elemi and Ralph sat in chairs in the front row and Orris worried at his hat as he paced the length of the nave. My father brought a cup to my mouth.

"Drink."

"Where's Dooley?" Both he and Pryn were nowhere to be found.

Kit paused before answering. "Something happened, Valora. Your amulet. He'll be okay, Pryn is with him now."

"What!" I shot up and pushed everything away. "I need to find him."

"Valora!" I stopped again at the sound of my name, but this time there was no mistaking who had called it out. Queen Elemi rose from her seat and drifted over to me. The Queen of the Selkies, both beautiful and deadly. The feeling of unease returned. "Before you cause the boy more harm I suggest you start telling the truth."

❧

I shoved my shoulder into the door of the temple and pushed it open before sprinting down the hall. The loose ribbons of my dress got stuck around my feet. I reached down and tore off the lower half, leaving me with a miniskirt wedding dress. I choked back my tears, overwhelmed with anxiety and the need to get to Dooley as fast as I could. I didn't want to hurt him. I didn't want anything to ruin this day.

Elemi had accused me of lying about the amulet, saying

that it had powers I wasn't letting on about. If anything she was the one withholding information. How could Kit have an amulet just like mine without some kind of dark magic at work? How could I know how the amulet around my neck worked when not even Pryn could figure it out? Of course, the only thing that was certain about the selkie was that they certainly did not walk in the light. Queen Elemi practically glowed with the same dark magic I felt in the Riparian. I only hoped that Kit wouldn't fall victim to her mother's corrupt nature.

As I neared the door Pika rolled towards me. I hopped over the fuzzy orange pikaki and pushed against the door. It didn't give. It was barred from the inside.

"Hello! Dooley!" I pounded on the door.

My father and Kit caught up with me. "Valora, daughter, you need to let Pryn do what he needs to do."

"But I want to know if he is okay. I need to know." My body crumpled in on itself. My father wrapped his arms around me. The last time he had held me that tight was the day my mother died. I couldn't handle Dooley dying, too.

"Go with Kit to her chambers. As soon as Pryn says it is safe, I will call for you to see Dooley." He stroked his free hand down the length of my hair and squeezed my shoulder.

"As soon as it is safe?" I gripped my temples. I couldn't believe everything had gone so terribly wrong. *Was this all really because of Aric?*

My father retreated, and Kit tried to usher me down the hallway. "Come with me. Come on, Valora."

Kit pulled against my arm, but my feet were rooted to the ground. She directed her gaze at me with purpose. Her eyes were pools of blue that deepened further and further until I was pulled into them.

"Come with me," she commanded.

⤳⤳

"Valora, why didn't you say anything about the amulet? What happened out there?"

The influence of Kit's gaze wore off quickly. It didn't matter if she was wearing her glasses anymore, I couldn't look her or anyone else in the face. "I didn't want to believe it mattered. I wanted to be happy, Kit. I wanted to marry Dooley today." My entire body burned as if it were wrapped in irons.

"You didn't tell Pryn or Dooley about your vision?"

"No, but I think your mother might know something about it." My pulse quickened once more, returning strength to my limbs.

"What do you mean?" The furrow in my brow reflected in Kit's dark lenses.

"Aric was underwater, and the last time Queen Elemi spoke of Aric she wanted him dead."

Kit tipped her head to the side. "A lot of people want him dead, Valora. Besides, I'm fairly certain I would've noticed if my mother had Aric as her prisoner."

"Are you so sure? How much time have you been spending with Mane lately?"

Kit winced slightly, her chin dipping down to her chest. She didn't need to tell me, I knew the answer to my question.

"It doesn't matter. I have no intention of going after Aric. What I need is to figure out how to rid the connection between us. This amulet has got to go."

The door opened and my father entered. He gave a hard and obvious swallow. "Valora, Dooley is conscious and ready to see you now."

I pushed past him and shot down the hall between our

rooms. I froze at the open door and watched as Pryn dabbed a wet cloth along Dooley's forehead. Orris was in the room along with a few of the Guardians that were once Hunters alongside me. Just like the time Kali had them all draw straws to see who would be saddled with escorting me on my first mission into the Riparian, their glowering was barely contained. Only Pryn's face remained neutral. Dooley was barely conscious.

"Is he okay?" I clung to the frame of the door wishing I could rely on it to keep my legs from going out from under me.

"Orris, you and the Guardians can go now. I don't think that your presence is required." Pryn gave a dismissive gesture.

"But that thing could go off again." Orris pointed at the amulet hanging at my neck.

"Everything will be okay. Leave us."

Orris gave a slight nod but refused to look at me as he left the room with the Guardians in tow. Orris and I hadn't gotten along for as long as I could recall, but after his brother died his manner towards me had softened. He definitely took to Dooley, though. Everyone did. I wasn't surprised that they were more worried about him than me. Especially since they all believed I had done this to him. *Maybe I had.*

I slowly approached the side of the bed. Dooley's skin had taken on a sickly yellow twinge. I searched his face and bare chest for signs of any wounds, but I saw nothing

"Did my amulet do this? What is wrong with him?" I asked Pryn.

Dooley's eyelashes fluttered at the sound of my voice. His eyelids parted slightly as he tried to smile. "I like the dress." He reached out his hand, and it dropped to his side before he passed out cold.

"Pryn, you need to help him." I reached out for Dooley but Pryn stopped me before I could touch him.

"Valora, I don't think your amulet did this. However, I don't think it's a good idea if you touch him right now."

"What do you mean?"

"Dooley's life force is draining. I don't know how else to explain it. You know when a fae is on Earth too long he loses his magic? Dooley is starting to lose his humanity here in the Realms. There was no way to foresee this. Aric is half-fae, the two of them are brothers, but Aric never seemed to have this problem. Of course they are both very different, and Aric had been taking magic to supplant his powers. I think the only solution is to take Dooley through the portal to Earth. I can try and see if that will help."

My legs felt gelatinous. I couldn't believe what I was hearing. When Dooley came through the portal to the Realms I warned him that he might never be able to return, and now Pryn was telling me he had to return or die. "I'll go with you.

"You can't. Your father's orders," said Pryn.

"What?! My father has never been the one to tell me what I can and can't do."

"He is your King."

"He is my father and then my King and even then the title means less and less these days." My skin tingled as a fine sheen of sweat formed across my brow. I heard the sound of someone clearing their throat behind me.

"He's standing right behind me, isn't he?" I asked.

Pryn nodded.

"Pryn, will you excuse my daughter while I have a word with her?" I refused to turn around at the sound of my father's voice.

"Of course." Pryn rose up from the side of Dooley's bed. He reached out and lightly stroked my forearm as he spoke in a soothing tone. "I will keep him safe, Valora. If anything should happen I will let you know immediately."

"Valora, will you please join me in the hall?" My father's voice was stern, and I knew before I could do anything I would have to face him.

I reluctantly let my father lead me out of the room. Pryn had told me that my amulet had not done this, but I wasn't convinced that he really knew. Obviously from Orris' reaction, I wasn't the only one who thought this was all my fault.

My father shut the door. "Walk with me."

"Why won't you let me go with him? It's not like I haven't been to Earth before." Everything had happened so fast. My mind could form no plan other than to try and reason with my father.

"You were sent to Earth before by Aric who had his own plans for you. I would never have let you go had it been my choice." My father's fingers were steepled before him as he stared straight down the hall. He had made his decision.

I continued to pace alongside my father down the hall towards the inner temple. "But this is not the same situation, Father."

"Valora, you will not go through the portal. The amulet that connects you to Aric is connected to a much darker magic. One that we don't fully understand yet. I need you close by me. What happened today was only a small example of its power, a power we don't fully understand. Sending you through that portal with it acting up the way it is would be like sending you with an unknown weapon strapped to your neck. I won't do it."

"But if I stay here without him it will kill me. I need to

do something."

He stopped, drawing in a quick breath before releasing it. "Aren't you listening? By staying here you are doing something, Valora. You are keeping yourself alive. I lost your mother to Aric's foul treachery. I will not lose you. As your King I command you to stay in the Realms. Pryn will take care of Dooley, and I am sure he will be able to return before long."

I stopped in the hallway, and my father continued to walk down the hall. He was done talking and I was done listening.

Kit passed him in the hall coming the other way and they exchanged glances. "Hey, what's going on? How's Dooley?"

"Not good." I told her what Pryn had told me and how I was forbidden to go with Dooley.

"Why not just go anyway? I could take you through the portal to Earth."

"My father isn't that stupid. He would have had the priests ward the portals against my traveling there. He isn't going to give me the chance to defy him because he knows I would."

"When are they taking him?"

As if in answer to her question sounds echoed down the halls. They were bringing him to the portal. I stood my ground. No matter what my father said I was not going to let my husband leave without saying good-bye. At least the man who should have been my husband.

A sudden realization hit me. I rushed forward as Pryn entered the chamber. "Pryn, you must complete the ceremony. You have to marry us before you take him to Earth."

"But, Valora, you know I can't do that while Dooley is

unconscious. He has to say the words."

"He did say them." He had said them many times, in my mind, in my dreams. He only wasn't awake to say them now before the one who cared to hear them spoken in turn in order to pronounce us married before the Goddess Varuna. If anything happened to Dooley I would never again find him in our afterlife if we weren't married before he passed on.

"Please. Please!" I tugged on the robes of the old priest much as he had tugged on mine the night I had dragged him out of the dragon's lair.

"It is not foreseen, Valora. You must wait. Be patient." He gently touched my wrist, and a brief wave of calm passed over me. White light emanated from the portal.

The others stood holding a stretcher with Dooley's limp form lying atop it. "Every second we wait he loses more of his life force, Valora."

I broke my grip on Pryn's robes and stepped to Dooley's side. I wouldn't stop them from taking him to Earth, not when that might save his life. I was just going to have to find another way to bring us together again.

Despite the looks the Guardians gave me I bent to give him one last kiss on his feverish lips before withdrawing into the shadows. Kit's small arm circled around my waist as I watched them all descend into the portal.

CHAPTER FOUR

I wasted little time feeling sorry for myself. The man who was to be my husband was gone and the only way I could close the distance between us was to find a way to break the spell of the amulet. My father gave me space after Dooley was taken. His plan was to go to Dell'Aria the next morning. But my plan wasn't the same.

"It's the only way." I sketched out my plan with Kit by candlelight in my room that night.

The empty space left in the bed where Dooley once lay was too much for me to bear, and Kit had agreed to a slumber party.

"It's not that I don't think I can take us there, but I don't think I can do it without my mom knowing where we are. Aric knows where you are because of that amulet. My mother knows where I am because of this one. The only time I feel free is in the waters of Lake Mavrovo and even then I'm not really free because it is my mother's domain."

"You've never cared in the past. I am sure Mane could attest to that."

Kit's cheeks flushed scarlet. "My whereabouts in the

Realms don't concern my mother, but it seems yours do. If we disappear together she will assume we have gone to the same place. Don't you want to keep this trip from your father?"

I rolled up the parchment and slid it along with the reed pen into my satchel. "I think I can give him a good excuse for wanting to visit Mount Elbrus." Again I rubbed the locks of Franca's thick blond hair in my pocket. "Will you come with me?"

"Yes."

It didn't take long to pack our provisions for the next day. I penned a message to be delivered to my father. The dwarves of Mount Elbrus had always been generous in their hospitality. I only hoped their shaman was up to seeing me once more.

The parting at the portal was tense the next day. The domed ceiling of the vast circular room felt as if it were pressing down upon me. The Guardians that accompanied my father stood silent next to the marbled columns that encircled the room. The King's will be done, except where his petulant daughter was concerned.

My father wanted me to continue on to Dell'Aria and take my place as leader of the Guardians, the new team of fae who were once Hunters. Our purpose shattered, like the light that cut through the individual windowpanes in the colenette, falling in crisscross patterns across my boots. My father had given me the burden of giving these fae a purpose. One that would carry them forth in productive lives of unquestioning servitude. My father neither liked nor appreciated my viewpoint on the matter. I agreed that I would do anything to protect the fae of Dell'Aria, my people. But how do you protect your people when you see yourself as the only real threat to them?

If the amulet which hung from my neck was truly a weapon like my father said, then I should be far away from all of them. But being close to Dooley wasn't a choice I had either. No, I needed to diffuse the situation.

Kit and I said our final good-byes to everyone. Elemi snaked her hands around Ralph's rotund belly as they disappeared into the portal. After I found out what was happening with Dooley, I wanted to find out what had happened to Ralph. Once such a proud and vibrant local sheriff and now he had been reduced to some pawn in Elemi's scheme. Soon Kit and I were the only ones that remained.

"Are you ready?" Kit practically bounced on her toes. Her long blue hair fell loose around her shoulder and her red rimmed cat-eye glasses sat propped on her nose. She carried a rucksack with all of her necessary supplies. She had impressed upon me that the selkie had a very specific diet, one I hadn't really had a chance to ask her about yet.

"Not quite." I dropped her hand and went to the window. The priests all said that Winter Haven was the closest you could be to the Goddess Varuna. I ventured a look out the window. In all of my mother's stories she had not been able to capture its beauty. The temple was massive and was the only building on the floating isle which was much higher in the sky than Dell'Aria or any of the other fae colonies. The isle was small, but its gardens seemed to go on forever. The mingling scents of sweet fruits and savory mosses danced in the ever present light breezes that floated through the open arches of the temple bringing with them a mist that cleansed and nourished the flora and fauna. It was truly a paradise, one that I was hoping to be a guest of my entire life.

"You'll be with him again. I know you will." Kit placed

her hand at the small of my back. Sweet Kit. The girl had been torn from her home on Earth and brought to the Realms at a moment's notice. She had more strength than I did in my little finger. I could learn a lot from her.

"I will make it my last mission to see that is so," I said. Before I could waver in my conviction I took hold of Kit's hand once more. I checked my pockets for the vials of potions I had snatched from Pryn's quarters. I knew Kit and I would need them as soon as we entered the fiery realm of Mount Elbrus, a living and breathing volcano which the dwarves thrived in, but whose environment threatened our very existence. Fae and fire don't mix. If my calculations were correct then we would be arriving in the same portal we had once landed in with Franca, Dooley and Ralph. And if that was the case, then I would need to have potion in my system before we even arrived.

I handed Kit a flask of the dark red liquid. "Take this. Once we hit that heat we'll be done for before they even have a chance at rolling out the welcome mat if we don't come prepared."

"To the Elysium and Acheron. The goddesses above and the gods below." Kit downed the thick brew in one quick gulp.

I paused with the vial half-way to my mouth as I pondered Kit's words.

"Well, why don't you take yours?" she asked.

"What do you mean, Acheron and the gods below?" The name Acheron seemed so familiar. I did spend quite some time in the vast library within the walls of the kingdom of Dell'Aria. But I recalled it as a passing reference, not something used in context so that I could have understood what it meant.

"It's just what the selkie say. I figured it was just an

expression. There's a lot of mumbo jumbo they say that I have no idea what it means." She handed me the empty vial and I placed it into my satchel. My fist clenched around the hilt of my blade. I had no intention of using it, but it felt good to have it by my side again.

Without time to hesitate any longer I quickly drank my potion. A cooling chill ran through my body, threatening to turn it to ice if we didn't get moving. As much as I wanted to talk to Kit about her mother's plans and the Acheron, it would have to wait.

"Every word has meaning where the selkie are concerned," I reminded her.

❧

I took Kit's hand and stepped to the edge of the portal, vowing to myself to return once I had Dooley with me. The swirling white light of the portal snaked out, encircling our ankles as we went down the stone steps towards the middle of the vortex.

I hesitated before we took the final step. Kit was the one whose powers could control where we landed after we stepped through this portal. I had been slow in my magic lessons, a fact that both Pryn and Dooley scolded me for.

I noticed Kit's face was drawn and pale. Far too pale. "Are you okay?"

Her hand locked tightly around my own, refusing to budge, as if her hand had turned to stone. She fell forward at the waist and pulled me along with her.

"Kit!" I screamed as the portal's light flashed from white to blue to red to green all around us, clinging to no particular direction.

"Kit, focus on Mount Elbrus. Focus on the fire."

Her hand was still locked around mine. A great and

terrible sound echoed all around us. Like a roar followed by pained screams. *Oh, dear goddess, please let her focus on Mount Elbrus and not Acheron.*

The light in the portal glowed green and we both tumbled to the ground. The trees surrounding us were lit with a soft morning light. It seemed we had gone through the same portal Kit and I had gone through the day before. We were supposed to be going to Mount Elbrus and we had ended up in the heart of the Riparian Forest. It was easily a day's journey to our destination.

Kit's body lay still beside mine. I put my hand to her forehead. She was ice cold. A shiver snaked up my spine. I never bothered to figure out what would happen if we didn't actually end up at Mount Elbrus after taking the cooling potion from Pryn's stash.

Both of our body temperatures were lowering in anticipation of the fires of Mount Elbrus. Instead we were in the damp forest of the Riparian. My amulet flared to life at my chest, burning brightly and returning warmth to my blood. But my amulet wouldn't help Kit and it seemed hers wasn't doing her any good.

"Kit, can you hear me?"

"So cold. Need to get warm." Her body shook, and despite the cold she sweat profusely.

I leaned closer to Kit and drew her towards me, hoping that I could help her stay warm. Kit nuzzled her nose into my neck. I stared right into her eyes which peered over the tops of her glasses.

"Need to get warm," she repeated just before extending her fangs and plunging them into my beating pulse. My reaction was delayed. The pain I had expected when she bit me never came. Instead a strange euphoria overcame me. The trees seemed to shimmer, and it wasn't until they did that I realized I was probably going to pass out. If Kit didn't stop she was likely going to drain me dry, but I was too weakened to stop her.

I heard the sound of something running through the trees. A blurry figure came blasting through, tearing Kit off me with one swift pull. I felt the pain then. I reached up to my neck and pulled away my hand which was covered in my own blood. Kit struggled against whoever had hold of her. That was the last thing I saw before I blacked out.

The aroma of meat cooking and the popping sound of wood on a fire slowly brought me out of my unconsciousness. I opened my eyes just a crack so that I could assess my situation. Waking up after you are passed out is never a good thing. I had no idea where I was and whether I was free or captured. I saw Kit, her shoulders covered in a heavy fur. I ran the edges of my hand along the cloak that covered my shoulders as well. Its soft fur likely belonged to one of the many creatures of the Riparian. Kit was greedily devouring a large hunk of skewered meat.

To her side was Mane, who had just added another log to the fire and was cooking some meat on a spit. He wore simple tan shorts with a loose vest made of buckrabbit fur. "Look who decided to join the land of the living."

I pushed myself up and became dizzy.

"Don't go too fast, you'll make yourself pass out again," he said.

"I don't think it was I who made myself pass out in the first place."

"Really?" Mane cocked his eyebrow and tilted his head. I wished I could slap that smirk off his face, but that would have to wait until I had regained some strength.

Kit threw down the meat she was devouring and dropped to my side. "Valora, I am so sorry. I didn't have any control. It was like I wasn't even me."

I waved her off. "I should have known better."

"Some lessons are best learned the hard way, right?" said Mane.

"Look, not that I'm not glad you showed up when you did – but how exactly did you know where we were?"

Mane never broke his gaze with me. "You know very little about the selkie. You know even less about the elves. We like to keep it that way."

"If you won't tell me how you knew we were here, would you like to tell me why you are here? Your people must wonder where you are."

"The elves don't function as one. I am free to go where I please." He pulled the meat from the fire and sank his teeth deep into the sizzling flesh. The juices from whatever beast it once was dripped down the sides of his mouth and he wiped them away with the back of his wrist.

"You seemed to be functioning as one the other night." Now it was my turn to smirk at him.

He leaned in towards me across the fire, the flames reflecting its red light in his eyes. "Yes, we come together for our rituals." The double-entendre was not lost on me, and I had to let him win this particular battle of the banter.

"Stop teasing her Mane, she's had a rough day." Kit pulled on his arm as she eyed the rest of his meal.

"Yes, I would much rather save my teasing for you." Mane snaked his arm around Kit's waist again and pulled her onto his lap. He tore the rest of the meat from the spit and placed it in her mouth. She giggled in delight. My heart ached at seeing them so happy, something I had known only recently with Dooley who was now on Earth in the hands of Pryn who hoped to heal him.

"We need to get to Mount Elbrus. Can you help us get

there?" I asked.

"Kit told me that was why you were knocked up with coolant." Mane paused as he stared at me. "Yes, I can help you get there."

"Thanks, babe." Kit threw her arms around Mane's neck.

❧

It wasn't until nightfall that I was able to move again. Kit insisted that we stay the night and start out in the morning, but I wasn't going to let any more time pass than I needed to. I was already running out of time.

Mane and Kit trailed behind me as I pushed through the dense forest, cursing at each branch that failed to break and instead snapped back into my face. I tried using my sword to cut through the worst of it but I feared my efforts were only dulling the blade. What I wouldn't give for a pair of wings that could easily fly me over all of this. Before we left I had Mane sketch out the route. We could make it to Mount Elbrus by daybreak if we hurried.

I grasped the hilt of my sword, glad to have it in my hands again. My new title was Guardian, but I identified more with my former role of Hunter. The heavy weight in my hand gave me some control. Magic didn't. Magic was controlling me right now and I didn't like it. Dark magic.

The moon was full and bright in the skies above the Realms, shining down on Underworld. I was hoping that the shaman at Mount Elbrus that Franca had introduced me to would remember me. The demon that shared its consciousness seemed to know more about this amulet, and it was the only lead I had.

The wind whipped through the trees and I could no longer hear the sounds of the forest around me. I stopped and realized that I could no longer hear the voices of Mane or Kit either. My amulet pulsed rhythmically. The red light of the stone acted like a beacon, and I certainly wasn't intending to draw any attention to myself in the middle of this forest. Last time I was here I had battled both ogres and trolls, and I was only hoping that I was up past their bedtime and not treading on their territory.

I tucked the amulet into my bodice as best as I could and tried to retrace my steps. Mane and Kit couldn't be too far behind. A deep moan cracked the silence. The sound mingled with the breeze making it difficult to figure out where it was coming from. I wanted to call out to Mane and Kit, but if I did and they were in danger it could make things worse.

The sound intensified and I realized I was almost to the source. Mane and Kit were still nowhere to be found. I got down on my stomach and parted the lower branches of a tree in front of me.

Through the space I created I saw them. Mane and Kit. She was bent at the waist and moaning with each stroke as Mane slid himself deep inside her, his hands gripping her hips for support. I was both angered and enthralled. How could they stop for this right now? But how could I say anything without thoroughly embarrassing Kit and myself now that I had seen them?

I only needed to wait them out.

"Like what you see?"

The voice was unmistakable, but then again impossible. I turned slowly and there, crouched beside me was Aric. I reached out my hand which passed right through him.

"Why are you here?" I whispered through clenched teeth.

"I was going to ask you the same thing, but then I saw

what you were looking at. Haven't you heard me calling for you?" He raised his eyebrows as if I was supposed to apologize for not rushing to his aid.

Aric was as delusional as ever. "Yes, how could I not?"

"Valora, I understand you are angry with me, but my life is tied to yours. If I die you die."

"I'm on my way to figure out how to fix that particular problem you have created for me." I found my hands closing around the amulet which was slightly warm to the touch.

Aric leaned forward and looked at Kit and Mane in the clearing. "He's quite impressive." He returned his gaze to me. "You can't fix it, Valora. If you separate yourself from the amulet, you die. If you separate the amulet's connection to mine, it ceases to work."

"So you say. You don't mind if I find that out on my own, do you?"

"Just don't learn the hard way, I beg of you." He gazed at the sky and let out a heavy sigh.

"Why doesn't Kali just help you? You took her with you."

"She is the reason I am in this predicament. I presume she is already on her way to Earth through one of the portals, if she is not there already. She always had only one goal in mind." He rolled his shoulders as if his shirt was making him uncomfortable, except that he wasn't wearing a shirt. A fact that was making me uncomfortable. Mostly because he could still affect me at all.

"Seems like you two had that in common," I said.

"That's where you are wrong, Valora."

Aric's image disappeared, and I turned to see Mane standing right before me, thankfully with his shorts on. He reached down his hand. "Can I help you up?"

"Thanks." I stood up as quick as I could.

Kit popped up from behind Mane's shoulder, her mass of blue hair a little messier then before. "You found us! Sorry, needed to take a little break. All better now."

I glared at Mane. "You do know we are on a schedule."

"More than you realize."

I ignored Mane and returned to the path I had been following. Aric's image had disappeared as soon as Mane and Kit had shown up. No one to confirm I wasn't starting to hallucinate. Kit scooted up to walk beside me.

"I have a knack for screwing things up, don't I?" she said.

"I would say yes except for the fact that all your screw-ups seem to start and end with me."

She placed her hand on my shoulder as we walked. "We'll get there by first light, I promise."

"Yes, we will."

CHAPTER FIVE

We traveled all night until we reached the base of Mount Elbrus. Finding it was the easy part, finding a way to contact those inside was a bit more difficult. I placed my palm to the rock, willing it to part before me. However, even if I made it inside I wasn't guaranteed a clear path to the answer I sought. Especially since to get the answer you really needed to know what your question was, and I still wasn't sure.

"Hey, can we take a break?" Kit sat down on a smooth rock, and Mane bent to massage her legs. What was it with him? I never knew the elves to be so amorous. Of course, I hadn't known too many elves. In fact, it seemed strange that we hadn't encountered even one other elf on our travels through the forest. The Riparian was said to be home to many of them.

I sat down on the rock beside Kit.

"So what is your plan?" asked Mane. For once he seemed to expect only an answer, not a reaction.

"My plan was we show up and they open up. I hadn't really planned past that." I reached inside my pocket and brought out the length of Franca's hair. "Dear, sweet Franca, how do I tell your people that I need help? How do I contact them?"

I put the hair to my nose and inhaled the scent of the fires inside the mountain that refused to release from her hair. Dead, but never forgotten. I remembered the first time we met. She had lumbered out from some inner tunnel in the mountain and proclaimed me free to face the wrath of a dragon that inhabited Mount Elbrus. A dragon whose skin I now wore as pants and a golden lined jacket. A beast of fire, just like the dwarves were beasts of fire. More at home in their mountain of lava then in the forest that surrounded it.

"If you require assistance, just say the words." Mane continued to massage Kit's leg. She looked as though she was about to drag him into the forest again and we didn't have time for that.

"Do your people speak to the dwarves?"

"For centuries. In Underworld you are either friend or foe. We are not friends but we do speak to one another." Mane stood up and approached the rock face. He placed his hand to the rock and his hand reddened as if it was hot. Seconds later an archway started to form, like bricks were being pushed out of the rock face itself. Torchlight came ablaze and a passageway revealed itself before us.

"You let us walk around in circles when you could have done that at any time." My wings twitched as I tried to suppress my annoyance.

"Not anytime. This is your journey. I'm only along for the ride." Mane looked from Kit to me and gave a snide wink, obviously feeling like himself again.

I shoved Franca's hair into my pocket. "We can't just go inside. I don't have any more of the potion."

"Then we wait for someone to answer the door." Mane sat next to Kit on the rock and interlaced his fingers behind his neck. He was ready to take a nap and I was running out of time.

"When will you people learn to listen? I don't have time for waiting." I set off through the archway and down the hall. Mane shouted after me and in a second I knew why. He hit the entrance to the tunnel and was repelled backwards.

"Only one can enter." He placed his hand at the invisible barrier.

Kit stood behind Mane at the entrance, her fingers pinching at the skin of her throat.

"Okay, then I'll come back." The archway darkened as I got closer to them. The images of Mane and Kit faded until I was staring at the mountain wall.

I wanted in, and I had gotten my wish. Aric's words about finding things out the hard way echoed in my mind and I said a silent curse to him under my breath. The heat wasn't too bad here but I knew in order to find the shaman I would need to go deep inside where the dwarves lived alongside the underground rivers of fire. I hoped that I would come upon a friend first rather than a foe.

As I felt along the sides of the tunnel in the dim light of the torches while my eyes adjusted, I tried to remember anything that might help me. The only thing that came to me was my memory of Dooley and our first night together – deep within the caverns of Mount Elbrus. Those memories weren't going to help me now.

My heart began to race and I tossed my satchel on the ground so that I could rummage through it. Desperation sat low in my gut, at about the place my mother's grimoire dug into my side. It was almost as if she liked to remind me that if I had only kept up with my magic lessons I could easily conjure a flame or some kind of protection spell right now.

I jabbed further into my bag and something sharp bit

into my finger. I looked down to see a small set of shallow bite marks and Pika who had apparently stolen away in my satchel when I wasn't looking.

"Your Uncle Orris was supposed to be taking care of you. He is going to be mad when he finds you missing." I reached down and patted the furry orange creature whose tongue lolled to the side of the mouth which took up its entire face. A vicious creature it was not. "Maybe you can help me."

I lifted Pika to my eye level. "I don't suppose you can understand me too well."

The pikaki gave a short yap in response.

"Well, it's worth a shot. Pika, I need some help. I need you to find a dwarf and bring him here. Can you do that?"

The pikaki yapped again. I set him down and he rolled off down the tunnel.

Time stood still as I waited. No sounds came from the cavernous darkness before me. The only light came from the torches which were set into the wall next to me. Torches which didn't seem to need any re-lighting. Magic. And then it dawned on me, this wasn't the work of the dwarves. They didn't deal in magic. Suddenly I wondered whose door we had knocked on. I had learned first hand that the dwarves weren't the only ones who lived within this mountain.

And that's when I felt it. Felt not heard. A deep thumping that shook the ground beneath my feet. Something large was coming this way and I was at a dead end with nowhere to escape.

The pikaki came flying towards me, yapping up a storm. It leapt up and hid its small round body atop my wings, peering out over my shoulder. I drew my sword in one hand and grabbed a torch from the wall.

"What did you bring down upon us, Pika?" The

vibrations caused dirt from the tunnel to rain down. "What did you do?"

The pounding stopped and I could tell that whatever it was stood just outside the circle of light cast by my torch. It was waiting there, in the darkness. Despite the heat my blood ran ice cold. Tendrils of smoke snaked in shadow across the crescent of light from the torch and I knew what I was facing. A dragon.

And I was probably wearing the skin of its kin. The dragon stepped one foot into the light, letting me see the size of its immense talons crusted with the blood of its last meal. I planted my feet in a wide stance and tightened my grip around the hilt of my sword, my training as a Hunter taking over any remnants of the fear that was more of a threat to me than anything.

"Let's get this started friend." I crouched, ready to get myself a little dirty. I was pissed and I needed something to kill.

The dragon continued into the light and a voice echoed in my mind. *"Only the King can order the slaying of a dragon."*

"Dammit Aric, stay out of my head. You're the reason I am in this predicament, in case you forgot." The dragon took another step. Maybe he hadn't yet realized that he had me against a wall. One puff of fire and I was his next barbecue meal, nothing I could do to prevent it.

"Let me help you."

"You've done enough." The dragon decided to test my resolve, letting out a focused stream of flame at the arm holding my sword. The bracer did nothing to prevent the fire from reaching my skin. I cried out in pain as my sword dropped to the ground. Pika jumped down my arm and licked at the ruined flesh. His strange orange drool seemed to hold healing properties for the fae.

I brought the torch in front of me and tried to move it back and forth to distract the beast as I reached down towards my sword. The dragon let out another flame at my feet, catching the sword and heating it up red hot. It fell to the ground with a thud and I fell along with it. Pika jumped off my arm and took refuge in the shadows. This dragon was enjoying playing with his food, and I would much rather he just get things over with.

"I asked, now I won't give you a choice."

The amulet at my neck flared brightly and I was glad I was lying on my back. The dragon walked forward, but its eyes had glazed over. It was no longer focused on me but on something else behind me. Hovering behind me was the glowing image of Aric, his wings outstretched.

It continued to lumber forward until it was standing just over me. I reached out, my fingers dancing across the pommel of my sword before I was able to grab the hilt. The heat bit through my flesh and I shouted out in pain before driving the sword upwards with all of my strength into the belly of the beast. I rolled to the side as its heavy weight came crashing down.

As I was catching my breath Mane and Kit came barreling around the corner. Aric's form had disappeared once more.

"Just in time I see," said Mane.

Kit ripped off her glasses and stared at the massive dragon lying on the floor. "Did you just kill that?"

"Yes." I hopped up and slipped my sword into its scabbard at my side. "Something I wish I didn't have to do. And how did you two get here?"

"Mane found us another way in."

"And it seems like you have found the answer to your problem," Mane said, pointing to the dragon's body.

"What do you mean?"

"The dragon's blood can offer you protection from the fires of Mount Elbrus. You only need to ingest it and then you should be free to roam for as long as you like."

Mane reached down towards my open satchel. He pulled out the two vials which had contained the cooling potion but were now empty. "Dragon's blood is very powerful." Mane reached the vials out, one at a time, and filled them before handing them to me. I slipped them into one of the inner pockets of my bodice. Mane's eyes gleamed as he regarded the pool of blood which oozed out from under the dragon's body.

"So I drink the blood and that's it?" All magic had a cost. The amulet hanging around my neck was proof of that.

"Count me in." Kit latched onto the dragon's hide with her fangs before I could stop her and retreated into her own world.

"Why is she so hungry? She ate so much last night I wasn't sure where the heck she was putting it all."

"She is selkie. She's been away from the waters of Lake Mavrovo too long. The amulet will keep her alive, but it doesn't feed the hunger building inside of her." Mane's eyes shined as he watched Kit feed on the dragon's blood.

"How do you know so much about the selkie?"

"How do you not?"

I ignored his question like he had mine. "I don't trust magic."

Mane stepped forward and cupped the back of Kit's neck with his hand. She detached from the dragon, her mouth bloodied.

"That should be enough. You don't need too much," he said.

Kit nodded and wiped her mouth with the back of her

hand. We all paused for a moment, the two of them waiting to see what I would do. I watched Kit to see if the blood caused any outward side effects on her.

Then I turned my attention to Mane. "Why don't you need it?"

Mane rolled his eyes. "Haven't we covered the fact that you know very little about the elves?"

I threw my hands up and plopped onto the ground. There was no way I was going to drink that blood. A dragon was a sacred creature. Killing it seemed justified to save my own life, but taking its blood was wrong.

Pika bounced over and licked at the wound my arm suffered from the dragon. I reached my hand up to look at it in the light. The pikaki's drool was disgusting, but you could hardly tell I had been burned.

"I suppose if you don't want to drink the blood you could always bathe yourself in pikaki drool," said Mane. Kit broke out in laughter.

❧

Every step was torture. We had sat there letting the pikaki drool over every square inch of me. It wouldn't have taken so long if Kit and Mane didn't have to stop so often for their laughing fits. Kit wanted to show me what I looked like in her mirror but my threats must have been loud enough because she put it away.

The pikaki drool gave my skin an orange sheen. I looked like a troll with wings, which only added to Kit and Mane's delight. As time went on I had heard every flying troll joke that must have existed and a few so bad I was certain they had just made them up right then and there.

Something was off about Mane, but whatever it was he seemed to make Kit happy and that was all that mattered right now. They would have their own battles to fight against Ralph and Queen Elemi if they ever planned on staying together. I doubted either of them would be as understanding as my father was with Dooley. The heel of my palm rubbed against my chest, trying to dull the ache that had settled there. I only hoped I was headed in the right direction and that coming here would bring me closer to seeing Dooley again soon.

We rounded a corner and squinted at the bright amber light that filled the cavern in front of us. We had been traveling in dimly lit tunnels so long it was a shock to our systems. Several dwarves rushed up to us and Mane spoke to them in their native tongue before I could even extend my hand in greeting, not that anyone would want to shake a hand coated in pikaki spit.

I recognized all the familiar landmarks from my last visit. Great basalt pillars glittering with fine-grained crystals dripped down from the ceiling. The dwarf children chased each other around the base of the pillar, their faces spattered with patches of black soot. One of the dwarves I recognized from my last visit paused from his work sharpening an obsidian blade on a grinding wheel and waved at me.

The shaman came to greet us as well, his hat teetering with trinkets and bobbles. "Valora, we knew you would return." His gaze quickly went to Mane. "He says it is nice to see you again, that it has been a long time."

"Are you talking about the demon inside you?" The last time I had seen the shaman a demon had spoken through him when he was in a trance-like state. He didn't seem to mind the demon much, although he was quite devilish. I suppose it gave the old man a bit of excitement. He only seemed to speak through him, he didn't control him.

"I thought he could only speak to you when you were in

a trance," I said.

"Very many things have happened since we last saw one another, Valora. Please, I invite you all to share my fire." The shaman chuckled and beckoned over one of the rotund dwarves to his side. "Please get enough cooling potion for Valora and her friend. Who are you, my dear?"

"Oh, I'm sorry, this is Kit. She came with us through the portal the first time we met. And this is her friend Mane."

"We know Mane. But Kit, my darling, you have grown so fast. The waters of Mavrovo have done you good. You are a woman now I see."

Kit's cheeks flared red, her eyes hidden behind her tinted cat-eye glasses.

"Yes, we met a few months ago," said Mane. He puffed out his chest. *Great, now the ego maniac was taking credit for Kit becoming a woman.*

"Also, bring a scrubbing tub and a handmaiden to help Ms. Delos remove the pikaki drool. I'm sorry, dear, but we are going to have to take a scrub brush to you. Your skin will definitely be red by the time we finish, but you'll live."

We all followed the shaman into the heart of the cavern which was dominated by a massive lava waterfall that cascaded into an open pit. The lava burbled and boiled, and dwarf children played upon the banks of the molten lake like selkie playing upon the beach. It was truly a different world. The heat penetrated even the thick layer of pikaki drool, and I was glad when the dwarf returned with the vials of cooling potion. Mane didn't need one and neither did Kit, but he whispered something into her ear and she giggled before accepting vials for the both of them. I suppose there were other things a cooling potion was good for.

Focus, Valora, focus. I downed the cooling potion as fast as I could. It was a thick brew and tough to choke down. I immediately felt its effects and gladly welcomed the sight of the scrub tub, eager to rid myself of the gelatinous orange masses that had formed in clumps all over my body. Pikakis were lucky they were cute and useful, because otherwise they would be utterly disgusting. Kit was playing with the fluff ball that had emerged from my satchel to squeals of delight from the children.

A dwarven woman made her way over to the scrubbing tub and dumped a bucket of hot water into it. The tub was no more than a wooden barrel with slats of iron holding it together. I slowly dipped one foot into the tub and then the other, careful to avoid touching the iron slats. Fae and iron are not a good combination. Steam rose from the water and as the cooling potion chilled my bones I was looking forward to it. The burns on my arms had disappeared thanks to the pikaki drool.

The woman set up a screen creating a barrier between the washing station and the rest of the cavern but still giving her access to the burbling pools of water that laced the edges of the reservoir of magma.

I slid off my clothes and hung them over the screen. I eased into the water, and its warmth melted away all the tension in my muscles. The low light hid my nakedness under the dark water of the tub. I looked up at the dwarven woman who held the brush in her hand and did a double take. Franca, my dwarven sister who had died in her efforts to help me, the one whose hair I carried with me, was now looking back at me. Only she was thirty or more cycles older.

"Hello, Valora, I hoped I would be able to meet you some day."

Franca's mother and I spent many hours trading stories about her daughter and my best friend. The rough scrubbing which was initially unpleasant turned to laughter and tears.

Joyful tears as Franca's mother regaled me with stories of an impetuous young dwarf, which was exactly how I had imagined she would be. At the end of our visit I begged her mother to take the lock of hair from me for herself. All that we had been able to deliver to her was an urn of Franca's ashes. She hadn't even been able to give her daughter one last kiss on the forehead. The least I could do was give her the braid. She finally accepted it before we said our tearful good-byes. She lovingly placed it in her pocket and I knew she would cherish it as much as I had. At some point I needed to let go of my dear friend, and this was the first step.

"I promise we will see one another again," I said.

"I dearly hope so. I would really love to see your wedding to this Dooley. He sounds heavenly," said Franca's mother.

Her choice of words made me giggle. Heavenly was the exact word I was looking for. "I would be honored to have you as a guest of honor at our wedding, Miss…I didn't even get your name."

"I am Franca's mother and will always be. If you'd like you can call me Mom."

Joyful tears threatened to break free. It had been a long time since I had been able to address anyone as mother, and Franca's mother was already like family. "I would like that." Franca's mother gave me a broad smile before turning and walking out with the lock of Franca's hair.

She had left a thick towel next to the tub, but I didn't want to get out of the water. I only wanted to let myself cry. As I gazed into the water I saw the reflection of my reddened cheeks. The sting of the scrub brush took hold. Suddenly it felt like my skin was on fire or itchy or both. It was unbearable.

I reached for the towel, and my arm smacked into Mane's shin.

"What the hell?" I dipped my body down under the water line. "A little privacy, please?"

Mane's gaze was all too direct given my circumstances, as if he could see right through the water. "Don't worry, hun. I've only got eyes for one little lady on this caravan. Though she seems to care a great deal about you, so that tells me I need to worry about you as well."

"Don't strain a muscle there. Wouldn't want that heart of yours to get too full of kindness."

"You have no idea." Mane's eyes blazed. Certainly a trick of the light.

"Did you have something to tell me when you came barging in here?"

He picked up the towel next to the scrubbing tub and held it out. "Yes, there has been word from Pryn about Dooley."

I leapt out of the tub and into the towel, practically pushing Mane to the ground. Finally word about Dooley. I only hoped it was good news.

৵৽

I barely had the towel tucked around myself when I scooted past the corner, using my wings to hover across the ground and spare my bare feet from the rough pumice rock.

Kit was holding the mirror she had from before and was talking into it. "You had a talking mirror with you?" I asked.

"Mom makes me keep one so she can keep tabs on me." In the reflection I could see Pryn, dark circles under his eyes.

I fell down beside Kit, and she handed the mirror to me. I took it tenuously, wanting to know what was happening with Dooley, but not wanting to hear any bad news.

65

"Valora, I wanted to let you know about Dooley." Pryn paused, clasping his hands together, and looking over his shoulder as the sound of screams came from the background. "He is fighting something, Valora. I have your Uncle Artemus here to assist me, but I am afraid there isn't anything we can do."

"What are you talking about?" I gripped the sides of the mirror so tight my hands ached. "You said that he needed to leave the Realms and that he would be better on Earth. What happened?"

"We could only guess that his human nature was the part of him that was suffering, Valora, but there is something else, something we don't know about. A magic stronger than I have ever seen warring within him. Neither the fae magic nor being home seems to have helped him." He wasn't looking at me now, resigned to the fact that Dooley's fate was hopeless.

"Fae magic?"

He answered with a small nod. "Yes, your Uncle Artemus thought perhaps that was what he needed. He went to the clinic without my knowledge."

"But that clinic was run by Aric. Didn't my father have it shut down?" Aric had housed all the magic that he had stolen at a makeshift clinic on Earth. The perfect place to hide it from the fae, and the place where he conducted experiments to see how he would go about restoring his mother's memory and my wings – a favor I never asked for or wanted.

"I don't think it was a high priority to him. He shut the portal directly in and out of the clinic and warded the entrance, but it wasn't enough."

"What do you mean?"

"Your friend Kali – your uncle ran into her at the clinic.

She was loading all of the vials into a truck."

"Kali is no longer a friend of mine." Despite the cooling potion, heat flushed through my body. Kali had done nothing but betray me. She always seemed to make things worse.

"She seemed to think otherwise. It was the only way your uncle talked her out of one of the cases of the vials of magic. He told her what was happening with Dooley and she gladly handed one over. But the rest is gone. She took it all and then disappeared."

"I am pretty certain I know what she is doing with it. You gave some of it to Dooley?"

He nodded again. "We did and it seemed to soothe his pain for a while but his condition has not improved. We only have so much and can only ease his pain for so long. I don't know what is happening to him, but if you want to see him, you will need to get here soon. We are at Dooley's cabin. I will stay here as long as I am needed."

"Of course, I'll be there as soon as I can."

"Valora, you will need to get your father to lift the wards. I know he has made sure you cannot pass through the portals to Earth, but I think perhaps he might let you now. I have sent a message to him and I await his response."

"I'll get him to lift them. Tell Dooley I am coming." I stood up and tucked the towel tighter around my body, realizing that I needed to find my clothing.

"I will. Travel safe," said Pryn. The mirror went dark.

"Can we use this to contact my father?" I asked Kit.

"Sure, I can try." Kit touched her finger to the face of the mirror and the image swirled blue and then red. The face of Queen Elemi appeared in the mirror.

"Where are you, Kit?"

"Oh, mother, I wasn't trying to contact you."

"I know you weren't. You didn't answer my question," she snapped.

Kit rubbed at the back of her neck. Mane ducked away, not wanting to be seen by the selkie Queen. "I just went with Valora to visit the dwarves. I was planning on coming home tomorrow morning."

"You have already been away too long. You need to return immediately."

"But, Mother, I'm trying to contact Valora's father for her. She needs to speak to him about Dooley. It's an emergency."

Queen Elemi shook her finger at Kit. "You are not to help that fae. Besides you wouldn't be able to contact him anyway."

"Why is that?"

"Because the coward has gone into hiding in his cloud city and shut down all communications with the selkie as he has declared war on us. Get to the nearest portal and I will bring you to Mavrovo now. Don't make me send an army for you."

"Yes, Mother." Kit shut the mirror, her mouth agape. "I don't know what to say."

My mind froze. Nothing made sense. Only a few days before, Queen Elemi and Ralph were in Winter Haven. If my father had any intention of declaring war on her he would never have let her come. "All you can do is return to your mother for now. I'm sure she is mistaken. There is no way my father would declare war on the selkie. Your mother was the one who proved that Aric was the one who had killed the Queen."

"Yes, but she also kept the Queen's body for many cycles while your people died. I was the one who convinced her to help. And she wouldn't even have been at the

68

wedding if it wasn't for me. Pryn gave me the invitation, and she insisted on attending."

"Go home." I stood up and clutched Kit's shoulders. "We will see one another again. The last thing we both need is an army of selkie coming through the portal and causing war with the dwarves."

Mane stepped forward from the shadows. "I will assist Valora. And we will see one another again."

Kit's eyes welled up with tears. "I really hope so."

"No one can keep me from you." Mane wrapped his arms around Kit and embraced her deeply. He ran his finger along her jawline and removed her glasses, looking deep into her eyes. "No enchantment, no magic, no Queen mother, nothing. Come, I will escort you to the portal." He turned to me. "I will return."

I nodded. At this point I wasn't sure how Mane could help me. I wasn't even sure what I was going to do. If my father couldn't be reached by a talking mirror I would need to travel to Dell'Aria, and I wasn't sure I had time to do that. And there was still the issue of the amulet around my neck. My father had warded me against traveling to Earth because he believed the amulet would pose a threat to me if I did. The next step then was obvious. I needed to talk to the shaman and his demon about getting it removed.

I quickly pulled my clothes on and went to find him. The shaman was sitting next to a fire smoking a pipe of beesroot. The honey sweet smell reminded me that it had been awhile since I had eaten anything, but my stomach sure couldn't handle anything on the nerves I was experiencing now.

"Come have a smoke with me, Valora. Calms the nerves," said the shaman. He reached into his hat of treasures and pulled out another pipe. He reached in again, pulled out a thick wad of beesroot and mashed it into the pipe with his chubby thumb, setting it alight with a stick from the fire.

The pipe was light, but the smooth wood took the pressure from my fingers as I rubbed at it incessantly. "My nerves could use some calming, but I also need your help in another way."

"Want us to look into the mist for you again?" The shaman leaned back and puffed smoke rings into the air.

"Yes, how did you know?" I took a long pull from the pipe and inhaled a cool breeze which washed away most of the tightness in my chest.

"I didn't. He did." The shaman pointed at his head to indicate the demon that seemed to enjoy speaking through him.

"I need to know more about the amulet. My father thinks it is a danger to me and won't let me go see Dooley. He's on Earth and is very sick. I need to find a way to get to him."

A booming laugh erupted from the shaman. "He's not the one you need to get to."

"What?" I saw the familiar red glow in the shaman's eyes. "Oh, it's you."

"How have you been, Valora? I knew you would seek me out eventually."

I pressed my lips together in a thin line. I knew I came here to deal with the demon, but I didn't have to like it. "Do I even have to ask you what I want or do you already know that?"

"Tough to know what you want when you don't even know yourself."

This demon seemed to be able to read minds. "Except I do know. I need to get rid of this amulet and my connection to Aric. I need to find another way to keep myself alive, and I need to find a way to keep Dooley alive."

"My, all in that order? You might want to be more concerned about your own mortality first."

"Fine, then how do I stay alive if I take off this amulet?"

"You can't."

"People keep telling me that, but with magic, all is possible, right? You said that the demon Aric made a deal with would know how to undo the spell."

"Yes, undo it. But that spell is keeping you alive. Such a dilemma." The shaman took a long slow puff from the pipe and blew the smoke into the air where it hovered like a cloud, refusing to dissipate. "I believe the answer to all your questions lies right in there." The shaman pointed to the cloud as a scene began to play within it. The same scene from my dreams. Aric.

"I won't help him." I folded my arms across my chest.

"Help him?" The shaman's voice had returned. "My dear, he needs to help you."

CHAPTER SIX

I furiously swept my hands through the smoke cloud willing it to dissipate before a wave of nausea hit me forcing me into dry heaves. The shaman placed his hand on my shoulder.

"You started the party without me." Mane was leaning against the basalt pillar, his arms folded in front of him and one foot crossed over the other.

"Dammit!" I threw the pipe to the ground. I undid the front of the towel that was still somehow wrapped around me and pulled it up over my head.

"What is wrong with her?" Mane asked the shaman.

"We told her that Aric is the only one that can help her. Apparently this is distressing to her."

Mane said nothing in return. I would have expected him to take the chance to kick me when I was down, but he remained silent. I raised my head from the towel slowly. Both Mane and the shaman stared at me.

"Shall we go solve your little problem?" asked Mane. The look on his face was sobering. He wanted to return to Kit just as much as I wanted to return to Dooley, and I was the one delaying things this time. The shaman shrugged and took another drag from his pipe.

"Why is it you want to be so helpful again?" If I was going to count on Mane I needed to know exactly what his motives were.

"Kit cares for you. She said you saved her life. I have never met anyone like her. She does things for me." Mane closed his eyes and clenched his jaw. He leaned over and held his hand out to me. "You helped her, I help you. Without you she would never have been in the Realms. And the sooner we solve your problem the sooner I can see her again."

I took his hand and let him help me stand up. "If we are going to do this you should be able to see her very soon."

"And how is that?" Now it was Mane's turn to ask the questions.

"Because Aric is being imprisoned by Queen Elemi at the bottom of Lake Mavrovo."

Mane and I went over the vision I had in detail. We worked out a deal with shaman for the potion we would need to survive under water at Lake Mavrovo and gave him Pika to watch over while we were gone. The stubborn mutt gave out a sharp yap as Mane and I drew close to the portal. "Now you be good and mind the shaman. He is your master while we are gone." Pika gave a whimper and snuggled into the shaman's coal stained robes.

Portal travel was becoming second nature to me. I almost felt like I might be gaining a few pounds around my middle from the lack of exercise lately. I wasn't sure what to expect if we were able to find and rescue Aric. The last time he and Dooley were in a room together Aric was handing me an axe to chop Dooley's head off, but that was before he knew Dooley was his brother. He had promised me he wanted to help me.

He wanted to help you, not him. Logic tried to force its way into my brain but I gave a strong push-back. I had no other direction I could turn at this point. Dooley was on Earth, the portals between here and there were closed to me, and I couldn't reach my father. And I couldn't keep ignoring the fact that everyone kept telling me that the direction towards my salvation lay in the hands of the one who had caused my doom.

The tightness returned to my chest. Yes, it all made perfect sense.

ॐ

My skin prickled with moisture making my clothes stick to my body. Each step became more uncomfortable as the cooling potion wore off. I followed behind Mane as he hopped from one rock to another with ease and wove his way down a side passage towards the portal. A few dwarves who were napping on chairs nearby paid us little attention as we passed. Apparently they weren't that concerned about our intrusion.

We reached the edge, the swirling red mist snaking out and tickling at our ankles. Mane put his hand up, stopping me in my tracks. "Queen Elemi knows you're here."

"Yes."

"She will know the second we enter the portal. We have a better chance of surprising her if we enter Lake Mavrovo from the surface. I'll take your satchel for you." Mane reached out and pulled the strap off my shoulder as he went the other way.

I grasped the strap, forcing him to stop. "No, no, no. When I was there with Kit it only took one touch on the surface, and the waters were swimming with selkie."

Mane tapped at his collarbone and gave a sharp tug at the strap. "That's because Kit is selkie, it recognized her. What do you think, that every time a pikaki drinks from the lake it sets off their alarms? They ignore most creatures because they're not a threat to them. Only selkie live underwater. Only selkie pose a threat to selkie, at least in their minds."

"So you're saying that we could just take a swim and no one would notice? But Lake Mavrovo is several days journey from here." Mane wasn't telling me the truth, but I did believe that he cared for Kit. Since I couldn't control magic enough to travel through the portals I didn't have much choice but to trust him.

"Any lake will do. They all connect to one another."

I dropped the strap and let him sling it across his chest then rushed to catch up with him. "How will we know where they are holding Aric?"

"We won't know, but I suspect you can find out." He motioned to the amulet.

"I have been trying really hard to keep him out of my head." In order to locate Aric I would have to let my shields down. Ever since Dooley taught me how to erect a shield around my mind I had used it to keep Aric out. But I didn't have to do it until we got close. I didn't need him in my mind any longer than necessary.

The shaman joined the other dwarves and Franca's mother at wishing us good-bye. Pika gave several more yaps, but he seemed content with the old shaman. He was, after all, a creature of the Underworld like the dwarves. Solid ground was where he belonged.

I embraced Franca's mother, and she handed me a satchel of dwarven goodies. We renewed our promises to see one another again. After everyone else had left, the shaman remained behind. He shuffled forth and whispered well wishes into my ear.

He reached to shake Mane's hand and abruptly pulled away. "We recognize you."

"Nice to see you again, old man," said Mane.

The shaman's eyes flashed red and I knew that it was the demon speaking and not the old dwarf. "You seem to be settling into your skin well after all these years."

"I wish I could say the same thing about you." Mane stood up straighter, his shoulders back and his feet in a wide stance as if he was expecting some kind of verbal onslaught.

The shaman waved his hand in dismissal. "We all choose our paths."

"We don't all get the option of choice." Mane leaned forward, and the shaman's eyes flamed bright in response.

I grabbed Mane's arm. "I don't know what this is all about but you need to leave it be."

"Oh, yes, you did have the option. Your choice was made before ever this was brought down upon you," said the demon.

The muscles in Mane's arm were rigid and the cords in his neck bulged. "I'm sure we will cross paths again." Mane gave a slight bow and took my arm, pulling me with him as we exited Mount Elbrus.

I pulled a cleansing breath into my lungs and realized that Mane still had hold of my arm. "Are we going to hold hands all the way to Mavrovo?"

He cursed under his breath and dropped my arm. He darted his eyes from side to side, looking for the best way into the Riparian and out of this conversation.

"So you know the shaman?" I moved so that I was standing in front of him. He could try and ignore me but if we were going to work together I needed to know what his story was.

"We are both creatures who have walked Underworld for many cycles." He reached into his vest and pulled out a piece of dried meat, ripping into it with vigor. As he pulled it away his lips were peppered with red dust. Mane's eyes closed, his head tipping back as he swallowed.

"Funny, you don't strike me as old."

He shoved the rest of the meat into his pocket. "And you strike me as very young." He knocked into my shoulder as he passed by me.

"Not as young as Kit." Mane stopped in his tracks but refused to turn around. His fists clenched and unclenched at his sides.

"There's much more to Kit than you know."

There's much more to you that I don't know. We trudged through the depths of the forest mostly in silence. He used a short blade to hack through the dense undergrowth. The last of the day was giving way to night as we reached a natural clearing. Waves of a small lake at its center reflected in the moonlight. The entire journey had been uneventful. The forest held no sign of elves or any other creatures for that matter.

I dipped my hand into my satchel which Mane had returned to me and munched on a handful of the spiny angelica nuts from Franca's mother. My stomach was unsettled, and I wasn't sure if it was because I was hungry or if it was something else. Hard to trust your gut if all it wants is food.

"What is the plan?" I think I blinked a few times when I realized Mane had stripped out of his clothes with only his loincloth remaining. His shorts and vest were folded tight and tucked in the waistband. The moonlight was bright enough for me to see the sculpted muscles of his thighs. He turned around, and I remembered the sight of him at the ritual. I think I swallowed one too many times because my mouth suddenly went dry.

"Getting ready to take a swim. You can go in wearing all of your clothes, but they will only weigh you down."

I zipped up the front of my jacket. The blade at my side was growing heavy, but there was no way I was going to be without it. "I think I will take my chances."

"Suit yourself."

I know I had seen Mane in comprising positions several other times, but with no one else to distract his libido I shied from his nudity.

"I'll just make sure I have everything strapped down okay." I busied myself with securing my satchel to my body.

Mane took a step closer to me. "You really have nothing to worry about. Despite what you have seen I share this body with only one."

"I don't want your body."

"Everyone wants it." He dipped his gaze and looked directly at me, a playful grin teasing at the corners of his mouth.

"You may think you are hot stuff, but you've never met Dooley. He puts that to shame." I pointed at Mane's loincloth stretched tight across his manhood which bulged against the fabric. My statement came out as unconvinced as I was. But it didn't matter. The only one I wanted was Dooley.

"Valora, I am waiting for you. Please hurry."

I pressed my hands to my temples.

Mane grabbed my wrist. "Is he speaking with you? What does he say?"

"Just as demanding as ever. Basically he wants us to hurry up."

"Ladies first. You will need to lead the way." Mane held up the vial of blue liquid in a toast to me and I did the same with mine. "To safe and quick travels." He downed it in one gulp.

As the thick potion hit my stomach all of the air pushed out of my lungs with a whooshing sound. I jumped forward into the shallow pool which seemed like no more than a glistening bog. The lake was only three feet deep if that.

Mane jumped in behind me and shot forward. I took an involuntary breath, and the coarse waters with all their grit and grime flooded my lungs. Mane swam over and put a hand around my amulet, dragging me forward by my neck. I struggled to free myself from him, and he held a finger to his lips. He pointed in front of him and whispered into my ear. "She has not seen us yet."

I froze in shock. My hand went to my blade. The pool we were in dipped down deeper in the center. At the bottom a yellowish ring of light encircled a large boulder. Sitting atop that boulder was what appeared to be an elven woman, her pointed ears peeking out from a flowing mane of bright red hair. But it wasn't an elf, it was a nereid. She was surrounded by her flowing white soul shawl. Destroying a nereid's shawl was the only known way to kill it. And we had one other problem. Men were powerless against the nereid as was evident by the stunned look on Mane's face as it turned toward us.

The nereid hadn't seen us before, but it saw us now. From the nereid's feet came its pet, a giant eel which swirled a tornado of water around the nereid before straightening out and coming towards us. Mane might not be able to deal with the nereid, but it went without saying that the eel was all his. Mane pulled a short metal rod from inside his loincloth.

"I knew that wasn't all you in there."

"There's plenty left, believe me, darling." He put one hand on each side of the rod and pulled, lengthening it into a lethal spear. "You might want to ask that nereid if she will let you borrow that shawl. And if she does let you, make sure you keep it."

I couldn't even laugh at his joke considering that if I did not succeed we would both likely be dead. The swirling tornado dissipated, and the eel pursued Mane. Each foe seemed to know his opponent. As the waters cleared I uttered the only thing that seemed appropriate at the time. "Shit!"

The boulder sat before me and the nereid was gone. I turned but it was too late. The nereid had her shawl around my neck before I could move. She put her feet into the small of my back and pulled the shawl tight against my throat. Of course, since I wasn't breathing air, she would have to pull really hard to cut off the supply of water to my lungs. But I was still at a disadvantage.

I watched Mane battle the eel as I struggled with the tightening cloth. He deftly plunged the spear into the side of the eel again and again, the water surrounding him turning red and reflecting in his eyes.

Mane turned towards me and froze. He was helpless and he knew it. The nereid had power over men and didn't usually have to defend herself. I wasn't sure exactly what Mane was, but he was definitely a man. The nereid's power of him was proof of that if nothing else.

I pried my fingers under the cloth of the shawl and was able to create a small space. "Did I ever tell you that I killed an echidna last time a water bitch like you tried to get between me and my man? Now it's your turn."

I slid my blade between my neck and the shawl and tried to push outwards. The nereid pulled, and the blade bit into my collarbone, but it also bit through the shawl, cutting it in two. As the shawl dissolved before me, so did the nereid. Both turning into formless water. But the damage was done. I grabbed at my chest as I watched Mane come towards me. The eel floated dead in the water. The red water. So much blood and I didn't know what belonged to me and what belonged to the eel.

Mane gripped his hand around my amulet and seemed to grit his teeth in pain. The amulet pulsed brightly below his hand and he screamed out, his face twisted and his eyes glowing bright red. There was no mistaking it that time. Mane had said there was something more to Kit than I knew. But I was right, there was more to know about Mane as well.

∂∘⩘

"What the hell was that?" My amulet had sucked a wave of power from Mane, and the ruined wound at my chest closed. But that was not what I was wondering about. What I wanted to know was how an elf's eyes glowed red. I didn't know much about elves, but that was certainly not normal. The only one whose eyes I knew went red were those of the shaman when the demon was talking through him.

"If you have two people in there I need to know now," I demanded. Time was short but not that short.

Mane quickly recovered. "I have no time to explain to you now, but I can tell you that the only soul in this body is mine. If we do not hurry then this potion will wear off before we gather Aric and we will both drown underwater."

The mention of souls and Mane had me wondering if the word Soulstealer really meant something more than the fable that Aric had made up as a cover story. "Would you drown?"

"This body would, yes. Lead the way, Valora Delos. Drop your shields and let Aric guide us to where he is."

I looked warily at Mane. If there were things I didn't know about him, what was I supposed to do? I had to remember that coming for Aric was my idea, and Mane was right. This potion wouldn't last forever. In fact, I wasn't sure how long it would last. I only hoped that Aric wasn't too difficult to find.

I placed my hands at my temples, trying to focus on the brick wall I had built in my mind. I pushed as hard as I could against it, and the wall slowly dissolved. Suddenly I was thrust forward into Aric's field of vision. I felt him heave a sigh of relief, but he said nothing. That was likely because at that moment he was facing the last two people I wanted to see and for very different reasons. The sparkling green-blue hair of Queen Elemi floated in the water partially blocking a figure which sat in the corner of the room. As the current moved her hair to the side I saw who it was. Kit was pleading with her mother, a pained stare on her face as she stole a glance at Aric.

"You need to let him go. He is connected to Valora. If you hurt him it will hurt her," she said.

"You think I care about the Princess when her father has declared war on us?" Queen Elemi bared the sharpened points of her teeth as she spoke.

"King Delos is upset because he knows Aric is connected to Valora, and besides, he is a betrayer of the fae of Dell'Aria." Kit pointed at Aric. "They are the ones who should punish him." Kit's pleas were obviously falling on deaf ears.

"Listen to that pretty little lady of yours, Elemi, she has a good point."

The Queen approached Aric, hit his face with a closed

fist, and I tasted blood in my own mouth.

"Why do you have to provoke her?" I demanded.

"Oh, hello my dear, so nice of you to finally show up when I am about to be executed. I thought perhaps before she did so I would let her know what I was thinking. You know, since I have been so close lipped these last few months here in her possession."

"I would not even be here if not for Dooley."

"Yes, yes, I know you want to save my precious little brother. I can help you with that as well. But the only way for me to do that is for you to get me out of here."

"Where are they holding you hostage?"

Aric stopped talking and let me see a picture in his mind. He was not bound, but the room he was in was impenetrable, and there were guards at all times. Large selkie who would pluck his wings off as easily as a small child plucked the wings from a fly.

"Just make sure that Kit is out of the way. I don't want her to get hurt," I instructed.

"That girl has a mind of her own."

"Then just shut up and don't get yourself killed in the next few hours."

"Yes, Ma'am."

I broke my mental bond with Aric and told Mane all that I had seen, including the fact that Kit was right in the line of fire. "We will get them both out," he said.

"You know Kit's mother won't let her get very far." I tried to talk some sense into Mane. The best plan would be to remove Aric and leave Kit. If Kit came with us it would only create a worse situation for her.

"There are ways of solving every problem."

"And creating new ones." Mane wasn't going to leave her here and I couldn't fight him. After all, I was trying to get to Earth for Dooley even though everyone was telling me to stay put.

We swam deeper into the eddies which ran at the bottom of the lake. A super-conductor ocean highway. The currents were strong, and I grasped Mane's arm before dipping my toe into the fast moving water. They swept us down and pulled us through a series of underwater passages. I once heard Queen Elemi say that all of these lakes fed into Mavrovo. I only hoped I heard right, because there was no map to guide us. The only thing I knew for certain was that Aric had gotten himself into a very bad position.

CHAPTER SEVEN

Mane and I were spit out from the underwater tunnel system and immediately tangled ourselves in a mass of deep red seaweed. Through the thick blades I spied my first glance at the nerve center of the Water Realm, the kingdom of the selkie ruled by Queen Elemi.

If I wasn't short on time I might be able to appreciate the wonders of Queen Elemi's kingdom more. At the center of the pool was a great gothic spired castle. A mixture of the fae temple and castle all rolled into one. According to Kit the selkie did not pray to the Goddess Varuna. They had no priests and from the look of it the only thing they revered was themselves.

It was breathtaking and fearsome at the same time. Sharpened black spikes sat atop the peak of each turret, and a large central spire rose up from the center like a giant blade. Parked around the base of the curtain wall were dozens of the black metal chariots that Queen Elemi had first ridden out to meet me in. The selkie swam beneath the portcullis which sat open. Mane was right, it didn't seem like we had set off their alarms.

"Okay, I got us here, now how do you propose that we get inside and get him out?"

Mane's eyes followed the traffic of selkie around the castle walls, their beautiful fish-like tails allowing them to swim through the water with grace, something we definitely lacked.

"I may have to sacrifice this body." I jerked my head back at his abrupt statement.

"I can't let you do that." I gripped his shoulder, my hand trembling. "Do you understand me? You are not going to sacrifice yourself for me. That has already been done and I don't think I can bear it again. No, I will find another way. There must be another way."

Mane reached down and put his hand over mine. "This body might be gone, but I cannot be killed, Valora."

"Is now the time where you explain to me how that works?"

He shook his head.

"I didn't think so. So you'll just have to listen to me. Besides, I happen to know that Kit likes 'that body' and would probably sink her teeth into me if she knew I had anything to do with you losing it."

"Yes, if I lose this body I will lose her."

"Then that is it. You keep that body, and we find another way."

We sat amongst the seaweed and watched the selkie, waiting to see if there was any pattern to their movements, something that might give us a chance to slip through unnoticed. As we did we saw a familiar wave of blue hair as Kit swam outside the castle walls. She seemed to have a direction in mind but then stopped dead in her tracks. Her gaze flicked briefly to where we had bedded down in the weeds.

"Does she see us in here?" I whispered.

"Her blood calls to mine."

"When did you two become blood brothers?"

"No kin would do what we did."

I held my hand up. "Forget I asked. I don't want her coming over here. The Queen probably has someone following her at all times."

Kit stopped and then swam back into the castle. She returned moments later and came towards us. As she passed by she dropped a small package before swimming forward into the eddy behind us which carried her into the underground passageways. Mane and I flattened ourselves in amongst the weeds as four large selkie followed behind her. Her bodyguards.

I unwrapped the small package and inside were two vials of liquid. A bright green-gold mix that sparkled with light. "I suppose Kit wants us to drink these."

"I was getting thirsty anyway."

"But then what do we do? We don't even know what this stuff does." Before I could say anything else Mane had uncorked the vial and shoved the contents into his mouth lest any disappear into the water.

His body shuddered and convulsed. I immediately pressed myself atop him to stop him from stirring up the water too much and revealing our location. I felt something growing beneath my stomach, against my thighs and down to my toes. Mane's face wore a slight grin. "I told you everyone wanted me." He flipped me over onto my back and floated into the water before me showing off his new selkie tail. The perfect disguise.

"Time to drink up, darling."

After I underwent the transformation there was still one slight problem. I had a selkie tail, but I also still had my short black fae wings. Selkie didn't have wings, and now I had both.

"What the hell am I supposed do now?"

Mane pulled some of the larger pieces of seaweed from the ground. "We'll call it a new fashion statement. He wrapped the seaweed around my middle, pinning my wings flat to my back, and tied it in the front.

If I had to breathe it might have been a problem. Good thing I didn't. Again I reached out in my mind to Aric. I could see that he was alone. Queen Elemi was nowhere to be seen, and that was because she was right in front of us. I slammed into Mane's back as he came to an abrupt halt.

"I know you." She pointed at Mane as I cowered behind him. Even with a tail and my wings hidden I was pretty sure she wouldn't mistake me for anyone else other than the daughter of the king who had apparently declared war on her.

"You don't know as much as you think you do."

I couldn't believe what I had just heard. The only thing Mane was going to succeed at was putting us both out of our misery very quickly. There was a pause where neither one of them said a thing. The selkie gathered around us in a large circle, all of them waiting on their Queen's command. We were surrounded.

"I'll have what you need very soon. There was no need to check up on me," said the Queen in a hushed voice.

"Then I'll report as such, dear Queen. You can hardly expect Ravanna to allow you to work in solitary."

"What are you here for?" Elemi's voice became clipped. She wasn't used to being the one taking orders.

"For your prisoner."

"I'm not done with him yet."

"Yes, you are."

❧❦

Mane didn't wait for the Queen's reply. He deftly pulled me around the side of him and hugged me to his front as he moved past the Queen, totally masking my presence.

"I need you to be quiet and not ask any questions right now," he whispered into my ear. "You need to tell me where he is."

I was surprised with the show of power and the declarations he had made before the Queen. I dropped the shields in my mind again. The room Aric was in was barren but familiar. He was still on the Peixes. The airship that had carried him away as his execution was ordered, but it was underwater. It was here somewhere.

"He is in the ship. It can't be far."

"Let him guide you, Valora. We are running out of time and air."

"I have already dropped my shields."

"Are you always this stubborn?" Mane blew a current of bubbles from his pursed lips. "Let him inside your mind. He has obviously let you inside of his, but unless you allow him to guide you we will never find him."

I wasn't sure exactly what Mane meant, but I knew that I didn't want to do it. Aric was a murderer and a liar. He couldn't be trusted, and yet I had to trust him with my life. "I'm afraid of what he'll do if he is inside my thoughts."

"If you are that afraid, he obviously already is inside your mind. You're more scared of your reaction," said Mane. He stopped in the hall and a wave of guilt blasted right through me. I had let him carry me in front of him, sheltered by his massive size, doing nothing while he was doing the actual work of getting us out of there.

I stepped back from Mane's grip and grabbed hold of

the amulet at my neck. The only way I could think to let Aric in was to make myself pretend that I trusted him. I tried to pull on a memory of a time when I had. The time we were in his carriage, before I had left on my first mission to Earth. He had given me my first kiss. At the time I believed he was infected with the Blight and I had vowed to bring him a cure. I couldn't have cared more desperately for him in any other moment.

Aric's mind sensed me and reached out. The tendrils of his thoughts wound around me, turning my decision making into his own. What he wanted I wanted. I took a few steps forward, stopping abruptly.

"Are you coming? We don't have all day."

Despite the graceful tail I wore I jerked down the hall, my mind shifting between my own control and Aric's. Both of us trying to determine where he was and where I was in reference to him. We finally came upon a spectacular set of doors. They shot upwards framing the high vaulted ceiling that rose sharply in front of us.

I placed my hand at the door. The wood was rough and dry beneath my palm, protected from the water by magic. "He is behind here."

Mane gently pushed me aside, put both his hands on the door and braced his feet against the floor. He pushed hard against it, the veins at his temples bulging with his effort. The door gave way but I wasn't prepared for the sight before us. "Seriously?"

"Looks like she has added to her collection. Damn! This is the sweetest ride I have ever seen!" Mane strode forward, pumped with testosterone at the sight of all the metal and machinery that dominated the wide open space. He pulled his hand along the tailfin of a vehicle which was carved in the image of the many motorized machines I had seen while

I was on Earth. "Do you know what this is?"

"A distraction. That is what we are here for." I pointed to the far side of the expanse at the Peixes which had seen better days. Its delicate wings were ripped to shreds. I choked back the emotion that welled forth. I had created a life for myself aboard that ship with Kali. Everyone else thought I was useless but aboard that ship, through my job as a Hunter, I had been able to prove them wrong. Now I had neither one. Father had deemed all Hunters as Guardians of Dell'Aria, and the Peixes lay broken and battered at my feet. Somehow it made it all the more real.

Mane followed my gaze and came to stand by my side. "He's in there. Let's go get him and get out of here."

The hull of the ship had broken in half. I could only assume that Aric had been placed in the room we had kept the prisoners in, a room which once held the sweet berries of Allbaruth. The name flooded into my mind, and I remembered stealing aboard the transport ship one day when I was very small as it made its way to one of the outlying colonies. I didn't dare move when the ship docked, but I hid behind a barrel of rice wine as the crew loaded and unloaded the goods we used to barter with. We gave them our ice fruits and they gave us the sweet voluptuous berries. I remembered the crew loading them and the ship taking off. As it hummed back into the port of Dell'Aria I stuck my hand deep into one of the crates of berries, relishing the feel of the soft skin and the juices bursting against my fingers. I didn't dare steal one for fear that they had counted them all, but I pulled my fingers from the barrel and relished in the juices as I licked them from my fingers.

Yummy.

I was pulled to the present again as Aric's voice echoed in my mind. The guards were gone, he wasn't bound, what was stopping him from walking out on his own?

☙◦❧

As we reached the door I noticed something odd. "That isn't the knob that was on that door." In place of the wooden handle that was once to the door to the cell where we kept the prisoners was a knob carved out of a jagged crystalline substance which only emitted a dull glow.

"The Queen has a sense of humor and she's smart," said Mane. "What was it the fae of Dell'Aria used to call your former King?"

"The Dragon."

Mane's lip curled as he spoke. "She has captured The Dragon with 'dragon's blood.' How appropriate."

"That's dragon's blood?"

"Not the same as what we recently encountered. It's the other name for this mineral. It's also called cinnabar or mercury. It seems she knows a little more about Aric then we do."

This was more information than I could handle at the moment. "Look, I am going to want you to explain this all to me, but…"

"Right." Mane reached out towards the doorknob, and I grabbed his wrist.

"Wait, won't it harm you?"

"Not in the slightest, and it won't harm you either. It is only a deterrent to Aric." The door swung open, and I caught the knob as Mane went inside. I gave a quick tug and it popped off in my hand. I shoved it into my satchel. If it was a deterrent to Aric there might come a time when I would need it.

Inside Aric stood in the middle of the room as if he was there to greet us for a cocktail party. His legs were still

92

wrapped in his white leather pants and the silken straps still surrounded his torso, the same as the day I first met with him in his Chambers. However, this time he also wore some contraption on his face which bubbled out the sides.

You'll have to excuse the mask, it was kind of Queen Elemi to give me a way to breath down here, but it's not all that nice to look at.

I spoke aloud. "This is Mane, a friend of Kit's. We are here to get you out because that is apparently what I need to do in order for me to see Dooley again. Don't think it means anything else."

Aric bowed deeply. "Of course not, princess. I'd never think anything different." The glint in his dark blue eyes told me another story.

We rushed into the garage and I felt a choking sensation, like I had eaten something and it went down the wrong tube. Mane clutched at his throat. "The potion is weakening. We will never make it to the surface before we drown."

This could be a problem. Aric's voice echoed in my head.

"Not a problem for you since you seem to have the breathing thing covered."

I won't let anything happen to you.

The doors swung open and Kit shot inside, barreling into Mane and wrapping her legs around his waist.

Now that is a greeting.

Shut it.

"Darling, darling, I missed you, too, but we have a problem." Mane gripped his throat and the same sensation seized me again. "We need to find a quick way out of here."

Kit held up a set of keys and pointed towards a sleek black car, tail-fins piped in red and a design on the front like a Cyclops eye. "The Edsel."

"Exactly how are we supposed to drive a car out of here?" I asked.

"The same way my mother got all these down here."

I reluctantly flopped down next to Aric in the backseat. Kit took the driver's seat and Mane slumped in the passenger side next to her. We were both starting to experience the effects of the oxygen leaking from our bloodstreams. When it was all gone we would drift off and not awaken. We needed to get out of there soon. My temporary fins began to unknit themselves.

"Are you going to be able to do this yourself?" asked Mane.

"Don't worry, I think the key works just as well as your magic." She winked at him. There was a story there for another day.

Kit put the key in the ignition and turned. Surprisingly the engine revved awake underwater. I knew that the selkie had strong magic, but this was nothing short of amazing. Kit placed her finger on the dash. "Shall we go visit Dooley?"

I clasped the amulet at my chest. *If only it were that easy.* "But, Kit, my father won't let me through the portals."

Kit plucked the red cat eye glasses from her head and slid them on. "Your father doesn't control all of the highways out of here."

She pressed the pedal down to the floor, and the car started to spin. The circular motion and lack of air made me dizzy. I lay back, and Aric's arm was there. He tugged me close beside him. I was beyond the ability to fight him. As I drifted off I felt the press of something around my cheeks. Suddenly I was able to breathe again. Aric had taken off his mask and placed it over my face. I looked over and he was holding his breath.

Take a few deep breaths. We'll be out of this soon.

After I took two deep inhales he brought the mask to his face and did the same before passing it back to me. Mane's eyes rolled into his head. The light surrounding the car reminded me of the lights I had seen when Kit and I were inside the portal. I squeezed my eyes shut trying to ward off the sickness in my stomach, and when I opened them we were back. The car sat in the driveway of Dooley's little cabin in the woods. Pryn sat on a rocking chair on the porch, his hands gripping the armrests. Uncle Artemus came flying out of the front door and abruptly halted.

I opened my mouth and realized we were still surrounded in water. Uncle Artemus ran to the door of the Edsel and pulled it open. Aric and I tumbled out onto the ground along with a torrent of water. He landed on his back and I landed on top of him. That's when Dooley walked out onto the porch.

CHAPTER EIGHT

I leapt off Aric as fast as I could and raced up the steps. As I approached Dooley he held his hand out, stopping me in my tracks. "What is he doing here?"

"It's a long story, but there was no other way."

"Are you certain of that?" There was no mistaking Dooley's anger. I could also tell he was terribly weak. I remembered the first time I saw him step out onto this porch in the light. He had exuded confidence and strength, now he was barely able to stand.

"Dooley, we need to get you to bed to rest."

"You didn't answer me."

"Of course it was the only way. What else would it be?" A thickness settled into my throat as the lies spilled forth. The truth was that I wasn't sure yet what good it was to rescue Aric. I only knew that everyone was telling me it was what I needed to do.

And perhaps you missed me.

I slammed the shields down tight in my mind.

"My brother can be very persuasive, especially where you are concerned." Dooley widened his stance and clutched one fist inside the other, cracking his knuckles.

Aric picked that moment to approach from behind me. "Looks like you healed well since we last saw one another, brother. Sorry about the scar."

Aric had tortured Dooley almost to the point of death. I had no idea what scars remained on the inside of Dooley from that encounter, but on the outside a thin darkened scar on the left side of his face from the corner of his eye to his cheekbone crinkled as he clenched his jaw.

Mane hopped onto the porch behind Aric. Thankfully he had slid his shorts and vest on. "Are we all glad to see one another again? I'd like to say we would love to stay and chat, but we don't have much time. In twenty-four hours we will need to return to the Realms." He looked from Dooley to Aric and back at me. His eyes widened slightly. "And this looks like a disaster waiting to happen."

I ignored his last comment. "What are you talking about?" Only twenty-four hours to figure out how to help Dooley and fix the mess I made. Great.

"I just had a quick chat with Kit and she won't last here for long. There are ways her stay could be prolonged but I would like to avoid the attention of the local authorities. We have a day." Mane's voice was final. "If your father did close the portals to you, Valora, you will be stuck here unless he reopens them."

A situation I was all too familiar with. But this time things were different. "Fine then let me be stuck here. I need to be with Dooley."

"I think it's time that I explain to all of you some things you will need to know going forward from here. You are all in a lot of danger, and hiding out here on Earth won't save you from it."

"Don't listen to that demon." Pryn stood up from his

chair and pointed at Mane. Uncle Artemus went to stand behind him, his salt and pepper hair matching the coloration of his wings which were spread wide.

"Demon? He's an elf," I said, not understanding why Pryn would say such a thing.

Mane's eyes narrowed as he stared back at Pryn. Kit scooted the dirt beneath her bare feet, refusing to look at me.

"A demon in elf's clothing," shouted Pryn.

"You're not really treating us all equally, now are you? Pryn, we had an understanding." Mane held his arms up and seemed to briefly study Dooley.

"We did, so long as your pursuits were the selkie girl and not Valora. You have crossed the line, Mane."

Mane's eyes glowed red. "I don't know anything about lines, old man. What I do know is that if you and your kind continue to keep the fae in the dark about Acheron and the gods below then you all will become their puppets. They will steal all your souls."

"Did you know he was a demon?" I asked Kit the question, but I already knew the answer. She hadn't so much as flinched after Pryn leveled his accusation. I couldn't keep the hurt from my voice. Kali had betrayed me, now Kit. I wasn't sure if there was anyone left that I could really trust.

Kit recoiled at the accusation in my voice. She took a few steps back from Mane, her full expression hidden behind her dark glasses, but her mouth stood agape. She raced down the steps and into the forest. Mane raced after her.

"Shouldn't we go after them?" I asked to everyone and no one in particular, but none of them moved.

Uncle Artemus waved off in the direction they had fled. "We don't need that demon's advice."

"Are you kidding me? You all just tell me, he tells us, that he is a demon and you don't care?"

They've done a lot alone in the woods, and they certainly didn't need your help. I glared at Aric who just couldn't seem to stop intruding on my thoughts. He gave a curt smirk, one that wasn't lost on Dooley. Dooley and I had been able to connect memories during rituals, but the amulet gave Aric the power to tap straight into my emotions.

"The only demon I care about is that one." Dooley jabbed his finger towards Aric who stood so close behind me that the tips of my wings fluttered against his chest. "This is my land. You need to get off my property. I don't care if you return here in a day to disappear back to the Realms but I will not spend my dying breaths in your presence."

"It doesn't have to be this way." The exclamation poured from my mouth before I knew what I was saying.

Aric placed his hands on my shoulders. "Yes, brother, we can all get along, can't we?"

I shirked Aric's hands off my shoulders, but not quickly enough.

A look of shock crossed Dooley's face. I might as well have slapped him. It quickly morphed into a wall of nothing. "Fine, then go along with him." He turned and braced himself on the door frame as his legs buckled.

"Dooley!" I rushed forward.

"Get her out of here!" he roared as he collapsed forward onto his knees. Pryn rushed to catch him by the arm as Artemus came to me. He circled his hand around my upper arm as he gently guided me away.

"My dear sweet niece, perhaps it is best if you find a place for Aric to stay and return here alone. Dooley's emotional state is being affected by his illness. I am sure he didn't really mean that he didn't want to see you."

But that was exactly how it felt. "But, Uncle, I came all this way to be by his side."

"And he will still be here in a few hours." My uncle guided me towards the car. "Return as quick as you can. You can't blame him for not wanting to be in the presence of this traitor."

Aric crossed his arms over his chest. "Great, so I'm infamous here as well?"

Artemus narrowed his eyes, his words coming out slow and pointed. "You are lucky that I have to abide by the humans' rules or I would carry out the King's orders of execution here and now."

"Yes, that and a little matter of, if I die your niece dies. Don't stress yourself out too much, Artemus. That vein at your temple looks like it is about to burst from the strain of all your restraint." Aric crossed his arms. I pushed him down the stairs towards the car, trying to put distance between the two of them.

I had never seen my peaceful uncle look so ferocious. The only thing keeping me alive right now was this amulet, and the only thing keeping Aric alive was the fact that the amulet was attached to my life force. But with a mouth like he had I wasn't even sure that would last for long.

Artemus shut the door behind him as he retreated into the cabin. My heart felt like it was bleeding inside my chest.

"What's the plan, my Queen?"

I pushed Aric firmly this time in the chest with both of my hands, causing him to take a few steps backwards. "You don't get to call me your Queen. You don't get to call me anything."

A few moments went by and I watched Aric's cool resolve melt before me. He sat on the hood of the car and ran a hand over his face, clutching his chin.

"I really didn't come to antagonize you, Valora. The only thing I have ever wanted is for you to be happy and to return my love. I know asking for the return of your love is beyond hope for me. You'll have to forgive me for the fact that my displeasure at that fact causes my comments to become crass. I still want for you to be happy." Aric delivered his speech in a monotone fashion. No inflections which would make me think he hadn't really meant what he said.

"I'd be happy if I found a way to cure Dooley."

"That I can help you with, but I am afraid that the only way I know how won't make you too happy."

Kit and Mane crashed through the brush to our left catching me off guard. Mane had Kit cradled in his arms and she was giggling wildly.

"I am guessing you found her all right." As Aric spoke, he brought his fingers to his long white blond hair and attempted to tie it out of his face. He was getting nowhere.

"Here, let me." I walked over and brushed my fingers through his silken tresses. I took the two long sections at the front and began to tie them in a lose knot.

"Yes, he found me." Kit jumped down from Mane's arms and slowly stepped towards me. "Valora, I'm sorry I didn't tell you, and I'm sorry I ran away. I've known about Mane, but there didn't seem to be any good time to tell you. I hate for you to be angry with me. I wasn't trying to hide anything from you. He's not bad."

"Don't tell her I'm not bad, you'll ruin my reputation. What she means is that I'm not evil." Mane slid his arm around Kit's waist and smiled down at her.

Mane still owed me a big explanation, but I would be blind if I didn't see that he definitely cared for Kit.

"What happened here?" Kit looked at my hands

wrapped around Aric's hair and then at Dooley's cabin which was shut up tight, the faded orange curtains pulled closed over the windows.

Aric's hair fell from my fingers. "We need to find another place to stay tonight."

"If you will let me, I can assist with that," said Aric.

"I'm not sure we have much choice at this point. Do you want to drive?" asked Mane.

"I would love to!" Aric grabbed the keys from Mane and the two let loose a series of claps and slaps which obviously was man code for "Sweet ride" or something to that effect.

Mane assured Kit that as long as she sat up front Aric should be able to drive the Edsel, her mother having imbued her with power over the car.

"Now don't do anything stupid," she advised Aric. "I need to make sure this car makes it back in one piece to my mother, or she'll kill me."

I leaned forward from the rear seat where Mane had just slid in beside me. "Kit, you don't think a little thing like stealing selkie potion or dating a demon might put you on your mother's naughty list?"

"Oh, she is definitely on the naughty list," said Mane.

"Forget I asked."

☙❧

Aric drove the Edsel down the winding roads that led away from Dooley's cabin and finally brought us out onto the main highway. The last time I passed through this way was in the backseat of Ralph's cruiser. My mission as a Hunter had given me purpose. Now I had been set adrift. Given the role as a Guardian, but of what? My father told me that the Guardians were meant to protect Dell'Aria but I couldn't even protect Dooley. Aric had offered to help, but his brand of help always seemed to cause more problems. Out of habit, I clutched at the amulet at my throat.

"I have already told Kit my story. Would you like to hear it as well?" asked Mane.

Aric kept his attention firmly fixed on the road, appearing downright nervous as the cars sped around us. Kit was arguing with him about how slow he was going. It was quite a comical sight.

"Mane, you have to know that Aric contacted a demon to forge the amulets we wear around our necks. Yes, the amulet keeps me alive, but it also makes me connected to Aric in ways I am not too happy about. Demons are kind of on my naughty list."

"Yes, I can see how you would feel that way. I'm not here to make you like me, Valora. But I do believe that you are owed an explanation. Should we part ways I would wish you well and never expect you to return the sentiment."

There wasn't much for me to say to that. I stared at Mane, willing him to continue on his own. If he thought I deserved an explanation, then he better get on with it.

"Right. I will try and keep my tale brief. Your priests have told you of the Goddess Varuna. You build temples to her and worship her birthplace at Winter Haven. But they have left out a very important piece of information. There are gods above in the Elysium, but there are also gods below in Acheron. Some call them demons, but this is all in one's perspective. I just consider it a different zip code. The gods above and the gods below have always been at cross purposes. Both are very powerful magic users."

"Where do you fall in all this?" Mane wanted to give me a history lesson and I just wanted to know where he stood.

"I was a demon residing in Acheron. While the gods of the Elysium are allowed free access to the Realms, we are cut off from it. The gods below were not happy with that. They have tried for centuries to find access to the Realms which owe them as much thanks for everything in Underworld, just as the Goddess Varuna is owed thanks for everything created in Overworld. But the gods of the Elysium made sure long ago that the gates between the Realms and Acheron would remain closed. It is said that is because of the strife the gods of Acheron caused in Underworld and the black magic that seemed to burble forth from their presence and those that worshiped them. Still, there are those that want the gates open and they are powerful. I disagreed with them. So I was banished into the body of a newborn elf. His soul was stolen from his body and destroyed and I was left to be trapped inside the infant and live and breathe within this form. This is why I told you that I would never die. But if this form is destroyed, I will be resurrected in the body of another infant and another soul will be stolen. I do not want that. All because I did not agree that the gates should be opened."

"Your kind are Soulstealers?" I asked. Aric had coined the term as part of his political rhetoric. Something to distract the people of Dell'Aria so that they wouldn't notice he was the one who was stealing the magic that cost them their lives. But he didn't actually steal their souls, not like Mane had just described.

"You didn't think I came up with that fancy term all my own, did you?" The car veered to the right as Aric looked over his shoulder at me.

"Watch the road!" Kit grabbed the wheel and straightened it out.

A heavy sigh left my chest. Dealing with Aric was going to be exasperating. "So if you leave this body the soul that it was meant for would not return?" I asked Mane.

"No. It has been destroyed."

I pressed my palm to my forehead. The shaman shared his conscious with a demon, and that was the first I had ever heard of such a thing. Now Mane was telling me that he was the only one in there. Therefore, his soul did belong to this body. He didn't steal the soul, someone else did. In essence he was trapped.

"Why not just destroy you?"

"You can't destroy a god." Mane leaned back against the seat and folded his hands behind him.

"First you were a demon, now you are a god?" All my life I had prayed to the Goddess Varuna. It was something all the fae of Dell'Aria did, something my mother had done. I had never imagined her to be corporeal other than when I gazed upon the statues that were erected in her honor in Winter Haven.

"It's all semantics, Valora. My soul is immortal. And that is the long and short of it."

"You still haven't explained why you said we were in danger here."

Mane sat up straighter. "I haven't had any communication with Acheron since I was banished. But I still know the signs. The ritual you witnessed a few nights before was my attempt to close the cracks between the Realms and Acheron, but I can't be sure if it worked. In fact, I don't think it did. I have been away from Acheron too long, and my magic isn't as potent."

Kit giggled.

Aric merged from one highway to another and seemed to be bringing us into the heart of the city.

"Seeing that hunk of cinnabar that Queen Elemi had used to trap Aric in his room just further confirms everything else I have witnesses recently in Mavrovo," said

Mane.

"How exactly did that hunk of rock keep me in that room? I couldn't get anywhere near the door," said Aric.

"You don't know your origins?" Mane asked. He tilted his head to the side and narrowed his eyes at Aric. "I thought for certain that you did with all I have heard about you. That your motivations were so strongly influenced by your mother."

"How in the hell would you know that?" Aric's sudden anger was barely contained. I only hoped we got to where we were going before he lost his temper.

Aric pulled off at the next exit, and the car dropped down onto a short road that faced the port of Seattle. Brick buildings dotted the waterway. Large ships laden with large metal containers trailed into the port. The purplish orange sky signaled the end of the day, reminding me of the sunsets in Overworld.

I wasn't sure how Mane could know about Dooley and Aric's mother. Dooley and I had many discussions about her which ended in Dooley telling me that I needed to stop trying to justify Aric's actions. Even though they both shared a mother, Dooley had never known her. He didn't remember when she had a memory. Aric had been several years older and remembered it all. His memory of Dooley had been erased, but he recalled everything about him once he knew. There was no reason Mane should know. Kit didn't know, I didn't tell her.

Aric shot daggers at me in the reflection of the rear view mirror. "I didn't tell him about your mother," I said, "so you can quit looking at me like that."

Mane placed his hands on the seat behind Aric. "So you do know? This is all very confusing. He knows he is half —"

"Half-fae and half-human, yes, I know," said Aric,

cutting him off. "Believe me, I know."

"Human? I suppose in a way you are correct. So then our description of your origins would have to be cut into thirds."

Aric pulled the car to the side of the road at a large brick complex. The front had clear windows and doors and inside was a grand foyer with artwork of half naked women plastered on the walls. Aric cut the ignition and faced Mane. "If there is something you know about me, spill it, demon."

"The cinnabar would never have any effect on you unless you were descended from the gods from above. From Elysium."

"You mean he is part angel?" I sputtered.

Mane raised one eyebrow. "You see, it's all words, isn't it?

CHAPTER NINE

We all managed to get up to the top floor of the building where Aric had long ago purchased a loft for his use during the time he was traveling between the Realms and Earth. He had sold enough of the magic to the locals to do so and then cut off their supply when it became clear he would need as much as he could get in order to gift me a true set of fae wings. He reached inside and flipped the light switch. The ceiling vaulted two stories high and was hung with lights that dropped down at various heights mimicking stars in the heavens.

"You see, angel," said Mane pointing to the sky.

"You seem to be missing something, Mane. His father was a King of Dell'Aria. He is part fae because his father was all fae. His mother is in a home here on Earth. She is a human. Where do you get that he is part angel in all this?"

Mane shrugged his shoulders. "I only know how cinnabar works and what I see when I look at him. The Elysium shines through him. And I know about intercourse, I can tell you about that."

"Tell me about that." Kit sidled up next to Mane.

"Really, you guys? Mane still hasn't explained how the Earth is in trouble."

"Cinnabar only comes from the realm of the gods below and here on Earth. It isn't found in the Realms. Also, Queen Elemi mentioned that she was on some kind of mission for them. She let us take Aric away because she thought I was from Acheron and checking up on her. I assume she will be very upset when she finds out from whomever she talks to that the gods below consider me a traitor."

"Hey, I am starting to like this guy. I am a traitor, too. Would you like a drink?" Aric swung around into the kitchen, reached underneath the black marble bar and brought forth a bottle of ice wine made from the ice fruits that grow only in Dell'Aria.

"How did you get that?"

"I didn't." Suddenly his genial expression changed to one of anger. He set the bottle on the counter and skirted around it, rushing towards a door off the main room which was shut. As he approached it his legs buckled and he fell to his knees.

"Damn you, bitch, I will kill you," he shouted at the door.

I pulled my sword and charged the door, kicking it inwards. There before me stood Kali, leaning over a counter covered in loose papers. She was muttering some incantation, and swirls of black mist circled the room like a whirlwind. They surrounded her then suddenly dispersed.

Kali's pale green eyes were even more brilliant against the lush jade color of the feathers of her wings. It had been so long since I had seen them I had forgotten how magnificent her wings used to be. Her hair was woven in slender braids covered at the ends with beads which clicked as she took a few steps forward.

I brought my sword before me. "Kali, I don't want any quarrel with you." She stopped and stared at me.

"I didn't mean to take you off guard. Valora, I would never attack you."

"Exactly what was it you did on the balcony the last time we saw one another, Kali? I seem to remember you grabbing for the axe in my hand and me almost plunging to my death into the crowd below."

"I wasn't going to harm you. I was planning on using it on his neck." She pointed to Aric who had risen to his feet again.

"Then what are you doing here?"

"Actually, Valora, this is a bit of a surprise for both of us."

"I would say it is nice to see you, Kali," Aric said, "but the last time we were together you were selling me off to Queen Elemi so you could come for what you wanted. I see that you got it. Did you happen to leave anything so that I could restore the memory of my mother?"

The tension in the room grew thick. "I'm afraid I had to use all you had. I did give a case of it to Artemus. He said he needed it to help Dooley." She turned to me. "I really hope it did help, Valora."

"You bitch!" Aric went for Kali, and she was gone. Literally gone. Wind swept through the loft, and I realized that a window that was closed when we came in was now open. I ran over and pressed my body against the ledge, seeking her out in the night sky.

"She wouldn't have taken flight out in the open like this."

"Are you kidding?" Aric stepped forward and peered through the window. "She has enough magic running through her that she could decide to become invisible and it wouldn't be a problem."

Aric sat down on the bench looking utterly deflated. Everything he had stolen had been stolen from him. He wanted desperately to return his mother's memory, and since he and Dooley shared a mother I couldn't help but sympathize with him.

Mane sat down next to him. "The magic she used was dark magic. Magic of the Acheron. You might want to get some air. It won't agree with you to be in the same room that ritual was performed in."

"Aric, I'm sure that they haven't used all of the magic on Dooley. And she is the mother of you both. How much will you need to restore her memory?"

"Just one vial." I was floored. Shocked. I walked over to the kitchen counter and leaned over, placing my forehead on the cool marble. All he needed this entire time was a minuscule amount. He had told me that he had continued his path of destruction because he wanted to present me with wings and until now I didn't entirely believe him.

"They share the same mother?" Mane gave a curt one note laugh. "Varuna certainly has been busy. This is very interesting."

"Is Dooley part-angel, too?" I mumbled, partly joking.

"No, I knew it the moment I saw him. Dooley is part demon."

∂∾ᔕ

My head shot up. "Are you kidding? That's impossible." Aric came up behind me and placed his hand on my shoulder. For once since everything happened I allowed him to comfort me.

"Don't worry, Valora, this demon has been making stories up all night. I'm an angel? Dooley is a demon? It all sounds ludicrous."

Mane folded his hands across his chest. "You don't need to believe me now, but you will eventually. I don't know exactly how it has happened, but it's true. And I think that the both of you are a big part of what's happening."

"You'll have to excuse me if I don't jump up and accept your explanation, Mane." I shoved my sword into my scabbard.

"You don't trust him?" Kit asked. "He has put his life on the line for you and you would rather trust the fae who killed your mother?" Kit's face wrinkled in disgust.

I brushed Aric's hand off my shoulder. But I didn't move or speak. I couldn't tell Kit that there was no way I was going to believe the word of a demon because that would mean that I was speaking ill of Mane and she was just a little more than attached to him. That much I knew to be true.

"Let's go to bed, Mane. They don't want your help." She tugged at his arm.

He bounded up the spiral staircase, following Kit to the upper loft.

"But what about Dooley? I need to get to him tonight. We were just supposed to drop Aric here and then go back. We can work this out."

"You can't drive the car without me, and I'm not going anywhere tonight, Valora. You'll just have to cuddle up with your other lover boy and see Dooley tomorrow."

Kit's words hit me like a slap in the face and were followed by a slam of the door upstairs. I was left alone with Aric, the cold breeze turning even cooler as the last of the light faded from the sky. Aric went towards the window and started to shut it.

"No, please leave it open." The cool breezes reminded

me of the nights in Dell'Aria which was where I wanted to be right now. My father told me that I shouldn't come to Earth, and he was right. Dooley didn't want me, and there was something terribly wrong with him. I couldn't deny that.

"You said you knew how to help Dooley. You said you would help him. How?"

Aric gestured towards the ice wine. "Would you like a glass? We might as well make good use of it. You're going to need it after I tell you what I'm proposing."

After Aric finished his explanation I swallowed the glass of ice wine and put it down on the counter. "Another please."

"Valora, you know it's the only way."

"There is no way he would ever agree."

"Then you would consider it?"

"I would consider anything that would help Dooley live, but I am not so sure he feels the same way."

"His love for you doesn't run as deep as yours does for him then?" Ever since Aric had revealed his proposal our conversation had been going in circles.

"You don't get it, do you, Aric? Of course, not like you ever have." I downed the second glass of ice wine and realized that it had been a while since I ate anything. I felt slightly dizzy, and Aric caught me as I teetered towards the large couch in the corner.

"Here, sit down before you fall over." He took my glass and filled it again before returning it to my hand. "Explain to me what you think I don't understand."

"Seriously?" I took another sip, letting the liquid courage take hold of me. "You destroyed the lives of so many fae. You killed my mother, even though I know that was not your intention, all because of your wish to bring me something that I would never have asked for if I knew what the consequences were."

One more sip and somehow I was transported to the time when Aric was my King and just being in his sight made me giddy. Even though my words were serious a giggle escaped my lips.

"But you didn't perform the treacherous acts. I did. I did it for you." He leaned into me and I smelled the same fresh rain and mossy scent I did the first time he was this near to me in his chambers in Dell'Aria.

I tried to shake away the fog that had settled over me and pushed his chest back. "But I would not have wanted you to. You never gave me that choice. You took it from me like you took my mother from me. And look what the result has been."

"Do not worry about Kali. I will chase her down and pluck those wings off her myself."

"Don't you see? She stole the magic to give her those wings. But if I had used the magic for wings it would have been stolen as well. Magic stolen from the people of Dell'Aria."

"Sometimes you have to do what needs to be done."

"But it didn't need to be done. That's just what I am trying to tell you." I was becoming a little sloppy. I was swallowing my third glass of wine and I still hadn't had anything to eat, but Dooley's rejection of me earlier stung and Kit's bitter words followed hard on the heels of that rejection. I wasn't sure if I was doing anything right anymore or if I knew what I was doing at all.

I pushed myself off the couch and stumbled towards the circular staircase. I had this urge to speak to Kit. I wanted to clear the air between us. I figured if I could fix anything that would be a good place to start. At the landing there was another staircase off to my right. I wasn't sure where it led, but I kept going up. I pushed at the door at the top of the staircase, and the cool wind of the outside hit my face. I had stepped onto Aric's rooftop garden. There were pots everywhere. Thin tendrils of willow wisp vine and ice fruit seedlings. In all the destruction that Aric had been responsible for, here he was trying to create life.

"I wasn't sure that I would ever be able to return to Dell'Aria after this was all over. I wanted to bring the things that I cherished back with me." Aric had followed me up the steps and slid his finger under the soft petal of one of the tender baby shoots of an ice fruit tree which had sprung from the earth.

"These can't grow anywhere but in Dell'Aria."

"They can grow when a fae from Dell'Aria tends to them. I have tried to come here as often as I could to make sure that the plant does not die. But it has not been able to grow because I am never here long enough to coax it out of its shell. It stays a tightly wound bud just waiting for me to give it the right attention." Aric fondled the tiny bud between his fingers and I felt as if I was going to burst.

Instead I tried to focus. "If we do this, what will that mean for Dooley and me?"

"I can't speak for my brother. I really only ever wanted you to be happy, Valora. To have everything your heart desired. Once upon a time that was wings and me." Aric hung his head. "I see that is not the case now."

"What you propose seems all too perfect. Something for nothing. Nothing is ever free. Not on this world and not in ours."

"Well, no. I cannot possibly anticipate how we will be affected, but it will save him." Aric took the glass from my hand instead of encouraging me to drink more. "Let's go inside. We can leave at dawn to go to Dooley's cabin."

"I want to stay up here. I want to sleep close to the stars. Maybe the Goddess will bring me the wisdom to choose the right path in the morning. Right now I'm not thinking too clearly." I lay down on my side on a wide chaise lounge and tried to get comfortable. I already had my eyes closed. Aric was no longer my concern, Dooley was. And my biggest worry was figuring out a way I could convince Dooley that the only way he could live was to follow Aric's plan. I also needed a way I could convince myself that it was a good idea.

I felt a downy cape descend upon my shoulders and was barely aware of Aric lying behind me. Perhaps it was best to let him believe he held a part of me. If he knew how I truly felt about him, I wasn't sure that he would be so willing to help Dooley, and I couldn't do this without him. That I knew for certain.

CHAPTER TEN

The next morning I awoke to the sound of Kit calling my name as she searched the house for me. She bounded through the door of the garden, carefree as usual. Seemingly unfettered by thoughts of any argument we had the night before. In a split second that look changed as she saw Aric rise up from behind me, propped up on his elbow and spooning me from behind.

"Not sure where you guys are at, but we are going to run out of time and we need to get to Dooley if we are going to see him before we have to return to Dell'Aria." She reached into her pocket and slid on her red cat eye glasses so I couldn't see her expression. The blue stone at her neck pulsed faintly.

"Is your amulet blinking?" asked Aric.

Kit touched the blue stone lightly. "Mane tells me it's because I haven't fed in a while and I need to feed or I will be too weak to make it through the portal. I was going to go out and find a little snack before we go."

"Why can't Mane help you out with that?" I asked. Mane was right. I really needed to learn more about the selkie. Kit

117

had been such a good friend to me, but I had no idea how to help her.

"Descendants of Acheron or the Elysium are strictly off diet for me. That much I was taught early on."

"Kit, can we talk really quick?" I asked.

"Sure, I have a few." Kit leaned up against the wrought iron railing, ran her hands through her long blue locks and twisted them into a bun on top of her head.

"I'll go see if Mane is up. Make us coffee or something." Aric quickly popped up from the chair and went downstairs.

"Can you possibly just boil some hot water for me?" I asked. "That coffee tastes like troll dung." Aric chuckled and descended into the loft below.

"What is it that you wanted to talk about?"

"I just wanted to make sure we're okay. Also, I feel responsible for you, Kit. Your father isn't here and I know he would expect me to be looking out for you."

"You have to know that you don't need to look out for me anymore, Valora. The Realms have changed me." She tipped her chin down as she spoke. "Totally and completely changed me. I'm not the young innocent girl you first met."

"I know that. Maybe I wish I had it together as much as you seem to. I'm about to get myself in a real bind here, Kit. Aric has come up with a plan to save Dooley. I know it's the right decision, I just don't know how to convince Dooley of that. And what if I'm being just as selfish as Aric has always been? Wanting to do anything to keep Dooley alive when it might be his wish to die?" I choked back on the last few words.

I looked up from my feet at Kit. All her limbs seemed to be frozen in place. She fell forward and caught herself on the railing just before she dropped head first to the street below. I raced to her side. The amulet blazed bright blue on her chest. "I think I might have waited too long," she said weakly.

"Do I call Mane for help?"

"Not enough time." Kit reached up and ran her finger against the throbbing vein at my throat. Her touch caught me off balance and I reached out to clutch the wrought iron railing. Big mistake. The iron sent a throbbing pain pulsing through my body.

Kit's mouth opened and she bared her fangs. Before she had a chance to enchant me with her gaze. Kit was so out of it now there would be no asking for favors from her. She had given me blood once to save my life. There was no question I would do the same. This was going to hurt even more than the iron.

I bent down closer to Kit's mouth and she shot up and clamped her powerful jaws around my neck. We fell backwards onto the deck, and Kit writhed atop me. It felt as if she might be devouring me whole. Blood gushed from my neck and from her mouth, trickling down my throat. I was swallowing my own blood. I knew that wasn't good, but there was nothing I could do to stop it.

The sound of a chair toppling over and our bodies hitting the roof must have alerted Mane and Aric because the last thing I saw was them at the top of the stairs. Aric had a jump on Mane whose face contorted in anger as he rushed towards Kit. The entire scene played before me in slow motion. Mane yelled out for him to stop but Aric wasn't listening. He ripped Kit away from me and she took half my throat with her.

❦

I heard voices in my head. They were arguing and shouting. It was not a good combination with the headache that I already seemed to have. My last physical memory returned to me, and I put my hand to my neck which I found wrapped in bandages. The inside of my throat burned hotter than the Dragonlands.

"Water." I managed to eke out the meager request and felt at my chest for the amulet. It was still there and intact. Why did I feel so horrible? I had gotten used to the amulet bringing me the power I needed when I'd lost my power. A feeling I didn't ever want to get used to. If I did I would be just like Aric.

I reached out and made contact with a cool glass that had been handed to me. A set of hands steadied me as I brought the glass to my parched lips. It felt like a millennium since even a drop of water had passed between my lips. The taste of my blood was still on my tongue, and I welcomed the cold liquid. One glass was followed by another. It was as if it would never be enough. My belly was full and bloated, but my throat was still on fire.

I opened my eyes and realized where I was. I wanted to laugh and I wanted to cry. The faded orange curtains flapped in the breeze. The shadow of a figure stirring a wooden spoon in a pot on the stove and the scent of the medicinal herbs used by the priests of Dell'Aria were all around me.

"Dooley?"

The figure holding my head came nearer into focus and dark blue eyes stared down at me. Sharp jagged eyebrows which weren't right. Couldn't be right. "Valora, it's Aric. You'll be okay."

In a second Dooley was also there, having abandoned the pot of water on the stove. He knelt by my side and took my hand in his. "I'm glad you're awake."

After gazing into the tired brown eyes of Dooley's face, the jagged scar at his temples, and the ends of his sun-kissed ringlets I noticed one thing that was very different. Dooley was wearing an amulet. One very similar to the one Aric and I had around our necks.

I looked at Aric and saw that his hung around his neck as well. I looked down at my chest. Mine was still there.

Sometimes you do what needs to be done. The same words used by Aric, but now it was Dooley's voice.

I tried to sit up, but neither one of them was going to have anything to do with it.

"Valora, you're still healing. You need to lie down," said Dooley. I surveyed the room and saw that Artemus sat in a chair in the corner, but Pryn, Mane, and Kit were nowhere to be seen.

"Where?" The question cut off in my throat.

"Don't try and talk, Valora." My uncle knelt beside the bed next to Dooley. "The others had to go. Their time was up and they had to return to Dell'Aria with the vehicle."

So the portals really are closed to me this time?

"Your uncle has reminded us that there are still things that need to be done here. It was best that we stayed behind, for now. We will find a way to the Realms eventually," said Aric.

"Best do so before the time comes when those come through the portals from the Realms in search for you," said Artemus to Aric. He turned his attention to me. "Valora, I have been here too long. I need to return to my post at the hospital. Now more than ever. I know you will be safe with these two. Your lives are tied together now, no use in harming one another. But you will have to work together. You are the one who is going to save us all."

I watched my uncle leave and remembered the first time I heard those words spoken to me. Pryn had whispered them into my ear as he caught me in mid-air, saving my life. I figured my duty as savior ended when Dell'Aria had been saved from the contraption Aric built to take its magic. But apparently that was not the case. My title as Guardian evidently meant something else. I was hoping that Aric and Dooley could explain it to me without getting at each other's throats.

However, the first thing I needed to know was how we all seemed to have matching jewelry.

"Your voice will return slowly, but it may take the day to heal. After the stone in Aric's amulet was split to make one for me the power to heal you was split as well. As I gain strength so will you."

Are you better now? Can we go back to Winter Haven?

"Hardly," said Aric. I realized now that whatever I tried to say to Dooley, Aric would hear as well. The amulets would insure that, no matter what, we could no longer have any secrets from one another.

I tried to ignore Aric. *I thought I would have to convince you to wear the amulet. I had no idea you would choose to wear it on your own.*

Dooley sat on his heels and hung his head. "I would never have chosen to wear the amulet to save my own life. But it was explained to me that the only way to save yours was to do so."

I was glad that I could use the excuse of not having a voice to avoid speaking. I wasn't sure what to say. I had never wanted to coerce Dooley into doing this for me. I had wanted him to do so willingly. He was now forcibly bound to Aric and me whether he liked it or not, and that was something I knew all about.

"Really you two, you act as if this bond is something terrible. There is no reason why we can't all just go about our lives like we did before," said Aric. He gave a sharp one note laugh. "Sorry, not even I can convince myself of that. No, actually you think I like being bound to the both of you? Your constant romantic mutterings in my mind?"

"I have not been thinking anything romantic," Dooley said through clenched teeth.

"Oh, well, then just her. What, you mean you can't hear that, brother? Oh, Valora, the things you wish to do with me. We'll just have to wait for the right time, my darling."

I jerked my head from his hands and slapped him full across the face. *Don't think just because our lives are tied together that I will let you spout lies about me.*

"That I heard," said Dooley. "Look, we can all learn to raise our shields, and this doesn't have to be a problem. Once we're healed I can teach you both to do so."

What was the other thing that we needed to do while we were here, before we can return to the Realms? I ignored Aric as he rubbed at the pink mark I left on his cheek.

Dooley stood up and brought back a small case of vials. They were all empty except for one. Dooley picked up the vial, and the coppery liquid roiled inside. He handed it to Aric who cradled it in his hands like a newborn child. "You are going to meet our mother."

Dooley and Aric wanted to wait until my voice had returned. By evening I was able to produce more than a few squeaks from my throat, and Dooley's color was back to normal. I wasn't able to get him to tell me what caused his illness. Pryn left before I could question him and Artemus had been no help. Dooley kept repeating that I would not want to know and that there was nothing to be done about it. He convinced me he was going to be fine, but we were anything but fine at the moment.

"When can we go and see your mother?" My voice cracked like a pre-pubescent boy. Dooley brought a plate and set it in front of me before joining me at the table. Aric had gone outside to gather some of the berries that were still left from the bushes that Brokk had planted.

Dooley laughed. "I think your husky voice is sexy. We can't go until morning when the home is open. Aric seems to know the schedule there. Apparently he went to visit her often even though she doesn't know who he is."

I put my hand over Dooley's hand. "How do you feel about seeing her again?"

"I don't know how to feel. I've never known her. My life was hard, Valora. Up until this point it was hard."

"And it's not hard now?"

"Not in the same way, no." Dooley stabbed his knife into the meat on his plate. "She left and I had nothing. I might as well have been living on the streets for all the guidance I was given by my foster family. They just collected the check and provided a roof."

Dooley had never spoken much about how he grew up. I wanted to encourage him, but I also didn't want him to shut down from too much questioning. "Ralph said he had a few run-ins with you when you were younger."

"Not even Ralph knows about all the things I did that I didn't get caught for." Dooley kept staring down at his plate as Aric entered with a cloth napkin bursting with fruit.

"Looks like your uncle must be taking care of the cabin. I don't know how else the plants out there could have stayed alive." Aric's hands were overflowing with the luscious berries. My mouth watered at the sight of the familiar fruit.

"Did you kill my father, Aric? Did you kill Brokk?" Dooley's accusation came quick and without warning.

Aric slowly set the fruits onto the table and stepped back. "You have access to my mind. Why not answer that question for yourself?"

"Because I want you to tell me." Dooley stabbed the knife into the table. I was only glad I had removed my hand before he did so.

"What good would it do to tell you either way? If I did, well, I don't think you can hate me more than you already do. If I didn't, then you have another mystery on your hands. That chapter is closed, Dooley. We have much bigger things to worry about now."

"Those things do not absolve you of your responsibility in this matter." It seemed any second I would have to break up another fight. I sure hoped that the rest of our days wouldn't be spent like this.

I jumped up between them. "Bigger things like finding a way we can all stay alive without these amulets. Because if we keep them too long I think we will all end up killing one another anyway, so how would they be protecting us then?" I suddenly realized that I was yelling and my voice was coming out full force. "Hey, I have my voice again." I went to the mirror and pulled at the edge of the bandage.

"Let me help you with that." Dooley jumped over to me and slowly removed the tape holding the bandage to my throat. My neck still had some healing to do. "We'll need to redress the wound. Aric, hand me that salve and a fresh bandage."

The memory of Aric cleansing my wound that day in his chambers came to the forefront of my mind. I couldn't keep it from him. He winked at me in the mirror and I could tell he knew what I was thinking.

I forced that memory away and another one popped in. One of waking up in Dooley's cabin with my arms and legs tied to the bed as he tended to the shotgun wound he had given me.

"You two played a lot harder than we ever did," said

125

Aric.

Dooley finished dressing my wound. "Why don't we go over the lesson I was going to give you about putting up the shields between our minds?"

"Good idea," Aric and I said at the same time.

⤚⥼

After we had eaten our fill Dooley gathered us around a wooden table at the center of the cabin. He placed a ceramic bowl in the center and set a box of matches alongside it. He passed us each a square of paper and a pencil.

"How is this going to be any different than closing my mind off to Aric?" I asked. The one piece of magic I had insisted that Pryn teach me was that.

"The difference, and I am only guessing, is that Dooley is actually going to teach you how to do it. You were never very good before, you know. I could always hear you. Some things I didn't appreciate, but those naughty thoughts of yours definitely made up for it." Aric leaned forward and pushed his fist under his chin, a slight gleam to his dark blue eyes.

Dooley clenched his jaw, but remained focused. "Before we learn how to separate our minds from one another we will cleanse our consciences."

"You're going to have to give me more paper, I am afraid," said Aric, smirking at me.

The table vibrated as Dooley placed his hands on the top, his anger roiling forth in an unexpected display of magic. "You may laugh at the Reiki rituals, but they are the reason Valora found within herself the memories which revealed your treachery and led her to me."

That shut Aric up.

"We will be performing the Burning Bowl Ceremony."

Dooley stood up and poured a bag of rock salt into the basin of the ceramic bowl, spreading his fingers through the crystals and smoothing them flat. He reached over and took a small candle, settling it down into the bowl amidst the salt. The bowl was a pale brown and had the Reiki symbols painted all over it. Dooley took his brush and dipped it into the inkwell, soaking up the fibers with a thick black ink. He traced five symbols, one atop the other, down the length of the paper. He completed each one deftly like he had done it dozens of times before.

"This is the Reiki symbol for distance, the Usui." He brought the paper to his lips and blew the ink dry. I couldn't help but stare at him as his lips pursed together. His deep chocolate eyes glanced up at me and smoldered with intensity, melting my insides. He reached out and placed the drawing atop the candle in the bowl. We watched as the center of the paper smoldered and then burst into flames. Flames as intense as Dooley's stare which seemed to burst with the fire of his passion every time he focused his gaze on me. The paper burned from the center to the outer edges, and Dooley bent his head in prayer. He whispered a few words which failed to reach my ears.

"Now you must each draw these symbols on your papers." Dooley set to work on a second set of three symbols and placed the paper in front of Aric and me. "This is the Sei He Ki. It means God and Man become one. It is also the gate to your subconscious. Sei He Ki means 'I have the key' or 'the mindset of those who don't fall apart,' and it eliminates negative energies." Dooley pointed to the paper in front of us. "This symbol is also used to break negative beliefs, addictions, emotional traumas and limiting emotions like anger, frustration or jealousy."

"You should find it particularly useful then," Aric said to

Dooley.

"I think we all could use a clearing of unwanted energy."

"When you say 'unwanted,' you don't happen to be referring to me?"

"I won't let you ruin this ceremony. Focus on completing the symbols." Aric gave in to Dooley and we each took our time to painstakingly draw each symbol. When I was done I noticed Aric was leaning against the wall half asleep, having finished long ago. So much for respect for religion.

"I'm done," I said. "What do we do now?"

Aric startled awake, sat up, and grabbed his paper.

Dooley shook his head slightly. "Take a quiet moment within your own mind and listen to your heart. Bring your new intentions to the forefront of your mind and burn your prayer in the fire, sending it to the Creator."

"To the Goddess Varuna?"

"He means to whatever God you pray to," said Aric.

I hadn't even thought about that. Dooley had grown up here on Earth and, of course, they would believe in other Gods here or they would have other Gods. Varuna only ruled Overworld in the Realms. She couldn't possibly have any influence this far away. Though every time I gazed into the sky I felt like I was still connected to her in some way. The sky was her Realm and my home. I suddenly felt very far away from the breezes that floated through the streets of Dell'Aria. I missed my father. I missed my life. I missed my people.

I bent over the paper, my hair falling forward. Everything seemed to gel and channel directly into my pen and onto the paper as I ignored the temptations of Aric and Dooley. *Be the Fae Guardian.* Four simple words, and I wasn't sure exactly what it entailed, but I knew now that was what I wanted. I wanted to guard the fae from whatever might harm them.

Aric and Dooley sat calmly with their papers in hand. I didn't want them to see or know my decision. Aric had done things I would never want in the name of protecting me. Dooley had done things he never wanted to do in the name of protecting me. I didn't want either of them to feel responsible for me anymore. It was time I stepped up and took the role that Pryn said had always been mine. I reached forward and dipped the edge of the paper into the fire, watching as the fire slowly licked up the side. I dropped it into the bowl as it burst into flames and watched it turn to ash.

As Dooley reached forward I wished I could know what he had written on his paper. Did he regret making this sacrifice for me? Of course he did. The real question was whether or not we could move past it and come together again.

As the last bit of ash burned away Dooley reached forward. He snatched Aric's wrist as the paper came nearer to the fire. "You would dare throw my name into the fire?"

Aric let the paper drop from his hand as he stared hard across the flame at Dooley. "The decision is not yours to make. It was mine."

Dooley took a deep breath and sat back. We all watched as the flame in the candle died out and the cabin descended into darkness. All that was left was the sound of our breaths. The air was peppered with the smoke from our burnt offerings and we inhaled deeply of our true intentions. The sound of rain pelting the cabin windows brought us all out of our reverie.

Dooley rose, and the wind began to beat against the windows. A flash of lightning came through the window and lit up the small space inside the cabin. Dooley reached forward and took the bowl from the table then ventured out the front door. Aric and I got up from the table and followed him outside.

The rain came down even stronger and battered against his body. Dooley's white t-shirt quickly became soaked and clung to the muscles of his back. I watched as he lifted the bowl to the wind, and the ashes were carried off into the coming storm. The lightning flashed again followed quickly by a thunderous roar.

As the thunder died down I suddenly heard another sound. But it wasn't erratic like the thunder. It was steady. More like drums.

∾∾

The porch light from Dooley's cabin shone into the forest. The sound of the drums was far enough away not to be a warning of an immediate threat, but close enough to perk our curiosity.

"Dooley, let's go inside and you can show us how to erect those borders in our minds," said Aric.

I was surprised that Aric suggested it. If anything he seemed to like being inside my thoughts.

I do, but there is something else trying to get to Dooley right now. Can't you feel it?

I reached out to Dooley with my mind and sure enough, just like Aric had said, there was something there that was trying to distract Dooley away from both Aric and me. Some kind of voice that beat like the drums through Dooley's head. I couldn't understand the words being said, but I could feel the effect of it. The voice was calling to Dooley.

I moved over to him and placed my hand at his back. He startled as if he were in a trance.

"Yes, let's go inside." Dooley responded to Aric's question as if there had been no disturbance.

"You heard Aric okay?" I asked.

The rain came down steadily from the sky. It dripped down Dooley's face and plastered his brown locks against his cheeks. "Of course I heard him. I just don't chose to respond to him as quickly as he would like." His tone was harsh at first and then he seemed to come completely into himself and reached out for my hand to give it a squeeze. "Don't worry, everything is fine."

"What do you suppose that sound out in the woods is?"

"Probably nothing other than some local tribesman praying to the rain gods to make it stop. Never works around here though."

My rain soaked wings were heavy against my back. Aric took cover under the overhang of Dooley's cabin. We all walked slowly inside and Dooley set about telling us how to keep out of each other's minds. It turned out it wasn't too difficult. It was all a matter of intent and purpose. However, we couldn't pick and choose who to let in and who to keep out. It was either all or nothing, meaning that if I didn't want Aric in my head then I couldn't have Dooley in there either. I rather liked knowing what Dooley was thinking, especially now that someone other than Aric or I might be trying to speak to him.

I took one of the cots and Aric and Dooley agreed to take shifts through the night to make sure we weren't taken off guard. Dooley thought the drums meant nothing, but Aric remained tight-lipped. There wasn't a way to ask his opinion without Dooley overhearing us. I had accepted my role as Guardian, but that meant nothing to these two. I kept my eyes cracked open as Aric took first watch and Dooley settled into the cot at the other side of the room.

Aric sat on a stool near the window and stared out into the moonless sky. His pupils grew large as he studied the darkness. It was rather interesting that he chose a place to live in the heart of the city while Dooley picked a cabin out in the woods. It just showed that they were two sides of one coin.

There was a lot to learn about these two and I hoped meeting their mother would help shed some light on the mysteries surrounding both of them. The strangest part about it was that I felt like I knew more about Aric than I did about Dooley. I knew more about my enemy then I did my lover.

Something was wrong with that. Of course I had known Aric my whole life. Aric turned from his post at the window and looked over at Dooley. He was fast asleep, the rise and fall of his chest a dead giveaway along with his arm which had fallen over the side of the bed.

Aric smirked. He reached up a finger and motioned for me to come over to him. I swung my legs to the side of the bed and tiptoed softly across the floor, trying not to wake Dooley.

Aric leaned over and whispered into my ear, "You are supposed to be sleeping."

I nodded and checked again on Dooley was still knocked out cold. "You think there was someone trying to contact him. Who do you think it was?"

"I am afraid the only one who could confirm my suspicions is the one who has returned to the Realms."

"You mean Mane, the demon?"

Aric nodded.

"I need you to explain to me why you think this. Stop keeping things from me Aric, it's driving me crazy."

"Actually all you want is for me to keep things from you,

Valora. You don't want to know the truth. You don't want to know how deeply sorry I am for what happened to your mother. You don't want to know the extent of Kali's treachery. You don't want to know how much I care for you. Because if you knew the truth about all of those things and you accepted it, then you might just have to confront your own truth. The truth that you still care about me."

Aric's voice was just above a whisper, but his arm was braced firmly around my waist as he spoke into my ear. My hand braced against his chest to keep us at a comfortable distance. Aric's heartbeat pulsed rapidly beneath my palm.

My breathing was heavy, trying to catch up with what he said like I was running away from it as fast as I could. He was right of course. He could see right through me even without the telepathy. He had always been able to do that. That was why he sacrificed everything to get me wings, because there was a time that perhaps I would have done anything for them. I had prayed to the Goddess Varuna. After I learned what Aric had done I stopped praying for a long time. Be careful what you wish for. The Goddess had granted my selfish wish, but at a price. And the punishment was that I didn't even end up with the wings and I still lost my mother.

In the end it was still all my fault. Aric's wish to return his mother's memory was a noble one, not selfish like the longings of some petulant child. I lifted my face and it was only an inch from Aric. His dark blue eyes locked with mine and he kept them opened as he stretched forward to place a feather light kiss upon my lips. I was frozen. Not wanting to push him away and not wanting to return his affections either. Aric ran a finger through one of my ringlets.

"Go to sleep, Valora." I stepped away from him and only then removed my hand from his chest. Without saying another word I lay on the bed with my back to him. There was a delicate silence between us that was slowly breaking.

CHAPTER ELEVEN

I wasn't sure what time it was when I finally fell into my dreams. It was a restless sleep, that much I knew for sure. Filled with visions of Franca and her blond braids. A speeding Edsel driving through the Riparian forest. And Aric and Dooley both lying on either side of me in bed. A night full of surrealism where all of my worlds were starting to collide. Even in my waking state I was having trouble keeping it all straight.

Dooley and Aric seemed to be in a heated discussion. Not because they were shouting, more because they were sitting on opposite sides of the table staring at one another intensely. I kind of wished they would yell at one another. But Dooley was too patient and Aric was too stubborn. Just which one would crack first was anyone's guess.

I slowly rose from the bed and walked towards the table. "So what's the plan this morning?"

They wouldn't stop staring at one another and it seemed something might really be wrong with them. "Guys, are you okay?" I reached out and touched both of their shoulders at once and suddenly the shields between all of us dropped to the floor.

Aric and Dooley had been fighting about me, but they had stopped once I awoke. Their words came flashing at me from both sides as their consciousness merged with mine. The intensity of their emotions blasted me backwards, and the floor connected with my backside. Hard. That seemed to snap them out of their staring contest.

"Valora, are you okay?" Dooley stepped forward and reached down to help me up.

"What the heck was that?" I rubbed at my tail bone which would probably have a nasty bruise in the morning. "The shields didn't work."

"It seems like you are a conduit between the both of us. You touched us at the same time and all our emotions flooded together into one big mix," said Aric. He cupped his elbow with one hand and tapped his lips with the other.

"Great. Note to self. Don't touch both of you at the same time." I regained my focus and brought up the shields between us. I knew they both had feelings for me. I didn't need to be reminded of it all the time. "It would be really great to know why this is all happening to us. Aric, you were the one who made the deal with the demon in the first place. Just what kind of deal did you make?"

Aric sat down at the table and rubbed his finger against the splintering wood. "I only paid attention to the term which specified that you would remain alive. Nothing else mattered to me."

"We really don't know what we are in for, then?" I asked.

"No." A simple answer with an endless list of repercussions. Though the look on Aric's face told me that he wasn't being completely honest with me. Of course, after our conversation the night before I was pretty sure I agreed with him in that department.

"When are we going to meet your mother?" I had started the day off with a bang, might as well continue.

"We'll have to have a short breakfast. The home opens soon. I was hoping to have Artemus join up with us before we visited her," said Dooley.

"What is your mother's name?"

"I don't know." Dooley hung his head. It was obvious that the prospect of this visit was taking a toll on him. I hadn't really thought about the effect seeing his mother would have on him after all these years. She had abandoned him, but not willingly. Her memory had been taken from her.

Aric reached over and placed a hand on his brother's shoulder. Dooley immediately relaxed his posture. I knew in that moment he was grateful for Aric, even if it only lasted a millisecond.

"I suppose we should get going. I wanted a chance to speak to Artemus anyway," I said.

After we had taken turns cleaning up and getting some food in our stomachs we went out and realized that there was no car in the driveway. Mane, Kit and Pryn had taken the Edsel back to the Realms the night before.

"Great, now how are we supposed to get out of here?" Just as I asked I heard the sound of a straining engine round the corner. The van was barreling down the road, its top speed seemingly super-slow. I could probably have flown faster than this van was going, and I didn't fly. It was a dusty brown color with an equally dusty orange roof and looked like a big box on wheels.

"A Vanagon!" Aric ran to meet the vehicle as it slowed to a stop, placing his hands on either side of the door like he was hugging an old friend.

"Since when do you know what these things are?" I asked. Immediately I remembered that Aric had a whole life here apart from his life in Dell'Aria.

Aric gently ran his finger down the faded chrome trim. "My mother used to own one of these when I was a child."

"Artemus!" Dooley clamped a hug around my uncle's shoulders as he leaned out the window.

"Are you all ready to go?" My uncle had left his life on Dell'Aria to live with the human woman that he loved here on Earth. He stayed with her until her years had taken her and he lived on as the fae tend to do. And then here I was committed in one way to Dooley, and in another to Aric. One in heart and one in mind and unable to distinguish which I wanted more. Which one I deserved more. Which one I knew more. My mother had told me the tale of Winter Haven which would dictate that I should be with Dooley, but why, then, was our marriage interrupted? Why had I been drawn into Aric's grasp once more? Because it was a test or because it was meant to be?

We piled into the Vanagon and Artemus pointed the car towards West Seattle where Dooley and Aric's mother lived. I wanted to be able to have a chance to speak to my uncle. I was certain that in some way he would be able to tell me what I should do. Or at least I was hoping for some guidance. Once upon a time Kali had been that guidance. I had trusted every word she said. Aric was right. I didn't want to know the extent of her treachery. A large part of me wanted to forgive her and place the blame on Aric instead. It made my choice easier.

We traveled down the road, and I was assailed with memories of Franca and the motorcycle I left behind at the cabin. "Can we make a quick stop at Camp Long?" If I was going to think clearly I needed to do it alone, with the powerful machinery of my motorcycle between my legs, not sandwiched between two over-protective men in the back of a Vanagon.

Dooley placed a hand on my thigh. "I think we should stay together."

Aric stretched his hands up and placed his arm around my shoulder. "Yes, I'm quite cozy."

"Dooley, you're going to give me a bruise." Dooley quickly released the death grip on my leg and I rubbed at the tender spot left behind.

"Just take a quick left up there, it won't be much of a detour." I leaned forward over the seat and pointed my uncle in the right direction.

It wasn't hard to find my bike. It was just where we left it. I placed my hand above what would have been the fuel tank and a pulse of energy surged from me into the bike as the engine revved to life beneath me. Finally I had some semblance of control. If things were going to happen, it was because I chose them to happen.

I needed the time in my own head before meeting the mother of Dooley and Aric, two men who had captured my attention for better or for worse.

૎•૏

I think my uncle circled the small community of West Seattle twice for my benefit which was good because I couldn't stop worrying about how much attention Aric was giving me and how much Dooley seemed to be ignoring me. He had every right to, of course. He was chained to Aric because of me. And I had let Aric kiss me, but what was worse was that I let him back into my head. I wasn't ready to look yet to see if he had ended up in my heart somewhere.

The Vanagon turned slightly right and before us rose a

large brick structure with a bell tower and traditional colonial brocade adorning all the windows and the quaint columned porch. Beautiful roses and daffodils splashed the grounds with color, not a weed in sight.

Artemus parked the van and I pulled alongside him. My uncle jumped out of the car followed by Aric. Aric dipped down and checked his reflection in the side mirror of the van. He murmured a few words, and his lightning shaped eyebrows formed into half crescents. He stood up, and his hand went straight into his pocket where I knew he was holding the last vial of magic that was left. All of the mistakes he had made were finally going to mean something.

We were lucky it was winter and wearing long coats wouldn't make us look like some kind of gang. Of course the fact that Dooley was only wearing a t-shirt still made Artemus, Aric and me look like his body guards in our long black trenches. We had to hide the wings somehow. Small glamours wouldn't drain our energy, but I wasn't completely well yet.

"Have you ever met their mother?" I asked Artemus.

"No, I've never had reason to come here. I believed Dooley when he told me the story of his mother's ailment. I had no reason to believe she was under any enchantment. Our magic can't heal human sickness."

We walked up the steps and the lady at the front desk immediately recognized Aric. "Aric! Oh, Varuna will be so glad to see you today. She has been asking about you."

I waited to see if my uncle had caught the name. His eyebrows knit together, and he pointed his finger at the nurse. "Did she just say…"

"Yes, Varuna." Aric cut him off with a look that said now was not the appropriate time to speak about it.

Aric and Dooley's mother had the same name as the

Goddess of Overworld.

Dooley glanced around, looking for answers where there were none.

"I've brought some other family to see her. I hope it's okay." Aric continued on as though there was nothing amiss.

"She seems to be in good spirits today. I just wouldn't press her too hard. She tires easily." The nurse handed Aric a clipboard which he signed and handed back to her.

"Of course, we'll make our visit short." We all signed in after Aric and then followed him down the hall.

I was the last to enter the room. There was an old woman sitting on a padded stool looking out the window onto a view of the waters of Puget Sound. She had long straight gray hair bleached by age. Her skin was slightly darker, like Dooley's was.

Aric stopped just inside the doorway and held a hand out for us to wait. For what seemed like a minute he stood there staring at her. Eventually he turned his profile to me and I could see the moisture in his eyes. His gaze drifted to a small crystal bowl filled with his mother's favorite butterscotch candies wrapped in bright yellow cellophane and he pocketed some of the sweets before finally approaching her.

Aric bent down on one knee, taking her withered hand in his. "Varuna, it's Aric. I've come for a visit."

A large smiled infected every feature of the woman's face, playing upon the laugh lines which showed she had lived a happy life. "Aric! I was hoping you would come and visit soon. It has been a long time, has it not? I tend to forget these days." She turned and noticed the rest of us in the room. "And who are all these people dressed in black? Am I late to my own funeral?"

Aric chuckled and patted the back of her hand. "Varuna,

these are my friends. They have come with me to visit you today. I hope you don't mind."

"As long as they don't mind me muttering on. Please, have a seat." She gestured to the edge of a small bed covered in a lavender quilt. "No use standing there unless you need to be going soon."

When we first entered the room it smelled of fresh linen. Now a different scent infused my senses. A warm earthiness contrasted with a bitter smoky aroma. I couldn't identify the source, but as I got closer to Varuna it seemed to increase.

I held out my hand. "So nice to meet you. My name is Valora."

"Varuna, Valora, all sounds the same, now doesn't it?" She spoke to Aric. "I like her and her name. If I forget mine again why don't you give me the name Valora instead."

"Sounds good."

Artemus grew pale as he sat on the edge of the bed and stared at Varuna. Dooley came forward and introduced himself, but the look on my uncle's face combined with the strong scent set me on edge.

I sat down next to him on the bed and whispered in his ear, looking on as Dooley smiled into the face of the mother he had never really met before. "What is it, Uncle?"

"They must not give her the magic," Artemus hissed through clenched teeth, staring intently at the wizened old woman.

"What are you talking about? There's no way I'm going to be able to convince them not to give it to her."

"Then you must be prepared to assist me once they do. We will have to erase her memory permanently, and I will need your magic to help me. I have been here on Earth too long, and I don't have as much as I need to complete such a spell."

142

I was about to ask him why when I heard Aric speaking to Varuna. "We have brought you a special treat today, Varuna. A medicine which will help you remember everything you have ever forgotten." He drew out the vial of copper liquid from his coat and held it up. It swirled in the light coming in from her window.

"It is meant to replace what was taken from you," said Dooley.

"Is that what you want?" asked Varuna. She placed her hand on Dooley's arm. Her dark brown eyes mirrored his own.

"Maybe we should talk about this." I stood up and took a few steps towards them, but their looks stopped me in my tracks. Both Aric and Dooley openly stared at me, disbelief clearly written across their faces.

"There is nothing to discuss," said Aric. His jaw was set firm.

"Artemus?" A sheen of sweat broke out on my uncle's forehead, his agitation becoming more obvious by the second.

"The vetiver. Can't you smell it?" He stood and paced the length of the small space, his hand rubbing at the back of his neck. "There is a dangerous combination in this room. As if only a small spark will set it to life, and I think that is it." He pointed at the vial in Aric's hand.

"I have given up everything so that she can remember again." Aric turned to Varuna, ignoring us completely as he handed it to her. "Yes, I want more than anything for you to remember again."

Varuna nodded and reached up gingerly for the vial. She gently clasped it as if it were something hot, and brought the edge of the glass tube to her lips. She drank it down and then all hell broke loose.

143

Artemus swept his arms across the room, and Varuna's screams went silent. Her mouth continued to open and close as she writhed on the floor where she had fallen.

Aric quickly scooped her up. Dooley reached out, and as his hand touched Varuna's arm he was rocked backwards by a wave of power. He clutched his head in his hands and grimaced in pain. I reached out to him as my uncle shouted.

"Valora, I need your help now!"

Dooley held a hand over his face as he waved me off with the other. "Go!"

Aric placed Varuna on the bed but the two of them could barely contain her. Their muscles strained as they held her arms and legs down. Things were falling apart fast.

And then it hit me. I closed my eyes and imagined the wind as it flew past, the ground coming closer as I fell without anything to stop me. But this time I focused hard on the writhing body of Dooley and Aric's mother, directing all my energy in her direction. Tension built within me like an arrow held taut on a bow. And then I let it loose. "Congelar no Tempo!"

I opened my eyes, surprised that it worked. Varuna froze in place. Aric and Artemus slowly removed their arms from her.

"It looks like Pryn has taught you a few things." Aric's glamour wavered and his eyebrows drew up into their more familiar lightning shape.

"What is wrong with her? You said that would restore her memory," said Dooley. He stumbled forward, eyes closed, pressing his palm into his forehead as he spoke as if he were in pain. As if the spell that had pulsed through the room hadn't only had a negative effect on Varuna but on him as well.

"It was supposed to. No, it had to have worked." Aric

was beside himself. He touched the back of his curled finger to Varuna's cheek and gave Artemus and me a pained stare. "What is wrong with her?"

"There is nothing wrong with her." Artemus pulled a hand through his short salt and pepper hair. "I have just realized why King Alastair would have conjured such a powerful spell to keep a mortal woman from remembering you and the fae. She is not any normal human. She is an oracle. The gods speak through her. And more importantly it seems she can channel them. The scent of vetiver is a warning. Smoke that rises from the earth foretells the coming of Acheron."

"So the fact that her name is Varuna isn't a coincidence? And what Mane said is true?" My heart seemed to freeze solid for a moment before it began to thud sharply in my chest. For a second I forgot everything else. The pieces were starting to fall into place.

"Are you okay?" Artemus rose from the bed and went to Dooley who was crouched on the ground, his head in his hands. My uncle reached out towards him, but Dooley crawled backwards, waving him off.

"You need to stay away. I'm fine. I'll be fine." Dooley growled as he pushed the palms of his hands into his closed eyes as if he was trying to rub away some vision he never wanted to see again. He grabbed the edge of the chair Varuna had been sitting on and pulled himself to standing, staring into the corner briefly before turning towards us. Something seemed different but I couldn't put my finger on it.

"Mane mentioned a name when he spoke to Queen Elemi at Lake Mavrovo," I said. Artemus seemed to know a lot about Acheron, a chapter of history that had been left out of all the books I read about the Realms as a child.

"I don't trust that demon," said Aric.

Artemus ignored my question as he studied Varuna. Her expression had calmed. "Let your spell go, Valora. Let's see what she has to say," said Artemus.

I released my hold, and she sat up in bed. Aric and Dooley took a place at her bedside. She placed a hand on each of their cheeks. "My two boys. I can't believe you found one another. That you both sit beside me now is proof that my life was worth living, even if I never got to know you. Even if I had to forget about you and about both of your fathers."

Her hands dropped to the bed. "But you must do whatever magic was done before and make me forget again. It is the only way to keep this world safe. Your father knew that, Aric. That was what he told me before he kissed me sweetly and left forever."

Dooley grimaced and dropped his head at the mention of Aric's father. He had a father, too, one that had been murdered and had never told him who he was. Varuna brushed her fingers against the back of Dooley's hand, making a small request for him to look up at her. "Your father was special, too, Dooley."

It seemed Varuna had much the same problem I was currently faced with. Her love had been split between Brokk and King Alastair. I wondered which one she would have picked if given the choice.

"Why would your memories be a danger to this world?" I asked.

Varuna looked up at me. Her eyes were a swirling vortex of blue and brown that threatened to pull me in. "I am blessed to have the Guardian in my presence. You will understand more than anyone. I am an oracle. I am the conduit between this world and the world of your gods. The gods above in Elysium and the gods below in Acheron. Just as you are the conduit between Aric and Dooley because of that amulet. But you also are the Guardian, something I could never claim to be. Something I wished I could have been for my sons." She reached out to them both, taking her time to stroke each of their cheeks and place a kiss to their foreheads. You could tell that neither one was a favorite over the other. She loved her sons equally. Varuna returned her attention to me. "I am lucky that they have found you."

"People keep saying I am a conduit, and I don't know what it means. Why is it that you call me the Guardian?" I asked.

"You know it is true. Do you not?"

Aric and Dooley both focused their attention on me. "I suppose so. But I don't know what I'm supposed to do."

"You'll know when the time comes. Now please, you must hurry and remove my memories. The longer my conscious stays awake in this world it is like a beacon which calls the gods and the fae to me. I cannot stop it." Varuna released her hold on Dooley and Aric and brought her legs up to her body's core, resting her forehead on her knees. She hugged herself and rocked back and forth like she was trying to contain what had sprung loose before.

"Mother, I could teach you to shield yourself. You can be safe from those that would threaten you," said Dooley.

She grasped his wrist and looked up at him. The skin bunched around her eyes as she gave him a pained stare. "No, it's not possible. Dooley, I have hosted two gods in my life. Both of them were with me when I conceived and gave birth to you both."

"Hosted or been possessed?" asked Artemus.

"We all have weak moments in our life. Sometimes we don't make the best decisions." She slowly dragged her nails

147

down her cheeks and her eyes began to glaze over. A memory, full of anguish, was clearly playing out in her mind. "They both gave me the option and I accepted it. Varuna and Ravanna. Both gods from your world, Valora. Both gods with interests which lie elsewhere. That was what I came to realize. I was given a choice the first time, but now that the door has been opened, there is only one way to close it. If I am to remain myself they could enter me again and use me against my will. I am afraid they will use any chance they can get. You need to make me forget so I am not a threat to this world or to yours."

Varuna reached her hand out to Dooley. "My dear Dooley, you and I barely had a chance to be together before I was taken from you. I am so sorry for that. I have to apologize. Once I realized that it was not only the gods of Elysium but also the gods of Acheron that could use me I agreed to King Alastair's wishes to remove my memory and to take Aric with him to the Realms."

"So Aric got to go to the Realms and I got a foster home full of people who hated me? How could you leave me without anyone to care for me?" Dooley tensed his body to ward off the shaking that I could see in his fists pressed into the tops of his thighs.

Varuna's voice fell to barely a whisper as she clutched her hands to her chest. "Your father was afraid of you, Dooley. I tried." She reached out but paused before her hand reached Dooley's cheek and brought it to her chest again. "At first when he learned that I was host to Ravanna when you were conceived, he wanted to dispose of you. I fought against his wishes. I would not let him harm you, but I could not make him take you. I blessed you as best I could and had to make the hard decision. It was best that your upbringing was without Ravanna's influence."

Dooley lowered his chin to his chest. Dooley had to realize that Brokk had spent his last years trying to make up for that mistake. After Brokk was banished to Earth he had clearly decided that his decision to abandon Dooley was wrong since I had found them living together. But if Ravanna was a god, why would he ever wish Dooley had never been born?

"Who is Ravanna?" I asked.

As I said the name aloud the scent of vetiver increased. Varuna's limbs went slack and the monotone voice that came from her mouth no longer seemed to be under her control. "The demon king of the underworld."

CHAPTER TWELVE

Suddenly Varuna's body stiffened and her eyes rolled into the top of her head.

"Please, do it," said Aric to Artemus. He wrapped his arms around his mother and held her down to the bed again.

"Valora, I am going to need your help." Artemus beckoned me over.

"But I don't know what to do." The words left my mouth and I knew they applied to more than just this immediate problem.

"You only need to repeat what I say. Here." Artemus took my hand and led me to the edge of the bed. Dooley stepped back. Artemus placed my hand atop his, and we touched Varuna's forehead. "Repeat after me. Demônios Fora. Lembre-se Nada."

I did so, and a surge of power welled between us, pouring down over Varuna. In an instant she was still. Her eyes opened. "Who are you people? Where am I?"

Aric lifted his head from where he had buried it into the bed beside her and swallowed hard. "You're safe. There are nurses here to help you. You suffered an injury and you've lost your memory. But you will be okay. We'll go get the nurses."

Aric rose up from Varuna's bedside and went towards the door. Artemus nodded at me and I followed behind, stopping to look at Dooley who was still staring down at the woman in the bed. Varuna was no longer there, she was again an empty shell.

"Are you coming?" I asked.

Dooley watched as the woman pulled the blankets to her chin and rolled away onto her side like he wasn't there at all. He focused on the popcorn ceiling and pulled in a slow deep breath, letting it out through pursed lips.

"Let's go." He walked past me and out the door.

We caught up to the others in the hall. "Are you certain that worked?" I asked Artemus under my breath.

"Not for certain, no. But it seems to have wiped her memory completely." Artemus pulled the collar of his coat up to cover the edges of his wings that had come loose.

"Yes, even the memories she had of me over the past several years," snapped Aric.

"There is nothing I could do about that. I tried to warn you."

As we reached the nurse's station Aric bent over and whispered into her ear. She nodded and went down the hall towards Varuna's room.

"We are done here. I'll have Artemus drop me at my apartment. I assume you want to go with Dooley to his cabin? You can fit him on the back of your bike, right?" Aric folded his arms across his chest.

Everything was happening so fast. "But, Aric, what about the Realms?"

"You really think I want to surrender to my executioners? I hardly think that would be in my best interest."

I put my hand on Aric's arm. "I also don't think that it would be in your best interest or in ours if we separate."

"And why is that?" asked Dooley. He placed a hand on my shoulder forcing me to look at him.

"Because we need to find a way back."

"We need to find a way back or you need to?" Dooley's anger seethed through his words and shocked me to the core.

"Just a few days ago you seemed happy to wed me at the chapel at Winter Haven and live out your days in Dell'Aria. What has changed?"

Dooley laughed. "You ask *me* what has changed? You go on a mission to save Aric and bring him before me, link him to me, and you ask *me* what has changed? I'll tell you what has changed, Valora. It is you. Because no matter what someone wants to tell me about what I am on the inside, I have always known. I have always fought against the evil welling up inside me. It's more than I can say for Aric. The one with angelic blood, and he is the murderer. Not me. It's taking all of my strength not to punch him in the face."

Aric stepped forward as we all stood in the parking lot of the Kenney. "I know, because you wouldn't want to wreck such a perfect face, would you?" Aric stood feet from Dooley. Dooley clenched his jaw and the scar at his temple, the one that Aric had given him, twitched with the extreme tension in his muscles. Dooley had always shown such restraint. He was even keeled, the one I could always depend on. Aric marched to the beat of his own drummer. His motivations were born of the crazy pathways in his brain that seemed to tell him whatever he did was okay. His justifications never made complete sense to me even if I could understand his reasoning.

I studied the hard asphalt beneath my shoes. I wished in that moment I could be airborne. In the sky. I wished I didn't have to be here on Earth anymore.

I heard his jaw snap before I saw the movement. I looked up, and Aric was cradling his face. Artemus had jumped up and was restraining Dooley who wasn't struggling. He had wanted to smack Aric across the face, and he had accomplished his mission. Blood trickled from Aric's mouth. All three of our amulets glowed red, and I felt slightly dizzy. Dooley staggered. The amulets were drawing power from Dooley and me to heal Aric's wound.

Aric took his time standing upright. "So how does it feel to hit yourself in the face?"

Artemus tightened his grip as he held Dooley's arms from behind. He practically spit venom at Aric's feet. "I would sever your head and sacrifice my own if I thought you would actually die."

I placed myself between them. "There is a reason we have been brought together like this. I know you don't believe it, Dooley, but you must trust me."

"You think I am blind? I know you let him kiss you last night."

Dooley's anger at Aric had really been anger at me, and I had no words for him. There was nothing I could say to erase what I did. Artemus dropped his hold on Dooley and retreated. "Perhaps it's best if we get going. It sounds like you all need some time to cool off and talk."

"Yes, but we are going to get this all straight tonight. You are going to make a choice tonight." Dooley pointed his finger at me. "Take Aric with you on the bike. We'll meet you at the cabin."

I watched as Dooley walked to the passenger side of the Vanagon and flung the door open. He got into the passenger seat and slammed the door without looking back at me.

Aric came up behind me and put his hands on my shoulders. "We could just go to my apartment. I doubt what he has planned for tonight will be pleasant."

"It might not be, but it has to be done. For you and for him." I took a deep breath and let it out. My warm breath fogged up before me in the cool evening air. "There are more important things on the horizon."

⊱⊰

Aric slung his leg over the bike and wrapped his arms around my waist. "Do you really need to get that comfortable?" I asked.

"Who said I was comfortable? I've never ridden on one of these things. I just don't want to fall off." I was glad that we were under the cover of night for a few reasons. First, neither Aric nor I had a helmet and that could get you arrested around here, and second, I wasn't sure that I really wanted Aric to see my facial expressions. I was finally able to bring up the shields between us, but he was still able to read me better than anyone I had ever known. Better than my own mother when she was alive.

"So why me, Aric?" I gunned the engine as I asked the question. Almost fearing his response. *What if he said something that made me waver in my commitment to Dooley?*

I sped up to the Vanagon which wasn't hard to catch. Its top speed was half that of the motorcycle which hummed with fae magic.

Aric's lips brushed against my ear as we sped along the highway. "Because we are the same, Valora. You and I would do anything for the ones we love. You will see soon enough."

I wasn't able to respond to him while I drove and I

didn't want to drop the shields. I was captive to his comments for the ride. Then again, I had invited them.

"You think that Dooley willingly took the amulet? Kit enthralled him before she left. It was the only way to keep you alive, but he wasn't willing to do it. He'd have let you die. Kit wouldn't let that happen. I wouldn't let that happen."

He sat back after that, keeping his grip around my waist. His words hit me as hard as Dooley's smack to Aric's face. I could understand Dooley's reservations, but I didn't think he would be willing to let me die. Either he hated Aric that much or he didn't love me enough. Either way there was a problem. He said he wanted answers tonight. Well, I wanted them also.

The Vanagon pulled up and Dooley hopped out. I pulled the bike in next to the driver's side window, and Artemus leaned out. "I will be by in the morning to check on you. I have to get to my job at the hospital."

The van disappeared, heading for the street, and Dooley stood in the driveway. I pressed my hand to the tank and the engine powered down, but Aric was still behind me with his hands clasped around my waist.

"Get off the bike, Aric." He squeezed me around the waist before he did so. Aric stalked to the front of the bike and took off the trench coat, tossing it to the ground in front of Dooley. He let his wings spread out wide as he stretched his hands to the sky, flexing the muscles in his arms and chest.

"Needed that stretch." He winked at me, a lazy grin crossing his face.

That set Dooley off again, and he ran towards Aric who shot up into the air and hovered just out of his reach. "Now are we going to play nice? I would hate to have to drain your powers again just to heal some wound you decide to inflict upon me."

Aric was having a good time giving Dooley a hard time, but I didn't like it. "Will you two please stop it? I can't stand it."

A sharp pulse through my skull dropped me to the ground. Suddenly there were two pairs of arms around me.

"Let's get her inside," said Dooley.

"Agreed." They cradled me up the stairs and laid me on the rug in the middle of the floor before I drifted out of focus.

I awoke in darkness, my vision slowly adjusting as the moonlight streamed through the window. I sat up and was slightly faint, like the time I had taken the amulet off. I felt at my throat. It was still there. "What happened?"

"I believe that is what you would call a power surge," said Aric. He stepped forward from the shadows.

"Why didn't it happen before then?" I pressed my hands to my temples.

Aric stared over my shoulder at Dooley, waiting for him to answer my question, but he only stared at Aric as he stirred a pot on the stove. They had obviously exchanged words when I was passed out.

"A power surge without release tends to run amuck. Am I right, brother?" Aric's eyebrows rose as he spoke.

"This is not my fault." Dooley's neck was stiff, the cords standing out as he restrained himself. He dropped the spoon in the pot and swiped a cloth across the beads of sweat on his forehead.

The woolen carpet was warm and scratchy beneath my fingers. I concentrated on that instead of the awkward silence that was building all around us. Aric moved to sit before me. Dooley mirrored his movements behind me.

Dooley grasped my hip in his hand and placed the palm of his other flat on my back. I took a sharp intake of breath. Aric didn't budge.

The cabin was cast in shadows. Aric's expression was hidden from me even though he was only a few feet away.

Dooley slowly removed my coat and tossed it to the side. "Stay here." He got up and went to the stove then took from it the pot of steaming hot liquid.

He lit a lamp on the table before sitting down on the floor to the side of Aric and me. "Take off your shirt, Aric."

In all the compromising positions I had found myself with Aric it dawned on me that I had never seen him without a shirt. Without speaking he took one hand and removed the white silken strapping which crisscrossed his body, allowing his wings to remain free.

Dooley swept his shirt off as well and both of them sat there before me. Their muscled chests mirrored one another. One dark and another pale.

"There is another ritual which I think will help all of us resolve this." Dooley placed his finger into the bowl and traced symbols onto Aric's chest.

He winced. "Couldn't let it cool first, could you?"

"Don't ruin the moment."

My mouth went slack as I watched Dooley paint the symbols on Aric's chest much in the way he had done with me when we were trying to access some of my early memories. My fingers ached to reach out to Dooley's muscled shoulder and trace the lines of his tattoos. Two of the most handsome men I had ever seen and both of them were shirtless in front of me right now. I winced as I pinched the skin of my forearm. I couldn't believe that this wasn't some kind of dream.

Dooley kept his eyes locked with Aric as he circled

behind me. They were like two hunters fighting over their prey. Waiting to see which one would pounce first. I wasn't sure if they were going to help me or rip me to shreds.

Dooley undid the laces on my bodice, his rough fingers plying at the flesh of my back as he quickly undid each one. Aric reached forward and unclasped the sides just as Dooley finished with the laces, and I was laid bare before him.

Aric didn't dare touch me, but his eyes ravished my body all the same. The glow of the lamplight revealed all his desires in the soft part of his lips and the flush of his skin. He kept his hands cupping my sides and eventually met my gaze as Dooley painted the symbols upon my back in long, slow strokes.

"Breathe," Aric whispered.

I pulled in a shallow breath, and my breasts came in contact with his chest, transferring some of the paint.

"Done." Dooley came closer to me, pressing his chest into my back. He wrapped his hands around my waist and linked arms with Aric, pulling me tightly between them.

"You both need to drop your shields," said Dooley.

I didn't feel like I could get any closer to either of them. Dooley's chest was pressed against my wings at my back, the warm paint acting as a glue between us, and my breasts were now crushed against Aric's sculpted torso.

Aric nodded and closed his eyes. I did the same. And then all the walls came down.

A flood of emotions hit me from both sides with more impact than the hardness of their bodies, but it also filled me with renewed energy. The amulets provided a certain dose of magic, but the linking of our minds seemed to provide a whole different level.

I let their intense passion flow through me and into the other. If they were ever going to get along they had to understand. They had to know everything.

Aric's lips sought out mine and the press of Dooley's hand into the small of my back willed me forward towards Aric. I let my mouth feast on Aric in a way I had always wanted to as Dooley's hands wrapped around my chest and fondled the sensitive peaks of my breasts. He laid small kisses at the base of my wings as I drew Aric's kiss deeper into my own.

Aric pulled away from me and exchanged glances with Dooley. I turned and met his smoldering brown eyes. There was no anger, only pure passion and emotion. He moved away from me, and I crawled towards him on all fours, my body aching with need as he lay down on the ground. I dropped my head over his, and he reached up, taking my mouth in his and cupping my breasts once more. His thumbs brushed over my nipples causing a slight whimper to escape my lips. Every nerve ending tingled and each touch enflamed the mounting desire within me.

Aric eased my pants down to my knees, exposing the rest of my naked flesh to the cool breeze coming from the open window. Aric's hand trembled over my backside and continued downwards, pressing a finger between my thighs, massaging my most sensitive spot.

Dooley continued to ply my nipples as his tongue caressed mine in increased intensity. He was able to sense everything, as was I, through the connection we had open.

I heard Aric's pants unzip, and I started to fall out of the moment. Dooley brought his hand to my face and cupped my chin. "No, you will do this."

Relieved and trapped. I thought I wanted this, but did I? Dooley reached up and pulled my mouth down to his then returned to torturing my breasts.

A gasp escaped my lips as Aric gently pressed his tip into

my swollen sex from behind. Dooley groaned, and I pushed back onto Aric's hard length which slid into my wet cleft without hesitation. Aric put one hand around my waist and reached the other hand down and around, coaxing me to climax as he filled me deeper and deeper.

My hand fumbled with Dooley's pants until I was able to reach inside and pull out his stiff member.

Aric and Dooley crested their waves of pleasure in my mind, and I caught up to them about the same time, allowing Aric and Dooley's fingers to pull at my pleasure zones as Aric pulsed deep inside me. All at once we thundered to a climax. My mind quivered with pleasure, exhaustion, fulfillment, and fear.

I collapsed down upon Dooley, and Aric quickly pulled up his pants. I still hadn't seen him fully naked, but there was no denying that I had felt him. On so many levels I had felt him. And so had Dooley. I wasn't sure what that would bring us in the morning.

All of my shields were down, and I was raw. I was scared to speak. Every nerve tingled with pleasure on the verge of pain. My mouth was suddenly dry. An immense thirst coursed through me, like the one I had when Kit ripped my throat out. *What had I done?*

A blanket quickly circled my shoulders from behind, and Aric handed Dooley a towel.

"Where do we go from here?" I whispered.

Dooley pulled his own pants on as I drew the blanket closer around my neck. "All that will depend on you, Valora. I told you a choice needed to be made tonight."

I fixated on Dooley's eyes. There was no flash of red, there was no demon waiting to pounce at me. Dooley was not like Mane, not like any other man I had ever met.

He sat there as calm as before. He had just shared me

with another man, but my heart was all his and he knew it. I knew it. Aric knew it. And that was when I felt Aric pull his shields up again. I did the same. I was more naked with those shields down then I ever was without clothes.

Aric walked to the sink, his wings draped down his naked back, and his white blond hair folded across his shoulder. He returned with two glasses of water and handed one to me. "You two can share that one. I'm going to bed."

He tipped his head back and let part of the glass of water drop into his mouth and the other half of it pour over his head. He shook, and the water splashed onto my naked shoulders.

"We have no quarrels." A question and a statement from Aric to Dooley.

"No," answered Dooley.

He nodded and went to the bed at the far end of the room. He lay on his side, his body curled up and facing the wall, his wings acting as his blanket.

CHAPTER THIRTEEN

I awoke suddenly in the middle of the night. I was nuzzled against Dooley's chest. He held me close to him on the small twin bed on the opposite side of the room from Aric. The calm and steady thrum of Dooley's heart beat tried to lull me to sleep. Then the sounds separated, and I knew I wasn't just hearing Dooley's heart. The drums had returned.

I slowly rolled away from Dooley and sat on the edge of the bed. Aric was still curled up on his bed facing the wall. I walked to the window which lay open and slowly parted the orange curtains. Somewhere in the middle of the forest the drums were sounding. If we had been in the Realms I would have dismissed it for elves, but here on Earth there was no such thing. Or was there? This whole cabin was full of supernaturals. Who was to say there weren't more of them camped out in the woods somewhere? But why, then, would they call attention to themselves?

Dooley and Aric slept soundly. The last thing I wanted to do was to wake one of them so we could face what we had done. The morning would come soon enough. But I also wasn't okay with just sitting here wondering if there was something waiting in the woods for me. The last time I had done that I ended up having to slay some goblins, and I didn't want any more surprises tonight.

I picked through the pile of clothes on the floor and found my gear. The dragon leather pants that Aric gave me slid on with ease. My wings tingled at the reminder of Aric. I felt less guilty than I had before. Aric and I had consummated the lust between us. He wanted more and I didn't. Aric's humanity had shown through tonight. Even with his wings it seemed his expectations were more of this world. But he had essentially lost everything today. His mother, me, and his home. I would have to watch him closely to make sure he didn't do anything stupid. I laced up the bodice and clipped it into place. If I didn't have wings to contend with I could have slid Dooley's shirt on. The night was warm, but I tucked my wings in and pulled the dragon leather coat on.

The hinges creaked as I eased the door open. I winced, but Aric and Dooley remained asleep. My sword and scabbard were propped up by the front door, and I grabbed them as I backed out of the doorway.

I shut the door and turned, freezing in place. The Edsel was parked in the driveway. Mane, Kit and Pryn had left some time ago and now the car was here, but no one was inside it.

After confirming that there were no sign of Mane or Kit I followed the sounds into the forest. Past the initial buffer of flora and fauna that surrounded the house the beat of the drums came suddenly into sharp focus. It was much closer than I had realized. It was as if there had been cotton in my ears before. I looked back and saw a faint shimmer that seemed to settle itself around the house, like the entire structure was sitting inside a soap bubble.

I reached out and passed through the shimmering field, taking a few steps towards the house, and again the drumming was muffled and seemed far off in the distance. There was something not right about this.

The magic doing this even seemed to muffle the leaves beneath my feet. I pushed past it and crept through the forest towards the pulsing sound. A scuffle to my left alerted me to someone else's presence. I looked up and almost didn't see him. Mane, sitting on a limb about ten feet up a tree, put his finger to his lips and pointed into the next clearing that he was watching from his vantage point in the trees.

I climbed up beside him until I could see what he was looking at. Through the tree line immediately in front of us was a circular clearing. The rhythmic beat of the drums was unmistakable. What wasn't clear was what I was supposed to be looking at.

"What are we hiding here for? There's nothing there," I said. As I did the drums stopped and Mane slapped his hand to his forehead.

Apparently I had just alerted whatever it was to our presence. Mane grabbed my arm and quickly pulled me out of the tree, dragging me behind him as he pushed through the brush and ran towards the house. No use being quiet this time. He skirted the bubble surrounding it and ran towards the Edsel.

"Get in the car," he yelled.

Our pursuers were invisible, but I could hear them. A gnashing and snarling that seemed to be getting closer. I jumped into the passenger seat beside Mane, and he turned a key in the ignition. The engine roared to life and he put the car in reverse.

"I thought a finger to the lips was a universal sign not to

speak."

Something clunked against the front of the car causing it to rock, but I still didn't see anything. Mane pulled the car onto the road and stopped for a second before throwing the car into first gear. Another crash rocked the side of the car as he rocketed down the road.

"Aric and Dooley…"

"Will be fine as long as they stay in the cabin," said Mane.

"Where, exactly, are we going?"

"To the city. Once I realized what Ravanna was doing I came straight back here."

"I understand that Ravanna is the demon king, but what does that mean exactly? And what is his plan?" I was starting to realize that labels didn't mean much anymore.

Mane shook his head. "Your people have always hidden in their cloud cities in an attempt to shield themselves from everything that happens in Underworld. But hiding does not make you impervious."

"My mother used to tell me that after the fae wars it was thought that it was the safest place for us. Are you saying that we were wrong?"

"Yes, and wrong for your ancestors to believe that keeping the truth from you would keep you safe. Ignorance is bliss, have you ever heard the term?"

I knew Mane was right. It was the reason I had pushed my father to make the peace treaty with the dwarves. They were no threat to us.

"We made peace with the dwarves. I think the fae are slowly coming to realize that they don't need to hide anymore. But it will take time. Our naiveté was not born overnight. It takes time to enlighten people." I knew because I was still trying to enlighten myself.

"Your mistake is not in trusting the dwarves, it is in not knowing everything that lies in wait for you out there."

"You keep saying that, but yet you don't tell me what it is I have to be afraid of. We already made sure that the conduit, Dooley and Aric's mother, has her memory erased. The gods won't be intruding here."

"What are you talking about?"

I told Mane about our visit with Aric and Dooley's mother. I didn't think I had ever seen him so caught off guard.

"Then this is something Ravanna has been planning a long time. I could tell you, but I think you need to see."

☙❧

Mane pulled into one of the suburbs of Seattle called Fremont. He parked the Edsel on the road, and I hopped out at the same time he did. Before us loomed the largest effigy of a troll that I had ever seen. "What kind of place have you brought me to?"

Mane laughed. "Oh, that? Makes me feel at home. Humans have funny ways about them. You'll find out soon enough. My apartment is around the corner."

"Am I the only one who doesn't have a vacation home on Earth?"

Mane tapped out a series of numbers onto a pad near the door of a looming brick building. "No, Kit hasn't found a place she likes yet. We're still looking."

"Are you joking?"

"Yes, even in the midst of an apocalypse you're still allowed to do that, I think. In fact, I think it is required to keep you sane. Follow me."

Mane led me down the hall to the elevator, and we took it to the top floor. The elevator opened and we padded down the thickly carpeted hallways until we reached the last door. I followed Mane into the apartment and, as he shut the door, I finally came to my senses.

"I need to alert Aric and Dooley." I sat down on the nearest chair and concentrated on dropping my shields. I hoped one of them was awake enough to hear me.

Dooley? Aric?

Was it all too much to handle, sweetheart? Great, the one person who responds to me is the one I least wanted to talk to.

No, Aric. I heard the drums again. Tell me that Dooley is there with you.

Still sleeping soundly.

Good, you two need to stay inside the cabin until I return. There is something out there. It's difficult to explain, but Mane is here with me now and I intend to get the full story from him. I'll be back as soon as I can.

You do realize that when your lover awakens to find you gone it will be hard to convince him to stay inside.

I'll leave my shields down. Just tell him to contact me and don't do anything stupid.

Do anything stupid. Why in the world would you think he would do something like that?

"I need you to see the texts." Mane passed his hands over what looked like a blank white wall. An archway appeared and through it was the largest expanse of books I had ever seen.

"If you wanted me to read a book you could have just told me what you need to tell me. Would have been quicker."

"Not quite." Mane reached up his hand and a large volume sailed towards him from the top shelf.

"Sit." He passed a hand over the archway we had come

167

through and it sealed, looking just like another shelf in the massive space.

I settled myself into a plush chair that was wedged in the corner between two stacks of books, and Mane knelt before me and placed the book on my knees. I reached out to open it, and he snatched my wrist.

"Place your hand on top. Close your eyes, and you will see."

"Okay." I set my hand on top of the smooth black leather volume. Words and pictures flooded my mind.

The beautiful Goddess Varuna and the Demon King Ravanna were at war with one another. The Goddess' wings glowed with such fierce light that I held my hand up to my eyes. The Demon King's skin was almost blue-black, and his eyes roared with a savage blood-red. They took turns trading spells against one another with no regard to those around them. Lands were laid to waste. Ravanna wanted his immortality and Varuna wanted to rule Overworld. Varuna got her wish, and Ravanna was cast down to Acheron. Ever since that time he had tried to find a way to escape the bowels of Acheron and seat himself as ruler of the Elysium, destroying Varuna in the process. And if Ravanna continued to rot away in Acheron, unable to have access to other sources of power to prolong his life, he will die.

Mane took my hand, breaking the spell. "The amulets the three of you wear were forged in Acheron by Ravanna himself. Everything Ravanna infuses with his magic he does for a purpose. I'm just not sure what it is where you three are concerned."

A chill ran down my spine making my wings tremble. "Are you certain?"

"Yes." Mane gave a slight nod. I couldn't tell if he had known this all along or had just come to the conclusion, but it didn't really matter.

"Then if he dies, the amulets won't connect us anymore?"

"Correct."

"Then let him die. You said there wasn't a way he could get up to the Realms. Why are you worried?" I was searching for a way to disconnect from Aric and this seemed to be the solution to my problem.

Mane crouched down in front of me, placing his hand over mine. "But he won't just die. Queen Elemi has been working to free Ravanna. I have seen it myself. It seems he has made false promises to the Queen that he will give her the ability to walk over the Realms with impunity. He has told her he would grant her and her people this request. She wants her freedom like he does. Why do you think she shacked up with that absurd human?"

"Ralph? Is he in danger?"

"Of course he is. All the humanity she has is due to her stealing it from humans. Without it the selkie are just monstrous creatures. Ravanna and Elemi are the true Soulstealers, not your lover Aric."

"He's not my lover." I pinned my arms against my stomach to make sure it stayed in one place. Everything else in the room suddenly became interesting. Everything but Mane.

He cupped my chin in his hand and forced me to look at him. "I am not the one you need to convince of that. And it doesn't matter to me in the slightest."

"But Kit…"

"Kit is different. She is half-selkie. She will always have to fight the demons warring inside her, but she has the power to do so. The amulet she wears is of the ancient selkies. Each Queen has possessed it. Its magic is of the

waters, not of Ravanna. Her mother, however, is different."
Mane's voice dripped with disdain when he spoke of Elemi.

"Is Ralph okay now?"

"He is entranced. He doesn't know the danger he is in. I
can't make Kit understand, but, honestly, he is the least of
my worries." Mane pulled a hand over his face, rubbing at
the stubble that had formed.

"What role do you play in all of this?"

"My role should be the least of your concerns. I am here
because I want to be."

Pryn's words repeated in my mind. I was afraid to ask,
but I had to know. "What is my role in all this?"

"If Ravanna is freed from his prison then you will be the
only one who can save us all."

"Why me?"

"You are the conduit. Both Aric, the son of Varuna, and
Dooley, the son of Ravanna, are connected to you through
these amulets. You draw on the powers of both gods,
Valora. Or you can learn to. You are the only one that can
stop them both from using the Realms and Earth as their
battleground."

"What do you mean, Earth?"

"Those creatures you couldn't see in the clearing? I
could see them because I am one of them. A demon. They
are already starting their rituals. My attempt to close them off
from the Realms has only meant that they are trying to get
through here first." Mane pushed himself up to standing.
"They must already have enough magic from Queen Elemi
to open a portal. The ones in that clearing were lesser
demons and held little power, but it is the beginning of
something much worse. If they succeed they will pour forth
and lay waste to everything in their path to access Varuna.
Anyone who is connected to her is in danger. If they draw

enough of her power she will be drawn down to them, and they will be able to challenge her in a fight to the death. And if the sky goddess dies, then the entire bowels of hell will pour forth and declare this world and the Realms their new Kingdom, and every creature left alive will be their slaves."

Mane stared into space, his voice resigned to the fate he laid out before me. It reminded me of the time I was told my mother had passed. I didn't want to believe that, and I couldn't believe this. This was something I could change. It hadn't happened yet. I could still be the Guardian.

"So it was true what Queen Elemi said about my father? He really has declared war on Elemi. How much does he know about all of this?" My hand went to the pommel of my sword and I worried at the silver tip. I had a feeling I would soon have use of it.

"I can't say for certain how much your father knows. But I know the priests have always had the knowledge that this was possible. They held the ancient texts in their temples after your fae wars."

"So Pryn knew this was coming?"

"He didn't just know. He wrote the book you hold on your lap."

❧

Mane and I spent some time going over what the plan would be. First we needed to make sure that whatever was making its way to Earth was stopped immediately. We couldn't fight a war on two fronts. Mane knew more about magic then I did. He was convinced that he could find the ritual he needed in the storage of texts he had amassed in his library. Some of the books seemed so old it was hard to believe that Mane was anywhere near their age.

I also needed to seriously brush up on my magic skills. I

still kept my mother's grimoire with me and spent the night flipping through it. Pryn was my teacher, but he was now in Dell'Aria and I wasn't going to see him again until I knew that Earth was safe.

I was supposed to be a Guardian of the fae, but it was looking more like I was a fae who was a Guardian of a lot more. I wanted nothing more than to have the amulets destroyed, but I also needed to live, and we still hadn't figured out an answer to that question. I needed Ravanna to stay alive, and I needed his plan to fail. And I wasn't totally sure how I was going to do that and deal with the fact that I had just had sex with two men. Two men that were connected to me on a level that my life depended on. If they couldn't learn to get along, I wasn't sure how we were going to make this work.

We worked well together last night. I played fair. Dooley's voice echoed in my head with words I would have expected to come from Aric. Inside this room I had no idea how time was passing outside. Mane had conjured up this magic hidey hole on his own and there were no windows.

A soft snore emitted from Mane where he had fallen asleep amongst some of the scrolls he was studying. *Seems even demons slept.* "Dooley and Aric are both awake. We need to get back."

Mane's head shot up from the desk and he rubbed at his eyes as he walked over to the wall. He passed his hand in front of it, muttering a few words, and the natural light poured through. "Looks as though it is daylight now. The demons will have dissipated. They can only do their conjuring in the night hours."

I saw a blur of blue hair as Mane was toppled onto the floor. My alarm quickly turned to joy as I saw Kit planting kisses all over Mane's face. Big bad demon elf didn't look so tough now.

"Babe, babe, I told you to wait by the portal for me. I don't want you wandering around these streets on your own."

Kit sat up and laughed. "Are you kidding? No one gives me a second look. Half the kids out there have multi-colored hair, and my glasses are a fashion statement. Even had one girl ask me where I got them. Plus I was bored, and the city transit works just as well as the Edsel in getting a girl around town." She pulled at the top of the tight fitting jeans she had somehow procured, but the iridescent scales along her hips still glimmered at her belt line. Kit smiled as Mane wrapped his arms around her and stood up, carrying her out the archway, her legs draped around his back. I stumbled over the book Mane had showed me as I followed them out. I bent down to pick it up and noticed that I had kicked the binding loose. Inside was a folded paper. I plucked it out and shoved it in my satchel to read later, leaving the large tome behind.

"Are we all going back to Aric and Dooley then?" I knew we needed to join up with them again, but at the same time I wasn't sure if I could face them.

"I think maybe you need some time alone with them first, don't you?" Mane looked right through me, and my cheeks grew hot.

"I think I have had enough time alone with them."

"You say that now." Mane sneered, his previous demeanor returning full force.

"What did I miss?" asked Kit.

"Nothing."

"Everything," said Mane.

"Let's just get to the cabin," I said.

"I have a better idea. I'll ask Artemus to go out and get

them. We are going to need to make a stop at a shop downtown, and we'll need to have them with us. This is something you all need to see."

"What, another supernatural creature with super special powers?"

"No, just a human." Mane tilted his head. "A very odd human. Dooley and Aric will be here soon. Make yourself comfortable. I'll just give him a quick call from the bedroom."

Mane continued to walk forward into the bedroom and kicked the door shut behind him. Kit's squeals of delight were hard to drown out. Of course in a moment I wouldn't be able to deny that I had just recently been doing the same thing. My two partners would be right in front of me.

I walked out onto Mane's balcony and shut the door to muffle the sounds. He had a beautiful view of Puget Sound and Gas Works Park. People passed by on the sidewalks with their little animals and it made me miss Pika. The sooner I could fix this problem the sooner I could be home. Winter Haven seemed like ages ago, and I wasn't sure if or when Dooley and I would ever make it back there now.

I stood on the balcony for a long time leaning against the railing and taking in the cool overcast air. My reverie was broken when I saw the Vanagon drive by on the street below. Artemus parked on the street. Dooley jumped out of the passenger seat and Aric out of the side door. So the two of them hadn't killed one another. That was a bonus.

I watched as each of them crossed the street. There was no denying that Dooley held my heart, but Aric practically had girls running into poles as he strolled across the street. He emitted the fae charm like no other. But the only one who had me enthralled was Dooley, perhaps because he only doled out a little bit of himself at a time. How was it that I had managed to attract the attention of both of them?

I walked inside and opened the front door before tapping gently on Mane and Kit's door. "The others are coming up. You two might want to get yourselves together."

I quickly popped into the bathroom and fussed with my hair, cinched my bodice tighter and took off my coat. There was no need to hide my fae nature as long as we stayed in the apartment.

I knew they had entered the apartment before I heard or saw them. I walked out to meet them.

"Hi, guys." I tried to be as nonchalant as possible but with both of them watching me, saying nothing, it seemed they were both waiting for me to say something that would mean something to them. "Kit and Mane should be out soon." Well, so much for meaningful.

"Aric, why don't you help me whip up some food for us before we go. I don't know about any of you, but I haven't eaten in a while," said Artemus who appeared behind him in the doorway. Dooley didn't break his gaze from me, and I noticed he had my coat in his hands.

"Put on your coat, Valora. We need to talk." Dooley held up my coat, and I slipped my hands into the sleeves. So much for stretching out my wings.

Dooley pressed his hand to my back and I took a sharp intake of breath as I recalled him pushing me towards Aric's embrace. "Put up your shields," he ordered, guiding me onto the balcony.

Dooley slid the balcony door closed, and I turned to face him.

"I question why you allowed that to happen last night," I said.

"Like I can keep you from something you want. It was better to happen in my presence. I knew sooner or later Aric would convince you to make certain that your feelings for him weren't real. Now you know."

"Do I?" I knew it was Dooley that I wanted, but there was something about Aric that I needed, and I wasn't sure what it was.

"He is more fae than I am. That is the attraction you have towards him. You have resolved your past issues, but the fae in him is strong."

"Then why don't I want to jump every fae's bones?"

"Because you have also cared for him in the past." Dooley pressed at his temples. "I didn't want to come out here to make you feel bad about last night, Valora. Last night was something you both wanted and both needed. If we are going to move forward from here to face whatever it is that we are fighting, you need to clear the air. Both of you."

He was saying all the right words, but it didn't make sense.

I took a step towards Dooley, closing the space between us. "What about you? How is your head these days?"

"Aching at the sight of you." He grabbed my arms, pressing his body into mine, and I knew exactly what he was talking about. He closed his eyes, leaning his forehead against mine. "I'm hungry, let's go inside." He broke his grip on me and turned away.

The echo of his warm breath danced across my mouth. He wasn't going to let me get any closer, and, despite saying that it was his intention that last night play out the way it did, I couldn't help but think otherwise.

CHAPTER FOURTEEN

The Edsel was too small for all of us, so we piled into Artemus' Vanagon after a breakfast of scrambled eggs and toast. A breakfast for all of us except Kit, of course. I worried about her ability to keep control of herself in a crowd.

"As long as it stays cool outside it shouldn't drain me too bad," said Kit when I questioned her. Mane sat up front with Artemus. Dooley and Aric were staring out opposite windows from the middle bench seat. Kit and I had the rear to ourselves.

"Are you telling me that you can't go out in the sun?" I looked out at what seemed like the typical overcast Seattle day and saw a patch of blue sky drifting towards us. It was overcast now, but not for long.

"It's not that I can't, it's more like it's a drain on me. And then I have to be a drain on someone else. I'm starting to get it all figured out." Kit reached up and put her hair into a loose bun at the back of her neck.

"You might want to leave your hair down," I said pointing to the marks on her neck.

"Oh, Mane, that little demon." She let her hair loose again and leaned over the seat in front of her, placing her head atop her clasped hands between Dooley and Aric.

"Little wasn't what you were telling me this morning, dear," said Mane from the front seat.

"Why don't you remind me again? I think I may have forgotten." Kit scooted her glasses to the edge of her nose and stared at Mane from over the rims.

His eyes flashed red, revealing the demon inside. "Don't tempt me."

"Too late."

Mane grunted and returned to watching the road. The exchange didn't affect either Aric or Dooley who remained focused on our surroundings.

"How is it that you two were able to get back here again with the Edsel?"

"Let's just say that I was able to convince Elemi to give it to me," said Mane.

"Kit, I think your mother might be up to something," I said. "I'm not sure that your father is safe."

"He is safe as long as he stays out of the way. But I know, Valora. I'm no dummy. My father needs to return to Earth. He can't stay with my mother. I think she only keeps him alive to appease me. She wants to use me to do her bidding since she can't stay far from Lake Mavrovo for long. If she gets her way that could all change." She twisted a length of her hair and bit down on it.

"Mane told me. Look, I need to see my father at some point. We have to know what he is planning so that we can make sure Ralph is safe. And what about the other selkie? They can't be all bad. If my father is planning an assault, are there others we need to rescue?"

Kit shoved her glasses onto her face and turned to me.

Her jaw set in a stern line. "If he knows of a way to defeat them, he needs to kill all of them. Every. Single. One."

I nodded. If Kit wanted all of her people dead, there was a lot I didn't know about what had gone on with her down there. Part of me felt guilty for bringing her there in the first place, but if I hadn't she would have been dead. Of course, that was my choice, not hers. I had made that choice for her like I had made that choice for Dooley. Maybe Aric was right, maybe he and I were more alike than I wanted to believe.

Would I make the same decision for someone I didn't care very deeply for? I hadn't been tested in that manner yet. I had no idea.

We rattled into the south end of the downtown district into an area called Pioneer Square. The buildings were smaller and dwarfed in comparison to the large skyscrapers that dotted the city in the center of town. It was as if I could stand on the roof of one of those buildings and have a conversation with the real Goddess Varuna. Maybe I could ask her what the heck I was supposed to be doing here.

Artemus maneuvered the van to a parking space, and we all piled out. We got a few strange looks, but didn't seem to be attracting any unwanted attention. With what I had seen around the city, I could probably walk around with my wings out and no one would look twice.

Artemus led us to a storefront with a sign outside that said "Zanadu" in large red letters. The building itself was a modest storefront, but its windows were packed with booklets of all sorts advertising creatures I had never seen before.

"What kind of place is this?"

"My son's comic book store," said Artemus.

"So, my cousin?"

"Not quite. He was my wife's son from a previous marriage. No blood relation. But he knows all about me. Once his mother, my wife, passed away we were all there was left for each other. His father passed away a long time ago. We see each other often."

"So, a normal human?" I asked.

"With not so normal interests. He has a particular interest in demonology. His mother was also a very unique individual."

Artemus pushed on the door to the shop, and the soft tinkle of a bell sounded above the door. The smell hit me before anything else. I came in right behind Artemus and put my hand on his shoulder to steady myself.

"When was the last time you saw your son?" I asked.

"A few days ago," he said. We all paused and listened to the lack of sound.

"The door wouldn't be wide open if no one was here," said Dooley.

"Blood, I smell blood." Kit whipped off her glasses and went charging past us towards the back of the store, Mane following close behind.

Everything in the store seemed normal except for the lack of people and the smell of death. I stopped in my tracks as did Dooley and Aric.

"What is it?" asked Aric.

"This is a trap. There is no way that no one would have come upon this shop before now." My Hunter instincts kicked in, but it was a little too late.

I heard Kit scream out and then Artemus yelling. "Keep her away. Valora!"

I rushed towards the back of the store and stopped dead in my tracks. Mane held Kit around the waist and she was clawing and biting at him. In the corner of the backroom lay a pile of three bodies which looked like they had been there for a while. Amongst a stack of overturned boxes was another body all by itself that Artemus was cradling. I could only assume it was his son.

"Bowen, what have you gotten yourself into?" He whispered the words as he stroked his hands through the young man's damp black hair.

I crept up slowly behind Artemus and realized that the man he was holding was still alive. Barely, but still alive. Artemus' voice rang shrill. "Valora, we need to help him."

I crouched down by his side. "What is it you need me to do?"

"He needs blood and magic. I'm not sure he can do with one and not the other. It will take a miracle. He has been here for several days from the looks of it."

Bowen reached up and touched Artemus' face with his bloodied hand, leaving a red streak across Artemus' cheek. I looked down and realized that he had a horrible gash across his mid-section. "Uncle, I don't know that we can save him."

"We have to try." His eyes were feverish with desperation, a look I was all too familiar with.

I nodded and sat down next to him, putting my hands to the amulet at my neck.

"No!" Both Aric and Dooley rushed forward to stop me.

"I need to save him, and I don't know any other way."

"Yes, but your actions with that amulet affect more than just you now. We are a triumvirate," said Dooley.

"He's right," said Mane. "There is another way." He brought Kit, who was kicking and fighting against Mane and her selkie nature, towards Bowen.

"Take your sword and make a cut on her wrist," said Mane.

I rose up and drew my sword. "I don't want to hurt her."

"She will heal quickly. I will make sure her blood is replenished. But hers is the only one that can save Bowen without harming anyone else. It's the only way. Don't look directly at her," warned Mane.

I nodded and looked only at Kit's arm. Dooley and Aric helped Mane restrain Kit and held her right arm out straight. I took my blade to the fleshy part of her mid-arm, away from her wrist, and quickly pulled the blade down in a sharp and shallow stroke. Blood welled up inside the wound and dripped down.

Mane positioned Kit's arm over Bowen and let her blood fall inside his mouth that Artemus held open.

Bowen made a choking sound, and Artemus closed his mouth down. "He's had enough."

Kit let out a whimper, and Mane pulled her away. Kit seemed frustrated that she was so close to her next meal.

Bowen sat up and then fell down again into Artemus' arms.

"I need to get her something to heal her. We will be back." Mane went towards the door and was suddenly forced backwards. "What the hell?"

"Trapped. Can't get out," muttered Bowen. He rolled his head to the side and opened his eyes, seeming to realize that it was Artemus who was holding him. "You need to get out. You can't be here when they come back."

I stepped forward and lifted Bowen's shirt. The wound had closed, but it was hard to say how much damage had been done and whether or not he would pull through.

Mane held Kit in the corner, but her humanity was rapidly disintegrating. Mane was no longer getting through to her. "Will she be okay?"

"She needs blood. If not, then we are all in danger."

"Why don't you open a vein for her, Mane? You seem to be good at exchanging fluids with her," said Aric.

"If you knew the seriousness of this situation, you would not be joking. There are only two here in this room that she can feed from. That boy who lies dying on the floor or Artemus. The rest of us, she will just kill to get out of the way."

"What?" I stepped forward and saw that sweat was beading on Mane's forehead as his muscles strained to keep Kit still.

"No demon blood and no angel blood."

"But she fed from me before."

"That was before you were connected to the demon and the angel."

Dooley and Aric. Demon and Angel. I would never have guessed that Aric could ever be considered an angel.

"I will help. If we are going to figure out what is happening here then we need her to be calm." Artemus laid Bowen gently to the ground and stood up.

"Artemus, the last time I offered up a vein to Kit she ripped my neck out. We don't have anything to heal you."

Artemus looked so much like my mother in that moment. His face full of the kindness she wore when she would tend to the sick. "My darling niece, your mother always knew that you would not follow in her footsteps. You have the heart of a warrior. She always said so. Don't worry that you are not her. If I do not do this, we all will die."

"But Bowen is near death already. If a sacrifice is about to be made…"

"Bowen may only be a human, but a human life — no matter how short — is no less valuable then a fae's life. And I will not let him be an unwilling sacrifice."

Kit became increasingly agitated, and Mane slammed against the wall as she tried to throw him off her. She reached up for Mane's throat and wrapped her hands around his neck.

"Kit, I have what you need." Artemus pulled his coat off, and his wings spread wide. I had never seen him like this before. His wings were a luminous white as Brokk's had been. Like my mother's had been. He tilted his neck as he walked towards Kit.

Mane strained to hold her back. "I don't know that you want to do this, Artemus."

"Come to me, child." Artemus held his arms out and Mane lost his grip on Kit. In a flash I saw Kit's mouth clamp down on his neck, a spray of red blood arcing across his white wings as he wrapped them around Kit and enfolded her. Keeping her tight against him. I stepped forward, and Dooley put his hand on my shoulder. Artemus had never intended to survive once he offered himself up to the selkie. But he knew his sacrifice would keep us alive. I just hoped that it wouldn't all be for nothing.

⁓⊰⊱⁓

When it was all over Kit lay weeping in the corner, her mouth and shirt strewn with my uncle's blood. I remembered my uncle when I was young. He so much like my mother. His sole purpose was to help and aid others. I wondered who would take his place at the morgue. How much longer would it be before our presence in this world would become common knowledge? What would that mean for the fae and for all creatures of the Realms?

But I couldn't worry about that for long. If we didn't figure out how to keep Earth safe then keeping our identities safe would be the least of our worries. My uncle lay dead on the floor. Several of the shop workers were piled up dead in the corner. Bowen was barely alive and still hadn't been able to make any sense. We were locked in this room by some kind of magic, and we were running out of time.

The storeroom was large enough to house all the back stock for the shop and a small front area where a computer sat on a small desk. The rest was taken up by long metal shelving which disappeared into blackness and contained row upon row of cardboard boxes and a few packs of bottled water. The lights only went so far. Aric and Dooley left to explore the rest of the stockroom to see if there was another way out.

I sat next to Bowen whose breaths were shallow but strong. A few times his eyes fluttered open and quickly shut again. But the wound at his stomach had completely closed, and I was certain he would survive. Mane left Kit for a moment and came over to speak to me.

"She feels horrible," he said.

Kit was curled in the corner sobbing into her knees.

"I know she does, Mane. So do I."

"I have tried to educate her on her nature. I have tried to warn her. But she is still very young and wants to believe that she has control over this. We will find a way, but until then she will be vulnerable to temptations like this."

"What about her mother?"

Mane spit on the ground. "That bitch hasn't taught her a thing. If anything she has made it worse. Making her believe that her true nature is nothing to fear. Her mother is all selkie. She has no idea of the difference between humanity and the selkie nature. And she doesn't care."

"But you do?" I didn't mean to question Mane's intentions, but the only thing I knew about him was that he was a demon in an elf's body. I had no real idea how he got there or what he wanted from all of this.

"I have lived inside this body for the past fifty cycles. When it was an infant I could do nothing but observe. It was very frustrating. I was a horrible child as a result. But that time taught me patience. I eventually gave in. Ravanna meant the sentence to be like a prison to me. In many ways it was, but I am grateful now. I only wish I never had to leave this body."

"But you told me you were immortal. Once this body dies you will be reborn into another." I gave Bowen another sip of water from one of the bottles of water.

"A problem I am trying to remedy." He pressed his fist into his chin.

I gave a slight nod before returning my attention to Bowen. Perhaps Mane believed that the selkie magic could help him. Queen Elemi obviously thought that the demons could grant her the power to be free of the confines of Lake Mavrovo. Maybe Mane thought he could be granted mortality. That was the question on everyone's mind. How did you kill a demon? Or a god? Soon, it seemed, I would need to know the answer to both of those questions.

"I'll go talk to her," I said to Mane. "Will you watch over Bowen?"

Kit held her hand out as I approached. "No, Valora, no. I don't deserve your words unless you have come to berate me. I'm a horrible person. I wish I was dead. But if I take off this amulet I will only end up killing everyone else because of the hunger."

I took a long slow breath and tried not to glance sideways at my uncle's crumpled body. "We are all out of our element, Kit. I wish I had known the extent of your condition. It seems like we have been playing a guessing game, and that makes things hard. But I know you didn't know either, so while I would love to blame you for what you have done, I know I can't. I also know that Artemus wouldn't blame you either. He sacrificed himself for his son. Without your blood he would have died."

"Is he going to be okay?" Kit watched as Mane held his hand to Bowen's forehead.

"I think so. So you see Kit, one life for another. It was the way Artemus wanted it. And whatever did this to Bowen and the others, that wasn't your fault. We had no idea what we were walking into. I am going to need you strong in case it comes back."

Kit sat upright. "I will kick the ass or asses of whatever comes through that door next." She wiped her tears from her face. "Thanks, Valora."

I reached out and gave her shoulder a squeeze. "Be strong. You can break down later." Words I was thinking applied to me, too.

She nodded, and I walked over to Mane. "Let me know if she is getting close to the breaking point again."

Aric came from one of the darkened aisles. "I don't know spells, but I do know that there isn't any way out there. I searched the entire south and east sides, and it is nothing but solid brick walls and boxes."

"Where's Dooley?"

"He hasn't returned? We decided he was going to take the west end to save time."

I dropped the shields in my mind and reached out towards Dooley. Aric did the same.

"He's here," said Aric. "But whatever was calling out to him before is here also, and I think it has finally gotten his attention."

∾∾

"A trap!" Bowen sat upright, his breath coming in sharp rasps and his body trembling. "Don't go down there!"

"Down here?" I pointed to where Dooley had gone. It looked just like another rack of stock which descended into darkness.

"Yes, please. You have to listen to me."

"But my friend is down there. I have to look for him."

"Your friend?" Aric raised an eyebrow at me.

"Cut it out, Aric, not now." Though I was well aware of what I had just said. Not as I was saying it but after the phrase had exited my mouth. Good goddess, calling Dooley my friend was ridiculous. But calling Aric anything more than that was the same thing. Ridiculous. And after what just transpired between us I wasn't sure what to think. I didn't go around having sex with my friends. I didn't go around having sex with just anyone. *So what the heck was Aric to me?* Something I did not have time to contemplate for more than a few seconds at a time. He was part of my escape which was also the main problem.

But now I had something else to deal with. Bowen had just seen Artemus and realized he was dead.

It took some time, and Kit did all she could do. She stayed out of the way. There was no amount of words from her that could have fixed anything about this situation. I kept the lines open between Dooley and me. It felt as if his mind was drifting, but I knew his body wasn't far. He hadn't left us yet. But I was running out of time to figure out just what Dooley had gotten himself into.

"Bowen." I touched his shoulder as he wept over Artemus body. "I know he was a father to you, but he died so that you would live. We are not out of danger. I need you to bottle up your grief for now."

"Yeah, hold it in. You can break down later. Right,

Valora?" Kit looked at me from where she was pacing in the corner. Her eyes were hidden behind her glasses, but her mouth went up in a vicious sneer.

"Mane?"

"I'll look after her." He walked towards Kit and did the only thing he could do. He pulled her towards him and undid her clothing as he pulled her down one of the other aisles.

"I suppose that will take care of them for a bit."

Bowen's mouth hung agape. "Are they really going to do what I think they are going to do?"

"I think your shop has seen much worse, and believe me, you would rather have them going at it then have Kit lose it and kill you. Since you, after all, are the only one left that could provide her with a meal," said Aric.

"How long do you think we have?" Bowen asked. The tremors in his hands were obvious as he clutched at his throat.

"Her amulet wasn't meant to allow her any extended visits, and this one is putting a lot of stress on her system. There is really no telling. What we really need to know is what we are dealing with. What harmed you and killed those people, and why are we trapped in here?" I asked. Bowen was the only one left alive who could give us the answers we needed.

"It was stupid. I told her she shouldn't have done it," Bowen was shaking his head again and looking at the pile of bodies. He stepped towards them and picked up the limp wrist of a young girl with pink hair.

"What did she do, Bowen?" Aric stepped forward. He wasn't going to let Bowen's grief get in the way of us getting out of here.

"All my research. All my notes. I had been keeping files

on my studies of demonology. Interviews of those I met over the years. Once about twenty years ago I met a woman who called herself Ravanna. She gave me the most complete information I had to date. A map or a plan on how her people were going to come to Earth. I hadn't given it much consideration. I interviewed a lot of crazy people over the years. But then the things she said would happen started to come true. It seemed like the stars were aligning, so to speak. I must have left my research open, and Lauralynn must have seen it. She was always bugging me about what I was doing. But I knew her interest came from somewhere not healthy. I was always in it to find out information. She just wanted an escape from her life. She had no idea what she was doing." Bowen pressed his open palms against his face.

"What did she do?" I wanted to allow him his grief, but Dooley wasn't answering my calls.

"I think she summoned Ravanna," said Bowen.

"What the hell?" Mane came rushing out completely nude.

"Mane! Get the hell over here!" yelled Kit from the darkened hallway.

"Wait." Mane's eyes glowed bright red. This man definitely didn't shy away from nudity. "What is this about Ravanna?"

Bowen took a deep swallow and continued his explanation. "The name came up more and more in my research. Online and in other places. So I kept a file. Eventually what I came to learn was that Ravanna was considered the King of the demons."

Mane spat out a laugh. "He is only a King in his own mind, one that wields power. A royal bloodline, he does not possess. But he will possess anyone who he thinks can help him get what he wants."

Bowen nodded. "I think that is what he did."

He went on to explain to us how he had come in to check on the shop and found Lauralynn in some kind of trance with a knife in her hand. The two other employees were already dead. He tried to free the knife from her hand, but she lashed out at him before turning the knife on herself.

"The last thing she said was 'Fucking waste of time' and then she plunged the knife into herself. I was already bleeding out. I tried to go out front and get away, but I couldn't. The doors seemed locked."

"I can sense it now. He has made this place one of his inner sanctums, sealed with many sacrifices," said Mane.

"He's here right now?" I blurted out.

"In a way. But we need to dispel whatever remains of him if we are going to get out."

"And just how do we do that?"

Bowen went into action. "I think I can help."

"Good, because I am needed elsewhere." Mane strode off down the hall he had come from.

Bowen shuffled through the papers on the desk, and a pain rang through my brain. Aric clutched at his head as well. We were both feeling the pull on Dooley.

"It feels like my brain is being sucked out through a straw. Can't that dweeb move any faster?" Aric banged on the ground.

Dooley. I reached out as far as I could with my mind, until only tiny threads held together my sanity. Strange images pierced my consciousness. Large grotesque beasts and flaming geysers of fire. And Dooley, walking quietly through it all full of wonder.

Dooley! In my mind I saw him turn to look at me, and his deep brown eyes flashed red. Red like a demon. *Wake up.*

The second voice was not my own, but Aric's. I looked

up. He was shaking my shoulders. Mane and Kit were clothed and were looking down on me.

"How long was I out?" I sat up and tried to ignore the throbbing pain.

"About fifteen minutes." A steady clicking drew my attention to Bowen who was typing away on his computer.

"What exactly is he doing that is supposed to help Dooley? And if I don't get answers in two seconds I am going in there after him no matter what is there." I drew my sword. The ring of the metal against the scabbard echoed through the stockroom.

"Just wait two seconds. I think I almost got this figured out." He continued to pluck away at his machine.

"Exactly what kind of magic do you know, human?" asked Aric.

"Oh, Aric, you're half human, you know," I said.

"Don't forget about the angel, darling."

"All words," said Mane.

"Okay, I think that I can just send a pulse through these lines and that should cause enough electro-magnetic disturbance for you to go in and get him."

"Go in and get him from where exactly?"

"He's at the doorway into the inner sanctum, and unfortunately for all of us he happens to have a very convincing key," said Mane.

"Meaning?"

"He is born of the oracle that Ravanna possessed. He is part of Ravanna born out in this mortal world. But he is not the only one who can access that world. If I ventured too near the door I could cause a problem as well."

"How about Aric? Wouldn't being part angel cause it to close?"

"Yes, but it could close him inside as well."

"So I am the only one that can go down there and get him?" I asked.

"Yes, you and Kit. But I don't think it is a good idea for her to assist you right now."

"Right. Okay, do what you need to do."

Bowen pushed a few buttons and all the lights got super bright then went dead. A set of emergency lights lit up the perimeter.

"Whoops, sorry. It will be a little dark, but that should do it."

"I'm going in." I couldn't wait any longer. Every second Dooley slipped further and further away from me.

I put my hand to the shelf and felt along the sides while clutching my sword. Stacks of paper and boxes brushed past my fingers and then something different. Heated stone. As I plunged deeper into the hallway, the concrete floor beneath my feet changed to dirt and I heard a shuffling as my boots scuffed along the ground.

When I reached what should have been the wall of the building I tripped slightly over something on the floor. I gained my footing and rose up slowly, realizing I was no longer where I used to be. The hallway opened into a broad expanse that was lit with a few torches. An immense doorway carved with horrific scenes of death and torture framed the wall.

Dooley had his back to me with both hands reaching up towards a large iron ring on the door. He could have easily reached it at any time, but he was fighting not to. Fighting as hard as he could.

❦

It took me a minute to adjust my vision in the low light. A minute before I realized what I was really looking at. The door Dooley was leaning against was not intricately carved. It was a plain wooden door which had been adorned with carefully drawn symbols. And I knew who had drawn them because he had drawn them many times upon my skin.

Something dropped to the ground at Dooley's feet. I saw the glint of the knife seconds before Dooley fell to his knees. As I rushed to him the light of the torches illuminated the symbols, and I realized they were drawn in blood.

I bent down and scooped Dooley's head into my lap. *Aric.* I tried to call to him through our connection, but nothing happened. "Aric!" I screamed as loud as I could. My voice echoed around me. They told me I was the only one who could come this far, but I didn't know what to do.

I tried to see where the blood was coming from, but the light was dim. I ran my hands down Dooley's arm and came back with a hand of blood. He had traced cuts into his arms in the same pattern as his tattoos. I looked up and noticed that almost the entire door was covered in the markings save for one space, the space that Dooley had been leaning against when I came up to him. The markings pulsed and a vibration passed through the floor.

If this space had been designated an inner sanctum for the demon King Ravanna then I was guessing that behind that door was hell. *Why the heck weren't our amulets working?* Dooley should have drawn power from me to heal but he wasn't.

From down the hall came Bowen. He had a cloth in his hand and he gave it to me. "The one with the wings told me to give this to you so you could wipe away the markings."

The cloth contained more blood. "What is this, do you know?"

"He sliced his hand open. And he told me to tell you it hurts, so would you please hurry up?"

"Sounds like Aric." I took the cloth and rubbed it over the markings on the door. They all became one large smear, but it seemed to be doing the trick. The vibrations stopped and the light stopped as well. All of a sudden I was knocked backwards. I slammed into a large shelving unit. I blinked and the door was all gone, replaced with a brick wall which was still smeared with blood.

Aric flew down the hall and landed in front of me. "Any doubt now who the angel is?"

"Aric, we need to see if Dooley is okay." The amulet at my chest lit up as did Aric's.

"I guess that gives us our answer." He drove a balled up fist into his chest. "Damn that hurts."

I crawled over to where Dooley was lying on the floor and brushed his dark brown curls away from his face. "How are you feeling?"

Dooley opened his eyes and looked at me, his expression grave. "Like I need to get outside and get some air." He staggered up and brushed past Aric and me.

I hurried after him. "Dooley, we can't get out, remember? We're trapped."

"Not anymore." He pushed open the door to the stockroom with ease and exited into the main store.

"Wait, Dooley, where are you going?"

He quickly turned around. His eyes no longer flashed red, but the look on his face told me that he was angry about something. "I need to get some air, and I need you to stop following me. I have the two of you in my head all the time. The least you can do is give me some space."

I felt the shields slam down around me. Aric caught up to me as I watched Dooley walk outside. He went across the street and into a store.

"Don't take it too personally. He has a bit of an anger

problem," said Aric.

"What do you mean, he has an anger problem? He is one of the most patient people I know, except when it comes to you, and that I understand." What I didn't understand was why he had just lashed out at me.

Aric looked at me with incredulity. "You have had access to both our most inner thoughts and you haven't even bothered to take a peek, have you? I mean, not wanting to know what is floating around in my brain where you are concerned, I can understand, but I certainly would want to know what Dooley was thinking if I were you."

"Are you telling me I have something to be concerned about? Look, I expect Dooley to tell me if he has something to say. I don't like this mind link any more than he does. I'm certainly not going to take advantage of it."

"Really? Because he has already done so with you." His fingers formed a steeple under his chin as he raised one eyebrow.

"You're lying. How could you possibly know that?"

"Because I have delved into his innermost thoughts, Valora. Why else do you think I would have gone through with having sex with the both of you at the same time? It was because I knew he wanted it. More like he knew you wanted it, and he wanted to see how you would react if he let you."

"So it was a test?" I practically choked on my words.

"Yes, and I think perhaps you may have failed."

It was all beginning to make sense. I hated Aric for bringing to my attention what was right in front of me. Of course it had been a test. Dooley had tried to throttle Aric only seconds before it had all happened. But there was still something that didn't make sense.

"Then why wouldn't I be able to sense his

disappointment. Until now he hasn't shown any anger towards me."

"Dooley has an inner sanctum of anger that is more impressive and foreboding than that door you just faced. He hides it well."

"How is it that you see it and I don't?"

"I don't know. Maybe it's one of my angelic powers. Or maybe it's right in front of you and you have been blocking it out because you don't want to see it."

Mane and Kit joined us in the front room of the store.

"You will need to clear out of here," said Mane. He held up the keys to Artemus' Vanagon. "I have the keys."

"What about you guys and the bodies?"

"Bowen is going to call in some favors from his father's associates. We're leaving a piece of Kit's mirror with him in case he needs to contact us. We'll stay behind to make sure everything is okay and then we'll meet you at Dooley's cabin."

"Maybe we should just go to my apartment. It's closer," said Aric.

"No, we need to close the doorway that has been opened near Dooley's cabin. Then we need to get to the Realms as fast as possible. Where's Dooley?"

Mane's question was answered as Dooley came from out of the store with a paper sack. He walked over to Mane and took the keys from his hand.

"Are we ready to get out of here?" Dooley didn't wait for an answer. He just got in the driver's seat and revved the engine.

Mane took hold of my elbow. "If he self-destructs he will take you both with him. You'd better watch out for him."

I nodded and quickly got in the passenger's seat as Aric

slid in behind me. The second the doors were closed Dooley peeled away from the curb.

"Don't you even want to know what is going on?" Dooley could be mad at me all he wanted but there were other things going on here, and I was annoyed that he was acting like a petulant child.

"I heard it all. Damn shields aren't working."

I took a second to test his theory. "But I can't hear any of your thoughts."

"I know. And I will keep it that way. But it takes a lot of concentration." His voice was clipped.

"Why don't you want me to know what you're thinking?"

Dooley reached in his pocket and pulled out a cigarette, propping it between his lips and then reaching in for a lighter. He clicked the lighter on and the flame danced in front of his eyes for a moment before he put it to the end and took a long drag on the cigarette.

"It's better for both of us that way." He continued to keep his eyes on the road as the van filled with smoke. I rolled down the window and stared outside. Aric was silent. Sitting in this car riding down the highway with these two men, and I had never felt so alone in my life.

CHAPTER FIFTEEN

We got to Dooley's cabin before anyone else. Dooley never stopped puffing on the cigarettes, and the second we stopped he took a big swig from a bottle in the brown paper bag he clutched in his other fist. He blasted out of the van and into the cabin, slamming the door shut behind him.

"I bet if we had sex right here he would come back out. You want to try?" Aric gave me a smirk. I had to admit, even though his jokes were distasteful, I'd rather have his jokes then Dooley's attitude.

"I can't stand this. When they get here I want to perform that ritual and leave here as soon as possible."

Aric's smirk drooped a bit. "I figured you would feel that way."

I took a deep breath, my wings bustling against the confines of my jacket. "I know you don't want to face what is coming your way in the Realms, Aric, but I bet that I could help with that. Besides, I can't really think of your reception right now. I need to find out what it is that my father and Queen Elemi are up to."

"I know." Aric kicked at a stone and sent it flying into

the brush. "Actually, I've known for a while that I would have to return to the Realms. Just as Dooley can no longer survive here for long, neither can I. And neither can you. I'm afraid this will have to be our last visit to Earth."

"What do you mean?"

Now it was Aric's turn to take a deep breath. "After these wars are over your father will certainly seal the portals permanently. If he wins he will have the power to do so. And he will see just how important it is in order to keep Ravanna from sneaking through."

"What if we kill Ravanna?" The thought had occurred to me when I found out that he was the one responsible for the amulets. Maybe if I hadn't been connected to Aric all these years I wouldn't have fallen into temptation with him and Dooley wouldn't be feeling so sorry for himself.

"You have lofty goals, but we have to think realistically."

The sleek black Edsel drove up the driveway. I could see Kit's blue hair in the passenger seat and Mane at the wheel.

As they pulled up I saw a flash of green pass through the bushes beside the car. I figured it was just the wind or a gathering of leaves. But in an instant I was proven wrong. Kali stepped between the bushes before Kit and Mane could get out of the car.

Before I could draw my sword Aric pushed me behind him. "You need to leave. You stole what you wanted, now get out of here."

"But I think I can help," said Kali. She really was beautiful. Her wings were a brilliant shade of jade green. But I was quickly shaken out of my reverie.

"How do you think you can help?" I really wanted to believe that Kali never meant to betray me. That it was all Aric's doing. But somehow I knew that was wrong.

You know it is wrong because it is wrong. Ask her how it all went. Aric's mouth was drawn into a thin line, a storm brewing behind his dark blue eyes.

Mane and Kit stepped from the car. "Do you need any help, Valora?" Mane held Kit behind him but I knew Kit was ready to come to my aid, and I knew Mane would be at her side.

"Why don't you all go in and check on Dooley. He wasn't feeling like himself, and I think I need a word with Kali."

She is a better liar than I ever was. And that you know is true. Aric stared Kali down. "If you harm her in any way, if she so much as sheds a tear, I will call upon every favor I have, upon the Goddess herself to bring her wrath upon you. There are no more chances for you, Kali Mirch."

"You think I don't know that?" she blurted out. I wasn't sure if Kali's reasons were self-serving or not, but I was willing to hear her out. For a second I looked at her wings and wondered what mine would have been like. Perhaps they would have grown long and black and I could have soared unnoticed in the night skies of Overworld. And for a second, the briefest of seconds, I understood her motives. But understanding and empathy or sympathy is not the same thing. Forgiveness is not automatic where understanding is concerned. It is only a bridge, and I wasn't sure I was going to walk across it. I certainly had made no such promises to Aric, though I'm sure he could have interpreted things that way. I tended to take our mind link for granted. It didn't matter what I said, he would know. Of course he seemed to know even when my shields were up. In fact he had stayed by my side this entire time.

"Thank you for speaking to me, Valora."

"You should know that Aric has told me nothing of your involvement. But I will know if what you tell me is a lie or not."

"Aric and I had a deal." She stepped forward and I stepped back.

"You can stay there and tell me." My fingers danced atop the hilt of my blade. This time my mind wanted to trust Kali, but my body didn't.

"He wanted me to keep you safe, but he didn't exactly define what he meant by that." She fidgeted with the dark green wings, pulling the feathers between her fingers.

"Seems pretty clear to me."

"It did to me, too, until he sent you to Earth without telling me. I figured it meant he wanted you to stay there." Kali took a tenuous step towards me and I stood my ground.

"So you closed the portal door?"

"Yes, but not before I had come through and taken care of Brokk." She retched slightly at her own words.

"I am not sure what has your stomach in knots now."

"We were...together before all of this. Before Aric made him go to Earth." She wiped the tears away from her face.

My skin crawled with an intense desire to be anywhere but here, but I had invited her to explain so I would listen. "I have to tell you this, Kali, you have a sick sense of commitment."

"I needed to have my wings again, Valora. I obsessed about it since the day they were taken away from me. You can understand, can't you? You have something every day and you take it for granted, then one day it is gone and you obsess over it? I know you can relate, Valora."

"You don't get to compare my mother to your wings. Not having wings doesn't kill you. I should know."

"Oh, but it did kill me, Valora. I died inside a little bit more every day until I felt like I was no longer a fae. When Aric send Brokk away I completely lost it. No one knew about us. Brokk needed to keep it secret because he was a priest, but he was the only thing that kept me sane. When he disappeared I found Aric searching through his hut. It seemed strange that the King was alone without the guard around him. That's when I saw Brokk's journal in his hands. I snatched it from him, we struggled, and a deal was born. I keep you safe and he would find a way to give me wings."

Standing before me was my best friend and my greatest enemy. She knew far too much about me for me to trust her intentions now.

"You must not have cared for him too much. You could have asked Aric to send Brokk back."

"That was not a condition he was willing to agree to. Brokk knew far too much about the machine. He went to Earth before the blight struck. He had no idea what was going on. I kept an eye on him though. I brought him ice fruits."

"Did you kill him?" I asked.

"No, I could never do that. I think that Aric was there the night Brokk was killed. I am fairly certain it was him."

"And Siam?"

"That was my doing. It was a desperate time for me, Valora."

"No more desperate than now."

Kali hung her head. "I know I can't expect you to forgive me, Valora, but I did make a vow to keep you safe. When I went for the ax it was out of anger towards Aric. I would never hurt you. Aric is dangerous, Valora."

"Thanks for the advice. Look, I really have enough to handle. If Aric killed Brokk I will deal with it. But I can't deal with you right now. We have work to do here tonight that is very important. We'll find our own way back. I suggest you do the same." I turned to go into the cabin. The important things, the important people I needed to deal with, were in there. Kali was obviously a waste of time.

"But, Valora…"

I spun on my heel and shoved my finger in her face. "My mother's magic runs through your veins to give you those wings and you dare ask to remain in my presence? Get out of here before I decide to become as murderous as all those around me seem to be."

Kali trod away into the forest. I remembered all those times she had stuck up for me. But she had made too big of a mistake. I didn't completely believe that she wasn't the one who killed Brokk. But if she truly loved him, maybe she didn't.

Inside, Dooley sat at the table. The bottle in his hands was half empty.

"He's going to puke," said Kit. "And I don't want to be here when he does."

I snatched the bottle from his hands. "You can be angry at me all you like, dammit, but we need to get this ritual done and over with. This is bigger than you and I."

"Actually, it isn't." Dooley snatched the bottle from me and took another swig. "It has everything to do with you and me and him." He pointed to Aric who was leaning up against the wall, looking overly relaxed in this situation.

I glared at Mane. "Have you been talking to him? Dooley, you know Aric doesn't matter."

Aric pulled a fist to his chest and feigned disappointment.

"Yes, he does. Do you not know what it is that I was told? Ravanna spoke to me, Valora. He used to speak to me all the time as a child until I was able to block him out. But he was speaking to me today, and I couldn't stop it." Dooley looked almost desperate.

"What does that have to do with Aric and me?"

"Why don't you ask him?" He took another drink and a long drag on another cigarette.

"Oh, the voices thing. We're going to talk about that now." Aric pushed off the wall he was leaning against and sat beside Dooley. He took the bottle from his hands and downed a swig before handing it back. "Really, it has always been more of a pain in my life thus far. Hasn't helped me at all. She's always trying to make me feel guilty. I tell her she picked the wrong half-fae. What can I say? She should be with Dooley, Ravanna should have been with me. But a piece of them is stuck in each of us by accident. I don't think either of them like it. Neither of us likes to do what they suggest."

"The Goddess Varuna speaks to you?" I was awestruck. It explained a lot of things. How he always seemed to know what I was thinking and feeling without needing to search out my mind. How he was always a step ahead of me. But he had devoted his life to chaos and self-service while Dooley had done the opposite and had tried to help others. But now Dooley, for some reason, was starting to succumb to Ravanna's words.

"What has Ravanna been telling you, Dooley?"

"The same thing he has always told me. That I need to open the doors. That I am the key."

"We can't let him get anywhere near that clearing we are trying to close," said Aric.

"We need him to close it," said Mane. He had remained quiet this whole time, and as he stepped forward I realized he was the only one who had ever ventured on the other side of that door.

"Mane, if it closes forever than you will be trapped." Kit stroked his face.

"What happens to me cannot be their concern. We have had our own discussions on this, and it is what I want, Kit. It is what's meant to be."

Dooley stood and made his way to the bathroom. Aric shrugged and followed him. As soon as the door closed, I heard the sounds of vomiting.

"What does Dooley need to do?" I asked. Dooley's condition was my fault, and I wasn't going to let my mistake be the reason this didn't work.

"Sober up."

I thumbed through my mother's grimoire as the sound of Dooley vomiting in the bathroom died down. The door to the bathroom burst open, and Aric came out and shut the door behind him. "I don't care what evil things I have done. I don't deserve any more of that." He plopped down on the table beside me.

"Did you really tell Kali to keep an eye on me?"

"Is that what she told you?" He propped his fist under his chin and leaned to the side, giving me the look that had once upon a time turned my insides to jelly.

"In not so many words."

"Then she also told you that it was she that locked you behind the portal here on Earth? I had no intention of leaving you here. As soon as I found out what she had done I had her captured. She threatened to expose our secret, said no one would ever believe it was her. I channeled the amulets' powers to reach you. The rest is history."

"She thinks you killed Brokk."

"I wish I knew who did. It certainly wasn't me, although I was here briefly. Almost ran right into that dwarf friend of yours."

"Queen Elemi did send an ogre after me. Maybe he did it."

"It could very well have been the ogre. Tell it to kill a fae, and it kills whatever is in front of it. Not too bright. So where is Kali now?"

"I told her to find a portal home, that we didn't need her help."

He nodded. "Probably was the best thing to do."

"Aric, are we going to be able to find a way home?" Aric stood up, went to the small icebox that Dooley kept in the cabin and came back with a small container and a spoon, handing it to me as he sat down.

"Eat this. You need some nourishment. Mane tells me that he can get us back in the Edsel, but if it goes straight to Lake Mavrovo, I'm not too excited about going into the war zone."

"Kit told me that if my father had a way to destroy all of the selkie, he should do it. She thinks they are all evil." I pushed the creamy pudding around with little interest.

"Well, I know Elemi is. She has known this entire time that it was I who was stealing the magic of Dell'Aria. It was only Kit and your involvement that made her decide to rat me out. Honestly, when you can't trust evil to protect evil." Aric took the spoon from me and scooped up a small bite, pushing it towards my lips. He didn't say a word, but tipped his chin down slightly in a silent command. I let him push the pudding into my mouth, and a sweet vanilla flavor burst in my mouth. I quickly took the spoon from him and shoveled in as much as I could. There was no telling when our next meal would be.

Aric stretched his legs out in front of him and crossed them at the ankle. His white blond hair fell down his back, and his downy blue wings rose and fell ever so slightly with each intake of breath. He looked everything like an angel. His blue eyes twinkled at me, and he smiled ever so slightly.

Kindly.

The door to the bathroom burst open and Dooley came out clutching the door frame for support. I felt slightly ill just looking at his condition.

"I think his hangover is making me queasy."

Aric gave a slight hiccup. "Our physical connection is growing stronger. I had not expected that."

"Hadn't you? When you first gave me this amulet, wasn't that the point? You wanted to own me?" Something inside me tried to push away the feelings that were welling up for Aric.

He grinned as if he knew exactly what I was doing. "You could never be more wrong, Valora. I wanted to save you. Without it you would have died. I won't lie. I've always wanted you to want me. At one time I know you did. I just wasn't able to get to you soon enough. Obviously my brother here saw to that. Isn't he just a vision of loveliness?"

Dooley was beyond hearing our words. He had obviously caused himself a lot of pain.

"Shut up, Aric," I said.

Aric stood up and stretched his wings. "If you're done praying to the porcelain god, we have some other ones who need taking care of."

"Mane, you said we needed Dooley to close the portal that is opening between here and the gods down under. What does he need to do?" I asked.

"Oh, I think you might know. In fact I believe you and Kit were witness to the ritual a few nights ago," said Mane.

I blushed slightly. Mane certainly was a sexy man. Demon or not it had been quite a scene to witness. "Does that mean we can stay here? You just need Dooley?" I wasn't certain I could handle watching that ritual again.

"No, actually it is very important that you are there. Kit

will stay here. I need to begin the ritual and I cannot do that and watch her at the same time to make sure she doesn't succumb to her carnal nature." His last words came out with a slight growl.

"Will you be okay, Kit?" I asked.

"Just call me jealous. But, yes, I'll be fine. It's night now, so there shouldn't be as much of a drain on my powers anymore. But you certainly will be drained when you come back." She winked at Mane and flopped onto one of the empty beds.

"Aren't we sleeping here tonight?" I asked.

"No," Mane slung a knapsack over his shoulder and threw another one at Aric who caught it with ease. "Tonight we spend in the woods."

⁂

We exited Dooley's cabin into the darkened wood. Kit had lain down to sleep before we went. The day had been a big drain on her. My Uncle Artemus was dead and had left behind a son who mourned him. I would have to contact Bowen again at some point to make sure he was okay. When you lose a parent you lose a part of yourself.

I was fairly certain that if I was a part of the ritual it wasn't going to be exactly like the one that I had seen Mane perform before. But it did explain one reason why Ravanna had not yet been able to pierce through into the Realms. Mane's ritual had reinforced the seal, but only temporarily.

Now they were trying to make it to Earth. My father was battling Queen Elemi to stop her from letting Ravanna and his demons destroy Underworld. I just hoped that if he wasn't able to do so the Goddess Varuna would send down her army to help the fae of Overworld fight and defend the Realms.

You really think she cares about the fae? Aric's voice echoed in my head. The thought had crossed my mind that perhaps Varuna was in this for herself as much as Ravanna was, but I didn't want to believe that. If it were true, what would that mean for the Realms?

"It sucks, doesn't it?" Aric was so quiet I hadn't noticed him walking beside me.

"What sucks?"

"Fighting someone else's war. It was one thing when the Fae Wars pit us against the dwarves and the elves and everything else in the Realms, or so I understand that is the way it was. Now we have to be in the middle between the Goddess Varuna and the Demon King Ravanna who is just mad because the Goddess won't let him live forever."

"You'd have her give in and grant evil a free pass to live on forever?"

"Be careful what you say. You do know that part of that evil lives within your fiancé?"

I watched Dooley walking beside Mane. "I can't believe it. I still can't believe it."

"It's funny how you love to ignore the obvious. A characteristic I have always found both oddly compelling and frustrating at the same time."

"So for now we stop Ravanna from entering Earth?"

Aric pulled his hair over his shoulder. "Yes, if he is going to wage a war against the Goddess it needs to be in the Realms. We don't have the weaponry or the people to fight him here. I'm afraid it would be quite messy, and this world would never be the same."

"How did this portal open anyway?"

"I was hoping you wouldn't ask that question. I think it has something to do with Kali."

"What do you mean? Why would she summon Ravanna?

I thought she had all she wanted once she got her wings."

"Oh, she did. But in order to reverse the black magic used to destroy her wings she needed to call upon a little black magic. Actually I am being quite modest. She used the magic sucked from thousands of fae over the past ten years to call upon a lot of black magic, and I have a feeling she did it in Dooley's backyard."

"Why would she come out here?"

Mane and Dooley came to a stop as the natural path of the trees dead ended in front of us. Mane motioned for us to be quiet. He gently pressed down on a leafy branch to allow him to see through. As he did, Dooley looked over his shoulder. Mane whipped around and took hold of Dooley by the shoulders. "Don't look through there, Dooley."

Of course Dooley did exactly the opposite. "Brokk!"

He shot through the tree limbs, and I raced after him. "Catch her," yelled Aric.

Mane caught me around the waist just as I saw what Dooley had seen. Brokk's body was lying in the clearing, much like it had the night I had first come upon him. It was all wrong. Sick. Wrong. There was no blood. Just his dead body in his bloodstained robes.

Dooley knelt beside him, took his limp hand in his own and cradled it to his cheek. "Brokk, father…"

A rustling came from the bushes, and Aric rushed past Mane and me into the clearing as Kali stepped from the bushes.

Aric stood beside me, and Mane loosened his grip. "I knew it was you out here."

"What the hell, Kali? What are you doing here?" I shirked off Mane's biceps and drew my sword once more.

"I can fix him." Kali's eyes were glazed over, like she had completely lost touch with reality. "I can bring him back.

I've been doing the ritual just as I was told. I only need to do it one more time. Just once more."

Mane dropped his arms from me and stepped forward. "Who told you of the ritual with the drums?"

"Do you really need to ask her such an obvious question, Mane?" said Aric. "She got it all from my loft. Everything I used to contact Acheron to forge this amulet was there."

Mane's eyes flared red as he stared across the clearing at Kali who was within an arm's reach of Aric. Dooley solemnly folded Brokk's hands over his chest and stood to face Kali.

"You have desecrated his final rest for some demonic ritual."

"I have been trying to bring him back for you, Dooley." Kali clasped her hands in front of her, begging for his understanding. But her pleas fell on deaf ears. I wasn't going to listen to her crazy gibberish anymore.

"You weren't bringing him back for Dooley, you were trying to bring him back for you," I screamed. "You have never done anything that wasn't for your own benefit. You may have fooled yourself into thinking you were being selfless, but you haven't fooled us."

"Yes, and I should know, considering I tend to do the same thing, darling. Really a dreadful move if I must say so," said Aric.

"But, Dooley, I only need to do it one more time and his spirit will be released into his body." Kali completely ignored our words, trying to appeal to the boy inside Dooley who had lost his father.

"You do that ritual one more time, and you won't just be releasing Brokk's spirit, you will be opening a portal to Acheron," said Mane. He stepped forward and tried speaking gently to her. "The only way to reanimate a corpse is through a ritual which cracks open the seal between the dead and the living. He wouldn't be Brokk anymore. He would be the first in the army of undead that Ravanna would unleash upon this Earth."

Kali took a few steps back into the brush. "But, I, I didn't know."

"No, you just thought you would go about trying to get what you wanted without considering the consequences. Sounds familiar," I said.

Mane looked at Kali, and his demon eyes flared red. "Put this body where you found it and then return to the Realms. You shouldn't be here on Earth any longer." Kali nodded. Whatever demon mojo was now in her blood responded to his commands. I was glad that Mane was on our side and wondered if he could do the same thing to Dooley.

Dooley stood protectively in front of Brokk's body, his fists clenched at his sides. Mane flashed his eyes again in Dooley's direction. "It will be okay, Dooley. She will do as I say. You do not need to worry about Brokk. Please let her pass."

Dooley nodded, and Kali quickly took Brokk's body, flew straight up into the sky and seemed to disappear.

"She has far too much magic flowing through her veins. I fear what she might do with it," said Aric.

"Don't ever do that to me again." Dooley stared at Mane. Mane's eyes flashed red and reflected in Dooley's but no words were said.

"We can discuss the hierarchy of you two demons later," said Aric. "Can we get on with closing whatever portal is here? My skin is already crawling with all the demonic energy here."

"Really? I don't sense anything." I tried to reach out into the space and discern what Aric was talking about. I got nothing.

"You wouldn't. You are the conduit. That through which both positive and negative energies flow and become the balanced force we are supposed to have. We need to restore the balance to this glen. That is why you need to be present," said Mane.

"What do you need me to do?"

"Take off all of your clothes and lie down." The three men surrounding me all stared at me intently. Mane bent down and arranged some jars and herbs atop the stump of a tree that had been cut down.

"I'm not having sex with all of you." My eyebrows shot up to the top of my head at the same time the words flew out of my mouth.

"Not me," said Mane. "I'm just here to bring forth the same energies that Kali did so that you can be the filter. Too bad, really." Mane's tongue flicked out and moistened his lips. "But you, Aric and Dooley will need to bond. Drop your shields, both physical and mental. I'm not saying you need to have sex. You only need to be flesh to flesh. But really, if the mood strikes you, then don't let me stop you."

Mane's eyes flashed red again, and a wicked grin spread across his face.

"Valora, we don't need to do anything you don't want to do." I was surprised that the comment had actually come from Aric and not Dooley who stood there looking at me like I was already guilty.

I dropped my coats and unclasped my bodice, letting it drop to the ground with little ceremony. I quickly did the same as I slid out of my pants, never taking my gaze off Dooley. I stood before him naked and with my shields up in full force. He tossed his white t-shirt to the side and dropped his shorts, standing bare before me.

Dooley walked over and pressed his naked body to mine, and I felt the press of Aric from behind. Dooley glowered at Mane. "Let's get this over with."

Dooley's coldness shocked me, and for the first time I thought I saw a glint of red in his eyes until I realized it was a reflection from Mane as he cast something using the ingredients he had brought. The naked flesh of Aric and Dooley should have made me warm. Instead I only felt intensely cold.

"Valora, if this is going to work you are going to need to drop your shields," Aric whispered into my ear.

I took a deep breath and let them down. Dooley's hate hit me like a ton of bricks. It had obviously been welling up inside him for some time, and in his weakened state he couldn't hide anything from me. It was as if the demon inside that Brokk had helped Dooley cage had been set free inside his mind and he couldn't stop it. A small growl emitted from Dooley's lips as Aric's mind tried to push back the hate with a white light that pulsed through me. I was indeed the conduit for balance between these two. I wasn't sure what that was going to mean.

"Brace yourselves, this is going to hit you all hard."

Mane chanted the final incantation, and a wall of energy hit me. Dooley pulled it towards himself and Aric pulled it back. The effort was clearly more on Aric's part as we were dealing with demonic energy and Aric was the only one who could bring it into balance through me, the one who connected him and Dooley. The Goddess Varuna and the demon King Ravanna were waging a little war inside my psyche.

If this was a battle, I was scared about what the war

would hold and just how we would all survive. Aric made one final pull and Dooley's mind returned to normal. The hate receded, and he was able to somehow pack it into the space where he had been able to hide it all these years.

Kit blasted through the trees and came to a stop in front of us. "Looks like I missed the show."

Mane stood up. "You were supposed to stay in the cabin."

"I was, but I kind of need you all to hurry. There is something you need to see."

❧

Aric handed me my pants and I rushed to pull them and my bodice in place. "What about the portal here? Is it closed?"

Mane nodded. "It is. I'm afraid it was easier than I thought it would be, though. I think it means that the portal may have opened elsewhere."

"Exactly why I need you guys to hurry," Kit hopped from one leg to the other like an anxious child. It seemed like just yesterday she was one. The Realms really did have an effect on those who were not entirely human.

Dooley was frozen in place, his fists clenched at his sides. "Are you okay?" I asked.

"Besides the fact that every time he touches you I want to kill him, yes, I'm fine." Dooley pushed the jars off the stump, and they fell to the ground.

Dooley's honesty was like a jab to my heart. He walked past Aric and me. Unfortunately now was not the time to discuss our feelings. I drew up all my shields. Something told me I would need them up soon.

"Dear Goddess, what have you done?" I heard Dooley shouting ahead of us before we came up behind him. The scene before us was nothing short of horrific.

In the same place I had found Brokk's broken body, Kali knelt with his body in her arms. Blood poured from her wrists as she rocked him back and forth. She touched his head, his cheeks. She caressed his hands and left smears of red wherever she touched him. We were all transfixed by the scene, but unable to move any closer. A sparkling red ring began to form around her and Brokk which wouldn't allow us to pass through. As each drop of Kali's blood hit the ground the brightness of the ring intensified.

Kali's words tumbled out of her mouth, her voice choked with emotion. "You're right, Valora, I did do it for me. I can't let him die. I have wings now. We can love each other again like we used to. I did the incantation one last time. It required blood. But soon he will be back and I will be okay. It'll be okay." Her wrists wept with blood. The skies seemed to feel the sadness and opened up. A light rain fell upon us all.

Mane took a few steps backwards. "I need to leave. We need to leave. He's coming." It was the first time I had seen the demon's normally confident facade shatter.

I didn't need to ask who. Dooley took two steps back as well. "Ravanna. He's coming for her magic."

The ground within the red circle shivered as a hand burst out through the earth beside Kali. She screamed, and a burst of red light shot up from the circle, creating a wall through which I could barely make anything out.

"If Ravanna gets Kali he will have what he needs to burst through into the Realms. Now I know why he wanted to come here so badly. It was because of all that magic Aric was storing here. It attracted him. Now Kali is infused with it. She's the key," shouted Mane.

"I thought I was the key," said Dooley.

"You were until you linked up with Valora and Aric. Now he has gone to plan B. We can't let him take her," yelled Mane. The ground at our feet quaked. Kit fell and looked like she was going to lose control again. Mane raced over and held her down.

Dooley looked at me. "There's nothing I can do. I can't enter the circle."

"Neither can I," said Aric.

The distorted shape of something twisting and writhing rose up from the ground around Kali who continued to scream and hold onto Brokk's body.

I pulled my sword from my scabbard and heard the satisfying sound of metal on metal. The weight of my sword felt good in my hands. Dooley and Aric nodded at me. We all knew I was the only one who could cross the circle.

It was time I was the Fae Guardian. This was the mission I had accepted. I pressed my sword forward through the wall of red light. The light traveled down my sword and spread up across my arm. It quickly enveloped me with a heat worse than that of Mount Elbrus. Before I could take a step forward the circle enveloped me and I was inside.

A half dozen swirling black arms snaked out of the ground and pulled at Kali. Pulled her down into a deep inky well of nothingness that had opened up in the ground.

I ran forward and grasped at one of the arms, but nothing happened. My hand passed right through it. But it seemed solid enough to Kali whose eyes were filled with abject terror. "Help me, Valora! Help!"

The hands were pulling at her wrists, at the places where she had been bleeding. Blood. I fished my hand into the pocket of my bodice and pulled out one of the vials of dragon's blood. I poured the vial onto my hand and rubbed it along the length of my blade and up each of my arms, bringing my fingers up to lick the ends off. The blood of the beast of the Goddess would certainly slay the demon.

I returned to one of the hands and grasped it. This time my hand came down on a length of hard blackened muscle. I brought my sword down, cutting one of the arms of the beast.

It let out a scream which I echoed. The amulet at my chest burned bright red and shot pain through me. A large wound opened up on my arm. A blast of heat threw me to the ground. The black mist went into a frenzy. I reached inside and locked my hand down on Kali's ankle. She screamed. I couldn't see anything, my vision was obscured by the thick dark mist.

Kali's screams receded along with the shadows. The red wall came crashing down. I lay on the ground bleeding from the arm clamped down on Kali's ankle, my other hand still clutching at my sword.

Dooley and Aric both ran forward, Dooley reaching me first.

"Now would be the time to pray, if you believe in that sort of thing," said Mane. He still held onto Kit. She seemed like she had gotten a handle on herself, but she sat with her mouth agape.

"It's okay, we'll figure something out." Dooley smoothed his hand over my hair. "We need to get your arm fixed. Aric, can you please help me with the body?"

"Of course," Aric stepped forward. "You need to let go of him, Valora. It's okay, you did your best."

"What are you all talking about?" I looked up and saw that in my hand was Brokk's ankle. Kali was gone and so was our best chance at stopping Ravanna.

CHAPTER SIXTEEN

At some point I must have passed out. My mind filled with visions of blackness on my hands that I couldn't wash off. Stained from the foul tendrils of the beast that had reached up and grabbed Kali down with it. I woke up, and the light from Dooley's porch was a welcome sign, a beacon of normalcy. My neck was sore from being at an awkward angle. My chest felt sore. Pretty much everything hurt.

I sat up and realized I was lying in the Edsel which was parked in Dooley's driveway. In the yard Mane and Dooley seemed to be arguing, though I could only hear bits of their muffled conversation through the glass. Aric stood with his back propped up against a tree and watched them go at it, but he obviously wasn't involved.

I was momentarily startled when a hand reached up from the front seat and clasped the head rest. The vision of the hands coming out of the ground and surrounding Kali too fresh in my mind. Kit's blue hair came into view, and she pushed her glasses onto her face.

"You're awake. How are you?"

I ran my finger over the solid red line on my arm that

had been left behind, but I wasn't bleeding. "Fine I guess. What's going on?"

"Oh, Mane is trying to convince Dooley that he needs to come with us, and Dooley doesn't want to go. I'm pretty sure that Aric doesn't mind if Dooley stays behind."

I jumped up and exited the car. Both Mane and Dooley fell silent as I walked over to them. The light from the porch cast Dooley's face in shadow. Mane stepped away as I approached Dooley.

"We couldn't have this conversation before. But we need to have it now. Days ago you were ready to come with me to Winter Haven and to confirm our bond at the temple of Goddess Varuna and now you want to stay behind? Is this because of Aric?"

In the darkness Dooley's features didn't move. Before I knew it he swung his arms up and around me, pulling me in tightly towards him. His mouth searched out mine in desperation. Our lips met, and again I encountered Winter Haven. Our bond hadn't changed but something else had. And I was about to find out.

Dooley pulled back and stared down at my shoulder, refusing to look directly at me. I reached out to tuck one of his curly locks behind his ear, but before I could he caught my hand and held it to his lips. The vision of his strong jaw went blurry as my eyes filled with tears.

"I need to stay behind. It's not good for me to be in the Realms when Ravanna could possibly use me to open up the door between his world and yours. I can't have that hanging over me. Mane and Aric will keep you safe. I have the amulet now. It should keep me from becoming sick."

Dooley held my hand fast as I tried to yank it away. He probably was afraid I would slap him with it and rightfully so. "Are you joking? Mane already told you that you're no longer a threat now that you and I are bonded."

"Which is what I have been trying to tell him again for the last thirty minutes," said Mane.

"But what you can't seem to explain, Mane, is why I was able to almost open another door in Bowen's shop. We were all linked then." Dooley had a point, but it wasn't good enough to keep him from coming to the Realms. Was it?

"There has to be an explanation." I clutched at the thin white cotton of his t-shirt. "Dooley, if you stay here I don't know when or if I will be able to see you again. Winter Haven is real. What we have is real."

"Yes, but I am a threat to your people." Dooley's voice dropped to a whisper as he clutched me even tighter to him. "You can't understand, Valora. You don't have voices speaking to you."

"She has us," Aric pushed himself away from the tree and walked towards us, into the yellow glow cast by the porch lights.

"Yes, I know, brother. And you know all too well how that has ended up." There it was again, his regret. I wouldn't necessarily do it again, but I didn't think that I regretted what came to pass between the three of us. It seemed Dooley definitely did.

"I don't know. It was a good time. I'd do it again," chided Aric.

Dooley's biceps clenched and almost pushed the air out of my lungs. "Are you trying to get him to hit you?" I looked at Aric who, even in the dim light, gave an air of quiet indifference, like somehow who was above this all. And perhaps he was in a way. He had a portion of the Goddess Varuna residing in him. He didn't have to fight against the power within him like Dooley did.

It was one of the things that had always attracted me to

Aric, the way he seemed overconfident. Like he could handle anything. His confidence made me feel good when the wellspring of doubt filled me up inside.

All at once Dooley dropped his arms from me and stepped back. "You will take care of her. That much I know. Valora, don't trust Aric with anything but your life. In every other way he will lie to you, but he would never risk harming you in a physical way."

"Unless she asks me to, of course."

Dooley retreated into his cabin, his hiding spot. The place where he had come so he could pretend like he was part of society without actually having to interact with it. Behind me the car sparked to life. Its engine rumbled and gunned as if it was at the starting line at some drag race. Kit still sat in the front passenger seat. She held her arms up like she had no idea what was happening.

"The car is going to leave any second. Sweetheart, Dooley has made his decision. It isn't a good one, but you definitely need to be in that car when it reappears in the Realms. Your friend Kali was the only one who knew how to open those portals by hand and we're running out of options."

Dooley didn't look back. He just kept going up the stairs, opened the door and walked inside. The door shut with a thud behind him.

Aric offered his hand to me. "He is right on one account. I will never let anything happen to you."

"And on the other accounts?" I took Aric's hand and gazed deep into his eyes for the first time in many months. Jagged lightning eyebrows set above the sparkling light that danced within the windows to his soul, a telltale sign of the Goddess Varuna who presided over the skies residing within him. I didn't know how I had missed it before.

"I will let you be the judge of that, Valora. I want you to trust me. It's the first step of many I hope to take with you."

"But Aric, you know Dooley and I — you and I can never have that."

"I don't want to have what he has with you." He dipped his head down and looked at me, looked through me like only he could. "I want something entirely different."

His finger stroked my chin and I was awakened to the reality that what Aric wanted he usually got.

Kit stuck her head out of the window. "You guys, I think this thing is going to go."

The lights on the Edsel flared brightly as it rolled forward. "Time to fly, sweetheart."

Aric put his arm around my waist. I swore I saw the orange curtains flutter in the window, but I wasn't sure. For all I knew Dooley had just said good-bye to me forever.

❧

Kit shoved the driver side door open and Mane jumped inside. The car continued to roll forward down the driveway.

"You will see him again, Valora." I wasn't sure if I believed Aric, but I also had no choice. I knew once this was all over I would find a way back to Dooley. I would convince him that he was not the demon he thought he was inside.

I ran towards the car and pulled open the door, jumping inside. Aric jumped in after me and shut the door.

"So how does this thing work?" asked Aric.

"It's like a portable portal," said Mane.

"Are we going to end up in Lake Mavrovo?" I shuddered. Coming face to face with Queen Elemi was the last thing I needed. She would gladly feed me to the demons she was trying to raise. Ravanna wanted immortality. Elemi wanted the freedom from her prison in the waters. I just wanted — actually, I wasn't sure what I wanted anymore.

"Hopefully not. I think I have it wired to go to Mount Elbrus. We are going to need some help from the dwarves and the elves of the Riparian. And we need to find a place to hide him," said Mane as he gestured to Aric.

Aric's mannerisms seemed to soften as soon as Dooley was gone. All of his deceptions had been aimed at helping me. He had refused to listen to the Goddess so that he could regain his mother's memory and to help me. Nothing had gone right for him.

"It isn't easy for me to watch you suffer such pain at the hands of my brother. He should not have abandoned us."

"Dooley could have gotten us killed, but so could you. You have a price on your head. If my father knew I was harboring you he would send the royal guard and the fae guardians after us all. You are both a threat."

"Then perhaps I should stay here, get to know my brother better." He opened the door as the car rolled along.

"No!" I pulled him inside, and he fell on top of me. The car continued down the roadway as a portal opened up beneath our feet.

A storm of light erupted within the car. Kit screamed out and shielded her eyes.

"Hang on, I'm not sure I got the spell quite right." Mane swiped his hand across the dash leaving a black smear and traced symbols into the paint.

"Those are the same symbols that Dooley uses." I said. The light surrounding the car turned a smoky black. I had a feeling we weren't going to Elbrus anymore.

"What are you doing, Mane? Where are you taking us?" demanded Aric.

"I can only take us one place for certain and then we will

have to find our way from there." The entire car shook violently.

Aric pulled me closer to him.

"The heat will affect you," Mane said, "but we will keep each other strong. I will get us out of this as soon as possible. Just try not to let the scenery alarm you."

And then it hit, the feeling of being sucked in through the portal. In one end and out the other. Aric held onto me, and I buried my face into his soft wings as they curled about me. The entire car came to a stop. I peeked through the dusty window and saw a stretch of dry desert. No life. No trees. No rocks. Just nothingness.

I tried to speak and my mouth ran dry. "I'm only part fae," Aric said. "This won't affect me as much, but who are you kidding? Both Kit and Valora won't last long out here, demon. You should have warned us."

"There wasn't time. Did you see the car move? We didn't exactly have time to pack."

"So you had no idea when this would happen?"

"Are we in the Realms?" asked Kit. "I've never seen such a place."

"And you wouldn't have. We are in the outskirts in the Ordos Desert," said Aric.

"Dragonlands?" I had read the chapters on the Ordos Desert many times as a young fae. They were my favorite, although I always got in trouble when my mother caught me reading it. She said it would give me nightmares. But the vivid coloring of the dragons that were painted upon the vellum left me only with wonder. Now I knew better.

Aric nodded. "Mount Elbrus is a few days journey east of here. But I suspect that we won't be setting off on foot. Had you always intended to give us over to Ravanna, Mane? Or was that something you came up with last minute after

Kali was taken and you realized our chances of winning this war didn't look so good?"

"What is he talking about?" I quickly drew my sword and pressed the tip of the blade against the underside of Mane's chin.

"He doesn't know what he is talking about. Always assumes the worst of others because he knows that if a part of Varuna didn't reside in him, he would be nothing." Mane tipped his chin up and gave Aric a vicious sneer.

"Then what are we doing out here?" I demanded.

"I told you." Mane's knuckles went white as he gripped the steering wheel. "I can only bring us to one place in the Realms. The gates of the Underworld. Kit brings us to Lake Mavrovo. You bring us to Dell'Aria. Franca brought you to Mount Elbrus. Are you sensing a pattern? I tried to override it, but it didn't work."

"But what are we to do out here, Mane?" Kit brought her hand to Mane's arm. She didn't know this was the plan either.

"You and I will go from here to Lake Mavrovo. They will journey to Dell'Aria."

"I won't go to Mavrovo." Kit crossed her arms and leaned against the seat of the car. Her hair was already plastered against her forehead.

"Can you take the both of you there now?" The scar on my throat throbbed in the heat, and I remembered one of the last times Kit lost control. Her mother's amulet wasn't good for long. That much I was sure of.

"You can't be left alone with him." Kit turned around in her seat to face me. "We can make the journey together. We can do this together."

The look on her face told me she was determined to continue by my side. The last time someone had done that for me they ended up dead, and there was nothing I could do to stop it. Kit would never make it across this desert.

"I can't have another friend's life on my hands. Aric will protect me. You don't have to worry about that." And as I said it I knew it was true. I thought the same about Dooley, but then he abandoned me. But then again, maybe what he had done was best to protect me. I wasn't sure if the heat was making me dizzy or the circular logic.

I could supposedly hear inside these guys' heads, and I had no idea what they were thinking.

"She's right, Kit. You would never make it across this desert," said Mane.

"And she will? This heat will kill her as fast as it will kill me." Kit leaned back on the seat. We didn't have much time left to argue or she and I both would pass out.

"No, it won't. I can fly us to safety quickly. It won't take long. But I can't carry everyone," said Aric.

"You two need to get to Dell'Aria and find out what your father knows. We need to get Ralph out of Mavrovo and to safety before Ravanna blows it sky high." At the sound of her father's name Kit's head shot up, her bottom lip quivering ever so slightly.

"Ravanna will destroy Mavrovo? But he and my mother had a deal." Kit's manner softened. It seemed that if her mother was the source of the treachery then she would gladly see her go, but the thought that someone would trick her into death wasn't such a good idea.

"I doubt Ravanna intends to give the selkie any of the power he is using. And he will need much more if he intends on knocking on the Goddess' door and taking his immortality. This has only just begun." Mane reached over and took Aric's hand. "We come from two sides of this battle. But just as you grew up with the fae, I grew up with the elves and consider the Realms my home. I don't intend to let any of these gods destroy it."

"I never considered the Realms my home." Aric straightened his back, his pride welling up inside him once more to his detriment.

"Better pick one soon. Either way, if we don't stop Ravanna and he becomes immortal it means a lifetime of hell for you here or on Earth. If you think he will stop at destroying the Realms you are mistaken. I once stood by his side. He feeds on power like you feed off her life force." Mane jabbed a finger in my direction. "And the drug is no less potent to him than it is to you."

"Take him to Pryn before you go to your father. Pryn will know what to do," said Mane. I nodded as Mane faced forward again. This conversation was over.

"We'll meet again. I will find you," said Kit. "I can always find you. It's the blood." Kit tapped on her teeth. As much as the idea of her being able to find me by the scent of my blood freaked me out, I also found a little comfort in it. Kit always seemed to show up when I needed her most. She had been a great friend.

I followed Aric out of the Edsel and watched as it sped down the dusty desert, a cloud of dust trailing in its wake.

"Is it safe to take to the sky?" I scanned the horizon. The sun was setting and I didn't yet see signs of any dragons. Perhaps we had gotten here just in time.

"Better now than wait to see if they wake up. Hang on to me tight. I want to try and make it to the tree line before dark."

I faced Aric and clutched my hands around his neck and my legs around his waist. He wrapped his arm around me and lifted his eyebrows a tad in my direction.

"Glad the seriousness of our situation doesn't seem to

be affecting your mood any."

"Nothing affects me more than you do." Aric crouched down before shooting up towards the sky. His wings spread wide against the horizon. The purplish light from the setting sun filtered through his pale blue wings making it easy to imagine Aric as an angel.

The light through his wings was momentarily blocked out as a shadow passed overhead.

Moments before I could say anything a tortured shriek rang across the sky.

"Aric, we have company."

❧

As soon as I noticed one shadow I saw others darting across the sky. I wasn't sure if the sun was getting lower on the horizon or if the sky was turning dark because of the number of dragons.

"Aric, they're everywhere." My voice trembled as I recalled the time a dragon had captured me in its powerful talons. There was no way I was slaying one of these dragons when I couldn't even let go of Aric to grab my sword. My breathing was labored, but then I realized that it was because Aric was holding me tighter against him.

"Just hold on." Aric's face was focused ahead of us. I dipped my neck back to see where he was going. We had traveled far in a short span of time. I could make out the trees. We were really close to making it. If Aric could just get to the tree line then the dragons would not be able to follow us into the dense forest.

Aric jerked us upwards as one of the dragons dove towards me. A hiss of fire escaped its lips as it cried out, frustrated it had missed. Our momentum was slowed, and it gave another dragon a chance to position itself in front of us.

The trees were coming closer and closer. Only a few more moments and we would make it.

Aric dove down to fly below the dragon's belly. Its sharp talons raked across Aric's back and down my hands. I screamed out in pain and let go of my grip on Aric but he still held onto me. Unfortunately now we were tumbling instead of flying. Aric's wings were damaged, and he was spinning out of control.

"Aric!" His face was full of pain as he tried to pull his damaged wing up to level us off. Behind us a legion of dragons formed an inky black line in the sky.

My back was struck with one tree branch, then another and another and suddenly instead of flying forward we were falling down. Hitting branch after branch. Aric had detached from me as we went into the trees. I struck another branch and clamped onto it with my legs, my hands a ruined and bloody mess from the dragon talons. As I dangled upside down I realized two things. One, I was still several hundred feet off the ground and two, Aric was on the ground, not moving.

I tried to use my small wings to get myself upright and on the tree branch. I dropped my mental shields, reached out to Aric and got nothing in return. There was a void where Dooley should have been as well. Though since he was still on Earth I wasn't too surprised about that.

Aric was awfully still. His body at an awkward pose, his wings sprawled out underneath him like Brokk had been when I came upon his body.

Oh, dear Goddess. He can't die, we need him to fight your war.

Is that all I am good for? Aric's voice returned in my head, but there was still no movement.

Are you okay? Again, nothing. The dragons circled overhead, but none of them could penetrate the dense canopy. I raced down the limbs as fast as I could, ignoring the pain of my bloodied hands.

I dropped to Aric's side, and our amulets flared to life as I took his hand in mine. My wounds knit themselves closed. They were still horrid, but no longer bleeding and I could bend my fingers again. Unfortunately it wasn't enough. It was as if with only the two of us we couldn't heal as fast as we could with Dooley present.

Aric's eyes blinked open. "Took you long enough to get down here."

I was unfazed by Aric's snark. "Get up, let me look at you." I pushed Aric up into a sitting position. He might have been conscious, but he was still weakened. We were both still feeling the effects of our injuries, but I pressed forward in checking Aric over. It felt good to rely on my training as a Hunter instead of the magic of the amulet.

"So do you think Dooley is feeling our pain?" he asked.

"You're the one who knows how these things work, not me." I inspected his wings. He had lost a section of feathers on one side, but the skin underneath had healed. "You look like you've been plucked, but no permanent damage."

Aric's shirt had been shredded by the dragon and was barely hanging on at the sides. "No, but this shirt will have to go." He ripped off the tattered pieces. Underneath the shirt, against his muscled back, he wore a leather harness.

There were two daggers set into the space above his wings. I reached up to the handle of the blade.

"Don't touch it." Aric's command was short and stern. "They're made of iron."

"You carry iron blades with you?"

"Does it surprise you? Every fae in Dell'Aria wants me dead, and I rather like living." He reached behind with both hands and made sure the daggers were secure.

"They want your head with good reason. Or have you forgotten that you killed their Queen? Your wife." I pushed off my heels and stalked towards the tree trunk. The shadows had lessened, but I didn't like being out in the open.

"You say 'wife' like that word has any meaning. You have always had choices, Valora. You have never lived your life like I have. I grew wings and was taken from my mother. I was given to that Queen as her consort, not as her husband. If you knew the humiliations I had to endure at her hands you wouldn't be mourning her death." Aric rose from the ground slowly. For an instant I thought he was going to fly at me. The storm brewed behind his eyes. His dagger-like eyebrows drew downwards with anger as his gaze pierced through me.

I stood my ground and stared at him. "No one deserves to be murdered."

"I wish I could prove you wrong." He softened his stance. "But I care about you too much to want to see the pain you will go through on the day you realize you are wrong."

"What, is the Goddess telling you the future now?" A blast of fire rained down from the trees above and cut a swath at my feet. A blazing wall momentarily separated me from Aric.

"Wait here. Stay to the trees." He crouched and bounded upwards to the sky, not quite as gracefully as he usually did. The only weapons I had seen on him were the two iron daggers, short blades. There was no way he would be able to defend himself from the dragon with only those small weapons and his injured wings.

I checked that I had my long sword at my side and climbed up the tree. My hands were sore from the slashing they had taken, but I had killed one dragon. Why not another?

Because no one deserves to be murdered.

My own words echoed back at me through the bond Aric and I shared. Dooley was still silent, perhaps unreachable. The branch above cracked and snapped as a large red dragon crashed through the upper boughs. I pulled myself flush with the trunk in time to miss its tail as it swung towards me before crashing to the ground.

Aric shot down from the sky after it and landed square on its chest. The beast didn't move. He reached down with two hands and pulled the daggers from the soft flesh underneath its arms. He had stabbed at the dragon's heart from each side with the short blade. Aric looked up at my perch in the tree, his white blond hair hanging down in his face.

"I told you to stay to the trees."

"Just where exactly do you think I am," I yelled down.

"Too far up. I need you to toss me your long sword. The beast is wounded, but it stirs below my feet." Aric stumbled a bit as the chest of the dragon rose and fell, the talons at the ends of its claws slowly closing and opening again.

I loosened my grip on the hilt of my blade and tossed it down to him. He caught it in one swift movement and plunged it into the heart of the dragon, turning once before drawing it out again. The beast gave forth one last squall before its head lolled to the side.

The shadows in the sky dissipated, but there were others drawing in. The shadows of the night and we were at the forest's edge. I knew the Riparian went on for days in many directions, but I had never been this far out. Aric was wounded and there was no way we were going to be able to fly anywhere tonight.

Aric seemed to sense my unease. "Come down here, Valora. We need to find shelter."

"I can't believe night is upon us again so soon." The tree groaned beneath my hand as I climbed down its battered limbs.

"Things change quickly in the Realms."

"It seems like the opposite to me. We seem to have stagnated for so long. For so many cycles living on Dell'Aria, isolated from everyone and everything. Earth changes in the blink of an eye."

"In the Realms just as on Earth there are small changes happening every day. It is anyone's guess which grain of sand will tip the hour glass the other way."

I reached forward and took my bloodied sword from his hand. "We're running out of time, aren't we?"

"I pray to the Goddess that we are not."

"You don't pray. You never pray."

"I do now."

Aric hopped down from the dragon and reached up to help me down. I took his hand. "You know I killed a dragon at Mount Elbrus."

"And I have killed two now, both for you, so I would say that I am still the worst of us both in Varuna's book. I'm sure you have nothing to fear."

"This is a red dragon. I thought there were no more left." I ran my finger down the brilliant burgundy scales which glittered in the fading light.

"There aren't anymore. I had to take out the worst of them so the others would flee. The red was the most fierce. He had to die for us to live." Aric bent down and gathered some tinder together to make a fire.

I brought my hand up as if it had been sparked by electricity and saw that it was stained with blood. Blood on my hands. I dropped to the ground and lay my cheek on the still warm belly of the dragon.

The dragon had raked its talons against Aric's wings. Wings he shouldn't have. He had shredded my hands which I had used to kill his brethren. Varuna's message was clear to me.

"Your heart runs too deep for your own good, Valora. Do you think that the people of Earth would think we are gods?"

Aric didn't seem to be making any sense. "Why would they think that?"

"Speaking as someone who lived as one for a while I can say that there are many who would. We come through magical portals. Fly like their mythical angels. Have powers that are beyond even our explanation. If we wanted to walk on Earth and proclaim ourselves gods, who would stop us?"

I wiped my hands on my pants as best I could. "We would stop us. It is known that if a fae spends any length of time on Earth our powers are taken from us. We would not have our magic if we weren't tied to the Realms."

"So you have been listening to Pryn's lessons. He taught me as well. Then think of this." He reached down and sparked the tinder with a pack of matches from his belt. It rose to life as it chewed away at the dead brush he had gathered. "Why are the ones we call gods - gods at all? Why are they not perhaps just beings from other Realms who have had a taste of what we have here and want a piece of it? We never see them. Perhaps they too would lose their own powers if they stayed too long in the Realms."

"If you believe that, why are you worried about them coming here at all?"

He picked up the amulet at his chest and thrust it out towards me. "Because I know more than anyone, where there is a will there is a way, and I fear they may have found it."

CHAPTER SEVENTEEN

I watched as Aric cut strips of meat from the dragon. I had been opposed to his doing so, but he was right. We had very little in the way of supplies and a long way to go. The fire blazed beside the body of the beast, either warding off predators or attracting them. I wasn't too sure. I had never spent a night in the Riparian before. Aric didn't scare easily. When he said he was afraid Ravanna had found a way to use the power of the Realms to gain his immortality, I believed him. More than that, I knew that we were in some way a part of his finding out. The amulets that Aric, Dooley and I wore were forged in the fires of his domain. We had been his test subjects and had proven that there was a way to live outside the rules you were dealt.

Aric shoved a portion of meat onto a sharpened stick and held it in the flames.

I tried to settle myself opposite Aric on the stump of a fallen tree. "Do you know why we can't hear Dooley?

"Maybe because he's there and we're here." I raised my eyebrows and set my mouth in a straight line as I stared back at him. "Or perhaps he has his shields up."

"I can't believe that he can keep both of us out of his mind. Have you tried to reach him?" I asked.

"Why would I want to do that?" Aric's words came out slowly, like thick syrup from a bottle.

"Because I want you to." I caught my bottom lip with my teeth. Even I couldn't deny that I was making it sound like I assumed that Aric would do anything I asked.

Aric pulled the stick out of the fire and handed it to me. "Eat this." He prepared another for himself. "You don't want to hear Dooley's thoughts right now. Trust me."

"So you have heard from him?" I scooted closer to Aric and closer to the fire. The cool night air kept me from becoming too hot. Aric was lucky. It seemed he got all the good parts of being a fae except for the fact that he was forced to leave everything he had known as a human behind. I suppose he didn't think he was so lucky.

"Look, Valora, Dooley is hurting and he is expending all his energy to keep Ravanna from taking over his body and his mind. The sooner we can shut this down, the sooner you can really talk to him and figure things out. The sooner he can figure things out."

"I didn't know Ravanna held such influence over him."

Aric pulled the stick out of the fire, stood up, and positioned himself in front of me, kneeling before me like he had that first day in his chambers when he tended to my wounds. The wounds I suffered now were on the inside. Dooley was fighting the demons within him, and I had no idea if he would win. *If he did win, would he even want me anymore?*

I was keenly aware that Aric could sense everything I was feeling, but I had lost the energy and the will to keep up my shields. I was mentally exhausted.

"Do you still have your mother's grimoire with you?"

The small book dug into my side where I stored it in the inner pocket of my bodice. I had gotten used to it and almost forgot it was there. "Yes, why do you ask?"

"Would you mind if I take a look at it? There is a spell your mother used to weave which I understand was simple, but I always found comforting as a child."

I reached under the bottom edge of my bodice and pulled out the leather bound volume. "She used to weave spells for you?"

Aric set the spits of meat against the log as he took my mother's grimoire from my hands. "I told you once she was like a mother to me as well. I meant it." He flipped through the pages, running his finger down the text. "I was never very proficient at magic, but I can manage simple glamours and — this, here it is."

Aric closed his eyes and furrowed his brow, his voice coming out in a steady, low pitch. "Revele o Coracao." He handed the book to me and I returned it to its place.

"What was that supposed to do?"

Aric held a finger to his lips. "Listen."

The deep thud of a drum sounded in the distance. I pushed myself up and placed my hand on my sword, looking around to see if I could tell which direction it was coming from.

A light touch grazed my hip as Aric moved my hand away from my sword and unclipped it from my belt, tossing it to the ground. "You won't need that." He took my hand in his own and placed it flat against his bare chest. The beat of the drum was keeping time with his heart. "Only we can hear the sounds that this spell weaves."

The sustained and languid tones of a stringed instrument layered themselves atop the percussion and built to a pitch that played in unison with my heart. A thunderclap sounded above and rain started to fall.

He caught me around the waist and pulled me closer, the music now becoming a part of us. My hands locked behind his neck as he swung me around, dancing to the chorus of instruments that had somehow risen from the quiet glen. The sound was near intoxicating. I got a step or two away from him and teased my hips from side to side, shutting my eyes and letting my chin tip to the sky. I opened my mouth to the falling rain.

Aric circled his arm around me from behind and touched his lips to the exposed skin of my neck, darting his tongue out to capture the droplets of water.

I spun around and Aric caught me, dipping me down to the ground and bringing me up again in time to the beat. Slowly the rain faded and with it the music like I was waking up from a dream that I didn't want to end, but I had no choice.

I sat down feeling slightly breathless. Something else besides our dancing was making my pulse race. With every ounce of strength, I tried to resist those familiar feelings I once had for Aric. I bit down on my top lip, my hands trembling as I clutched the tops of my thighs and took in several deep breaths.

Aric reached forward and took a spit of the cooked flesh, the other having dropped to the ground. He pulled a small piece of meat from the stick and held it to my lips. "You must eat something, Guardian."

His eyes burned with the same intensity they had in the few intimate moments we had shared together. I parted my lips and allowed him to place the meat on my tongue. I drew the light and sweet flesh into my mouth, savoring how it practically melted as it traveled down my throat.

"I never expected it could taste so wonderful."

Aric smiled as he reached forward and pushed a loose strand of hair behind my ear with the back of one finger. He trailed his hand down my shoulder and across the top of my wing. An unexpected vibration ran down my spine, into my stomach, and between my thighs.

"It's interesting all the things about the fae anatomy. Our wings are meant for so much more than flying. Are you going to share this?" Aric eyed the cooked dragon's flesh in his hand. "Mine seems to have fallen in the dirt."

Something stirred in my belly and curiosity got the better of me. What if Aric was right? What if the gods were just creatures from other Realms? Then what did the magic of Winter Haven mean? Dooley seemed to discard me so quickly.

I reached forward, pulled a piece of the meat from the stick and brought it to Aric's mouth, pausing just before I placed it to his lips. The fire crackled to life beside us and danced shadows across Aric's pale muscled chest. I waited for him to take the meat from my fingers, but he didn't move. He only stared at me with his dark blue eyes.

"I won't ever force anything upon you again, Valora. I'm done fighting. You do this, you do it of your own free will."

No tricks. His voice echoed in my mind.

I pushed the meat forward to his lips and they parted, allowing me to place it onto his tongue. He waited for me to draw my finger away before closing his mouth. Aric tipped his head and shook his white blond hair back and forth before looking at me again. His hair fell over his shoulders. He swallowed deep. "So good."

He ripped off another piece of meat, this one larger, and offered it to me. "Are you ready for more?"

I took his offering and sank my teeth into it without breaking eye contact with him. The meat once again melted on my tongue, sliding down into my stomach and filling me with renewed vigor. "Enough talking."

I pushed the stake aside and straddled Aric's lap, letting my legs wrap around him as I pushed my tongue into his mouth and he returned the favor with vigor. Our shields were down. My mind glimpsed his hunger and the enticing and delicious delicacies he wanted to bestow on me. A gasp escaped my lips.

He's using you, Valora.

I pulled away from Aric as I heard Dooley's voice.

Really, brother, you choose now to show up?

Isn't that what you intended?

Aric leveled his gaze on me. "You are a delight that I want, very badly. But he is right, I knew the only way to draw him out of his cocoon was through you."

"You said no tricks." I pushed myself off of Aric and sat on the ground.

"There weren't any. My actions served a dual purpose. One of which, I knew, would work against the other. But I have only ever wanted to give you what you wanted, Valora. You have to know that by now. And a large part of you wants him. Those fantasies of mine cater to the other part and will always be available to you." He ran a finger down my cheekbone, tracing the length of the chain of my amulet and barely grazing my breast though the fabric of my corseted bodice.

I took a sharp intake of breath, and he let his hand linger awhile longer. The voice of Dooley playing in my head and Aric's finger playing upon my breast made this feel like the time I had taken them both in at the same time. Like the time that had gotten me into trouble in the first place.

I sat up and separated myself from Aric. *Dooley, are you okay. Is everything all right?*

Everything will be fine.

His response was short and clipped, but not without sincerity. *Are we okay?*

The expanse of time subsequent my question and his answer ripped open, sending me into a spiral of self-doubt, longing and want. A place I never wished to visit and never wanted to be again.

You only have to have faith. I could tell his response was canned. Faith was something not even he believed in anymore. *What is supposed to be, will be.*

"He still fights his demons." Aric looked up at me from his seat on the ground.

I shut my shields down tight, bringing them around me as strong as I could. "He can fight with demons. Tonight I will wrestle with an angel."

☙❧

The morning came too quickly. A euphemism for a bigger problem. My follies with Aric had been mind-blowingly satisfying. He knew it. We both knew it. I awoke wrapped up in his naked body, his wings acting as my blanket. My mind in one place, my body in another. I kept the shields up the entire time, keeping Dooley from my emotions, but it was only a matter of time before he knew everything that had transpired between Aric and me, alone.

"Thank you."

Aric was awake and staring at me with lazy eyes. We barely slept the night before and today we had to set off on our quest to seek acceptance from my father and confirmation from Pryn that Aric really had a part to play in saving the Realms after he had tried to sabotage Dell'Aria.

I slowly pushed free from him and quickly gathered my clothes and my dignity. "I don't…"

Aric held up his hand. "No need to explain. You don't know if what you consented to last night was because you had been hurt by Dooley or because you have feelings for me."

I slid my arms through my bodice and fastened it up tight. "I'm not sure what came over me last night."

"Could have been the dragon flesh. It is a bit of an aphrodisiac you know." Aric propped himself up on his elbow as he lay naked on his side, his leg bent so as to hide the fullness of his anticipation. He had been insatiable last night, his touch so delicate and yet ruthless in drawing out every twinge of pleasure from me until I collapsed in exhaustion. And I let him.

I took a deep breath as these thoughts played upon my mind and therefore in Aric's mind as well. "So this is something you knew about when you fed the flesh to me? It must have been why."

"Hmm." Aric nodded, a slow smile crossing his face before he rolled away from me, giving me a glimpse of that pleasure once more before he reached for his pants. He stood with his backside to me and quickly pulled them up, his wings draping down his back. He tucked a lock of his white blond hair behind his ear and padded towards me. I recorded every minuscule movement, somehow unable to stop staring at him.

"We have far to travel today. I think it best if you let me fly us as far as I can. The dragons will have gone into their lairs for the day. We can't waste precious daylight." He circled his arm around my waist and pulled me against his naked chest. A hot and wet tear fell down the side of my face as I laid my cheek against him.

"He'll never forgive me."

"He won't blame you. He'll blame me. You can blame

245

the dragon's meat. Everything will be okay." He brushed his fingers through my hair.

"But it wasn't just that."

Aric brought a finger to my lip and gave a soft shush. "It was all my doing. That is what he will know. I give you my word."

And a deal between Aric and me was struck without any more words. The truth of the matter was that I was attached to both of these men on such a deep emotional and physical level that separating out their own wants and desires from my own was becoming increasingly difficult. The only way we would all know the truth would be when we were separated and had the choice to go our own way.

"Are you ready to go?"

"What about your harness and knives?" I asked. The weapons lay discarded atop the remnants of Aric's shirt.

"I won't need them where we're going and I don't want to risk hurting you."

I looked around the clearing that had been the setting of our debauchery, in the shadow of the carcass of the great red dragon. If I wasn't sure if I was going to hell before, but I certainly would be going now, whether to fight demons or become one myself I wasn't sure.

I wiped away the errant tear with the back of my bracer. "Ready."

Aric crouched and jetted upwards towards the sky. In the light of day I could clearly make out the isles of Overworld. Amongst them was Dell'Aria, once the only home I had known. But the world had since grown much bigger.

"We're going to go to Charnac to see if we can get word to Dell'Aria of our approach without alerting the Guardians of our presence and causing them to shoot arrows at me."

"You have friends there?"

"I wouldn't call them friends, but I would call them associates and thus far they have been unaware of the price your father has on my head."

"When was the last time you called on them?"

"Who do you think manned the Peixes? I had one of them there to steer it, but as soon as we were clear of the storm they flew home, leaving me with Kali and her treachery."

I clutched tighter to Aric. I hadn't wanted to think about Kali. I forced her image out of my mind at every turn. But the truth was, she was now the key. Dooley had exiled himself to Earth and Ravanna had Kali who was infused with the magic of thousands of fae. I could only imagine that whatever happened it was too late for Kali. There was nothing any of us could do now to save her.

We'll come from below.

Their sentinels will still see us.

That is what I am hoping for.

Aric flew closer and closer to Charnac. The light pierced the transparent scarlet crystals that grew out from its underbelly.

What is that?

Proustite. You wonder where your sword was made? Likely here. They have rich deposits of it. It is the only reason anyone is still here anymore.

What do you mean?

You'll soon see.

As we got closer I could see that Aric was flying towards an inky black cavern. He reached it and set us down quickly on the floor.

"Stay close to me while we're here."

"Are you worried that the fae of Charnac will defile the

daughter of the King of Dell'Aria?"

"Your station means little to these pirates."

"Why do you call them pirates?"

We inched forward into the darkness. Aric held fast to my wrist. "Because after the Fae Wars that is what they became. You think Dell'Aria was shut off from the outer isles because of the Blight? They were long ago shut off from the isles by your former Queen because we are the only ones who have been able to rebuild. The rest of the islands remain without. Magic can only conjure so much. She cut them off because she didn't wish to impart any of the riches of Dell'Aria to the rest of the fae of Overworld."

A light flickered at the end of the blackness before us and slowly drifted towards us. "Aric?" The voice of a woman.

"Don't worry. That is likely who I was hoping for."

The light drifted closer and I could see that the person holding it was fae. A very drop dead gorgeous fae.

"Calliope!" Aric dropped my wrist and greeted the fae goddess who stood before us. Her long hair was decorated with red, orange, and deep yellow braids adorned with complimentary ribbons. Her bright red wings hung down to her waist, and even in the dim light I could see that her eyes glistened with the same golden color as Pryn's.

She eyed me over Aric's shoulder as he hugged her tightly. "Looks as though you have brought a wayward princess with you. You know her head is worth even more than yours these days. You really are risking a lot."

"I appreciate your hospitality." Aric stood to face her. "We only need to use your mirror to contact Dell'Aria, and we can be on your way."

"I hope that is not all you came here to use. Follow me." Without addressing me directly she quickly turned and sauntered down the tunnel.

"Let's go." Aric grabbed my wrist and we continued after her.

What exactly is she expecting from you?

Do I sense a little jealousy?

I would give him no such satisfaction.

She is likely expecting from me some of what you had last night. You can't believe that I would have anything else to bargain with these people. I couldn't bribe them with magic like I did Kali. Magic is not what they are lacking. The Queen is lacking companionship. These pirates just don't do it for her.

Calliope is the Queen of Charnac?

The Queen of a dying isle, but yes, the Queen.

Does she know you kill Queens?

Very funny.

I wished I was being funny. But nothing about this was funny at all. Dooley was on Earth. Kit and Mane were likely fighting to rescue Ralph when he didn't even know he needed rescuing. My father was waging a war with Queen Elemi in order to keep Ravanna from entering the Realms, and I was canoodling with the pirate Queen of Charnac and Aric, her former lover and my current lover. I dropped my free hand to my side. At least I still had my sword. One made with silver from the Charnac mines. I felt like perhaps I might need it soon.

We continued to walk. The dirt beneath my feet turned to stone and the light from the candle held by Calliope was joined by torches that were set into the wall. She blew out her candle and placed it into a small alcove without slowing down her pace. As the light continued to grow so did my view of the Queen. She wore light brown pants, made of the skin of some beast, which hugged her curves tightly. Her small waist was bound even tighter by a saucy orange corset which traveled up her body and ended at a generous bosom made more so by the tightness of her dressing.

She faced Aric again. "I hear your successor has started a war. Are you jealous?" She took Aric's words right out of his mouth. For the first time she looked at me and offered only a wink. Calliope had stopped just on the other side of a large wooden door. The end of the line.

"War was never something I intended."

"You certainly are good at causing a stir."

"Something you seem to delight in." Aric's hand once again dropped from my wrist and it was as if I was no longer there. I might as well have been one of the shadows which danced in the torchlight against the tunnel walls.

I stepped forward and offered a hand towards Calliope. "I am Valora, daughter of King Delos of Dell'Aria."

She turned slightly, but refused to look at me directly. "Yes, I know who you are. And if you are smart you will keep any further introductions to yourself." She turned her attention to Aric. "Has this one even been outside the castle walls before?"

I drew my sword and she caught it with one hand, clenching her fist upon the blade. Blood welled up between her fingers and dripped down her knuckles. "You dare turn a sword on me made of the silver from my own mines? You are stupider than you look. Lucky for you that you learn this now, because if you try that out there you will be eaten alive."

I pushed forward on the blade and watched Calliope flinch. "Dear Queen, the only thing you need to worry about is getting us in communication with Dell'Aria. The rest I can handle."

Calliope dropped her grip on the blade and pressed her bloodied hand to Aric's bare chest, painting a red swath down his muscled stomach. "I mark you to protect you. She is on her own."

She lifted the wooden bar holding the door in place and kicked it outward with her foot. The light flooded in and blinded me temporarily. As I regained focus I wondered if my mind was playing tricks on me. The scene before me was nothing like the bustling town of Dell'Aria. Our streets were lined with merchants. Our fields were ripe with ice fruits and other delicacies. The castle stood like a beacon on the horizon. What lay before me now was almost as desolate as the Dragonlands. The only difference was that it was peppered with fae who were entering and exiting from large gaping mines, pickaxes dangling from their shoulders and grime coating their bodies. Everyone moved with a purpose, and Aric and I looked grossly out of place. I was beginning to regret getting on the Queen's bad side.

Stay close. Aric's voice echoed in my mind, but he didn't need to remind me.

Calliope strode towards the blackened remnants of a building where two fae stood at the doorway, the richest thing I had seen thus far. It was pure silver, no doubt, and covered in intricate carvings. The two fae at the door saluted Calliope as we got closer.

Is this the Queen's castle? I could hardly believe that after all these years Charnac still looked as though it had been in a war just yesterday.

Yes, what is left of it.

꧁꧂

Calliope pushed the silver door open with ease, and it shut with a thud behind us.

"The mirror you seek is in my bed chambers." Calliope tugged at one of her braids as she drank in the sight of Aric's bare chest.

Aric reached his hand behind his neck, his bicep flexing in the process. "Keep all your valuables there, I'm guessing."

"You've suckled at the teat of Dell'Aria's riches too long, Aric. What is valuable here is silver that we can trade and sell for food. We work day and night, and one day we will return to our former glory. But that day is long off."

"Then why keep the mirror?" I asked.

Calliope spoke over her shoulder as we reached a crumbling set of stairs. "She asks too many questions."

I followed behind, and my foot shot through a rotted board, throwing me off balance. Aric caught my elbow, helping me up to the next step.

"Oh, did I forget to say, step where I step? Sorry about that." Her apology dripped with sarcasm as Calliope took a crooked path up the steps. When we reached the top she swept the curtain aside, and we followed her into a small room. She was right, it was nothing like Aric's chambers had been. It looked more like the hut I had shared with Kali except it held only one bed. A round table with several stools around it sat in the center. On the walls were threadbare tapestries which covered the blackened stone. The ceiling above us opened up to the sky. This fae colony was on the brink of starvation, and Calliope had helped Aric escape from Dell'Aria. Was it because she despised Dell'Aria so much? It worried me that she might side with Queen Elemi in this war if that was the case. What could Aric have possibly offered her to convince her to do such a task for him? I swallowed hard remembering his talents in the bedroom.

Aric took a seat at the table and Calliope brought forth a cask of wine with several goblets from an alcove behind one of the tapestries and set them on the table.

Her face tightened as she spoke to me. "Are you going to sit, or are you going to refuse my most gracious hospitality?" I walked towards the table.

"I don't need any of your wine."

"Afraid I am going to poison you, or are you unable to handle the ice wine?"

"You have ice wine? Where did you get that?"

"Had a few visits from a fae of Dell'Aria. Her name is Kali. Do you know her?"

Kali's treachery continued to build. At this rate she would have more black marks against her than Aric, and that was saying a lot.

Aric took a glass from Calliope. "They were once very close."

Calliope nodded. "Hard when your closest ally betrays you, isn't it? You see, I used to be very close with the Queen of Dell'Aria." She took a swallow of the wine and wiped her mouth with the back of her wrist. "But there comes a time when you need to cut your losses. She abandoned the rest of the fae of Overworld, so I relieved her of her head."

I choked back a mouthful of wine. "You killed the Queen of Dell'Aria?"

"Who did you think did it, silly girl?"

"Oh, dear Calliope, the whole of Dell'Aria thinks it was I. You see there is the small matter of the Queen's head ending up on Elemi's doorstep, and she made a rather grand show of presenting it to my feet and accusing me of being a traitor." Aric swallowed the rest of the wine and reached for the cask to pour himself another.

Calliope put her hand over his wrist. "You didn't tell me. This was not our deal. You gave me safe passage into the city to kill her, and I was to reward you with a favor. You were never asked to take the blame."

"You think Charnac would be enjoying such riches if I sold you out? Calliope, Dell'Aria would have sent the Guardians to wipe you out just to appease its people."

"You will not sacrifice yourself." She locked eyes with Aric, and I could tell that she cared for him. This was more than a deal to her. "We will activate the mirror, and I will tell her father myself that I was the one who did it. You will be welcome in your home."

Aric stood up so fast he knocked his stool to the ground. "You will not." He pulled the wine cask to his mouth and drank a large gulp straight from the cask before setting it with a splash on the table.

Calliope's golden eyes seemed to sparkle as she stood slowly to face him, her bright red wings in stark contrast to Aric's pale skin.

Aric didn't take his eyes off her. "Valora, please take this cask and wait outside. I have some things I need to discuss with the Queen before we leave here."

"But the mirror…" My voice trailed off on its own.

The two of them looked as though they were going to rip one another apart. I retreated from the room. Aric could handle himself, that much I knew. And I would only be right outside if he needed me.

I parted the curtain and leaned up against the wall, hugging the cask to my chest. I took another drink and quickly realized that it had been a while since I had eaten anything. The stairwell tipped slightly, and I dropped to the ground to avoid falling to it. My back pressed into the dingy tiles, but my blackened wings wouldn't show the filth and I had little choice in caring.

No sound came from the room. I leaned over and parted the curtain slightly to peer inside. Aric came around the table without breaking his gaze from Calliope. His hand went to the crest of her corset and he gave a quick tug, loosening her breast from its holds. He rubbed his thumb across her nipple and took the back of her neck in his hand, pulling her mouth to his.

Aric's battle strategy was clear. Seemed to be a recurring theme for him. I let the curtain fall and my head fell against the stone wall, a bit too hard.

"Ouch." I felt for a lump on my head and looked up to see another fae. It didn't seem like he saw me. He studied the steps before him and swung his burgundy wings out to the side to keep his footing steady as he traversed the stairway. His hair fell across his face which was bathed in shadow. His foot hovered above the step I had put mine through.

"Not there," I was able to get out before clamping my hand down upon my mouth for fear that more than my voice would come out. I was suddenly and severely nauseated.

The figure froze on the step and looked up towards where I was seated. I realized that since I was sitting in the shadow I probably seemed more of a threat to him than he was to me at the moment.

"Who's there?" the man commanded.

The Queen had warned me against telling anyone who I was. "Just a guest of Calliope. She had to talk to my...brother and so I was just waiting here until they were done."

A scream came from behind the curtain, but it was one of obvious pleasure and not distress.

The man chuckled. "Yes, well, knowing Calliope they could be awhile. Why don't I offer you a more comfortable place to sit while you wait?"

The man's face was unreadable, but his dress indicated

that he was likely someone of the Queen's Court. He didn't wear the filth soaked garb of the people of Charnac. Though his clothes were not fine by any means, tattered by overuse and threadbare, they were not in the style of a commoner.

"Might I ask who is offering me their hospitality?" A small hiccup escaped from me as I pushed myself up the wall to test how well my feet stayed beneath me.

"The name is Henryk. I am part of the Queen's Guard. I had matters to discuss with her, but it certainly can wait." Calliope started to make sounds I wasn't in the mood to hear. Henryk's face caught the light. A long raised scar ran along his cheek from the corner of his eye to his ear. I shuddered involuntarily, and the sickness welled up in my stomach again.

"Certainly, well, if it wouldn't be too much to ask, perhaps I can bother you for a scrap of food. I fear I've had too much wine on an empty stomach."

Henryk chuckled and came towards me, traversing the rest of the way up the stairs. His black hair hung in unwashed strands around his face, and his neck was coated, not with the grime from the mines but with the dust and dirt of everyday. It made me think twice about asking him for food. "Of course. Let's go downstairs." He lent me his arm, and I steadied myself as I walked down the stairwell in front of him, making certain I stepped the same way down as I had stepped up.

As we reached the landing my stomach lurched again and I knew I wasn't going to make it. "This way." Henryk directed me to a small room off the landing and the smell from the water closet was the last thing it took to do me in.

Henryk held back my hair. I wiped my mouth as best I could and turned to thank him. It was then that I knew I was really in trouble.

CHAPTER EIGHTEEN

Henryk ran his finger down the copper chain and pulled at it enough to loosen the amulet which now swung freely at my neck. Although it was only worth my life it probably looked like it would fetch a good amount of coin.

I tried as best I could to pretend it was nothing and tucked it inside my bodice as I stood up, but it was too late and I never was good at card games.

"I know who you are," he said slowly.

And just when I didn't think it could get worse, it did. *Aric, I need you to stop what you're doing. I'm in trouble.* I sent out the silent plea knowing that Aric likely had his shields up, but there wasn't much else I could do.

"The amulet isn't worth much, just an old trinket my mother gave me before she passed away. You know, I'm a lot better now that stuff is all out of my system. I don't need to bother you for any food. Thank you so much for your help."

I stumbled over my words as I tried to move past him, but he wasn't going anywhere. He stood in the doorway of the water closet and the only thing at my back was the mess

I had just made. There was no way out.

"I have little interest in your jewelry, Valora. What I do have interest in is the price you will fetch when the King of Dell'Aria realizes we have you here. He won't be able to ignore us any longer." In an instant he took hold of the chain around my neck and gave a quick twist, closing off most of my airway.

I struggled to free his hand from my throat as he pushed his face closer to mine. His sour breath, the breath of someone who has gone too long without food, assaulted my senses. "But I think I will have a little fun with you before I hand you over. Calliope seems to be enjoying herself and I never get to have any fun."

All the synapses in my brain fired at once. I burned with a hatred for the stagnant man before me, for the crimes my own people had inflicted upon Charnac to cause him such hatred of me, and for men in my life in general who seemed to think they could take what they wanted when they wanted it. No. More.

I leaned back as Henryk's hand was busy undoing his pants and quickly brought myself forward, knocking my head against his. It was enough to catch him off guard, but he also still held onto my amulet. He staggered and the chain at my neck snapped as he fell to the ground with it in his hand.

I pulled my sword and brought it before me, clasping it in one hand and reaching out with the other. "Just hand me the amulet and we can forget this ever happened. You don't want to do this."

"The hell I don't." His eyes flashed with anger as he quickly flipped himself onto his feet with the aid of his wings and raced towards me.

His body was blind to my sword. It was the only reason

I could think of later. The only reason why he would have rushed so quickly upon it. I took two steps backwards as it sank through his middle, and he looked down in shock. He fell to his knees, and my amulet clattered to the floor at my feet.

I reached down for it just as another scream rang out from Calliope's room, but this one was not from pleasure. I peered around the corner as Calliope swept the curtain open. She saw me at the bottom of the stairs. Henryk's body was just around the corner out of view, as was my sword which was slick with his blood.

"Something is wrong with Aric. He just collapsed." She spread her wings and glided down the broken stairs. I dropped my sword and went to her. I didn't need her to see that I had just killed one of her men. She put her hand around my waist and flew to the top of the stairs.

"Your mother was a healer, right? You can help him." Aric lay inside on the floor, his face pale and his breathing shallow. He reached one hand out to me and clutched his amulet with the other. I did the same instinctively, before realizing it was no longer around my neck, it was broken and lying next to the body of the man I had just killed.

Calliope licked her lips with cautious hope.

"I'm sorry, I can't help." I ran past her.

"Coward! Just like your father!" she yelled out.

I was hoping she would be concerned enough about Aric that she wouldn't leave his side right away. I only needed seconds. I traversed the rickety staircase once more and turned the corner, scooping up my sword and the amulet in one swift movement.

So swift in fact that it caught the two guards hovering over Henryk's body by surprise. I raced past them towards the silver door. The amulet sprang to life in my hands, gleaming bright red and draining me of my energy.

Dammit Aric, only take enough to keep yourself alive. I'm running for my life here.

I didn't know if he could hear me, but the amulet continued to burn bright. I reached the silver door and pushed against it. The guards were the two who had been standing outside, and there was no one now. The land before me was dry and barren. There were few places to hide. The only place that I could see losing those who chased me was a place I feared losing myself, but I had no choice.

I sheathed my sword, tucked the broken amulet into the front of my bodice and rushed headlong into the silver mines.

჻

At the entrance to the mines was a stack of baskets and coverings made of brown cloth food sacks. Now bare of food they were only good at keeping out some of the black soot. I grabbed one of each as I fell in line with the others entering the mines. The fae of Charnac really were of meager means. The day had become late afternoon. When I entered the mines I was temporarily blinded by darkness.

I quickly pulled on a sack and accidentally bumped into another fae walking in front of me.

"Watch yourself. No need to be in such a hurry." My vision adjusted as the fae in front of me turned. I tried to shield my face as best I could. Even with the disguise I was grossly out of place. This fae's face was weathered and cracked from the dry, arid landscape. I couldn't tell if I was talking to a man or a woman. The bulk of the rucksack around the fae's form and the multiple baskets slung across the shoulders of the fae completely obscured anything other than this fae was here in the mines to work.

"So sorry." I briefly fell out of line and pretended to drop my basket. I reached my fingers into the dusty earth and wiped my hands across my forehead, cheeks, and down both arms. I swept them down the lengths of my pants and made sure that the sack covering my body also hid all evidence of my sword.

I picked up the basket, slung it across my shoulder and took a quick peek at the entrance of the mines. Hints of purple and orange streaked the sky, signaling nightfall. I couldn't worry about Aric now. I was in the thick of it and the only way out was in.

I got in line and followed the rest of the fae to the carts which sat on silver tracks leading into the mines. They all piled in, several to a cart, body next to body. This was an occupation of necessity. There was no one here who enjoyed their job. That much was painfully clear.

I piled into a cart along with two others and made sure I held tightly to the edge.

"Looks like we got a new recruit. This your first time in the mines, girl?" The grungy face of another fae stared back at me. They all looked identical except this one who was abnormally plump for the starving fae of Charnac. The fae next to her was more stick-like and androgynous. But the fae I spoke with had plump curves which definitely signified she was a woman.

I nodded. "Yeah, not feeling so well today, either." I didn't need to lie about that. The adrenaline was wearing off and my stomach reminded me that I still hadn't eaten. Whatever was in my stomach was still on the floor of the Queen's water closet along with the body of one of her men.

"She looks green around the gills. Hoping she doesn't lose it in here. Last thing I need is to start my shift covered in someone's daily rations." The thin fae's voice revealed her sex as she pushed her tightly fisted hands into her hips.

"No, I'll be fine." I waved away her concern and quickly planted my hands at the side of the cart as it pitched forward into blackness. The carts were loaded with fae who all stood their ground as the carts gained speed. I was the only one huddled down clutching at the sides. *Way to blend in, Valora.*

I tried as best I could to stand up in the cart as it gained speed.

"Plant one foot forward. Lean into the curves. You'll be fine." The rotund fae woman patted me on the back, and I had to swallow the bile that rose in my throat.

"For Charnac!" she yelled as she thrust her pickax into the air. The other fae echoed her cry. "Charnac. Charnac."

I reached into the basket at my waist and brought up my ax, mimicking the cry of these soul-worn fae. After several rounds of the chant the cart picked up speed. The chanting seemed to keep in time with the carts as the wheels clacked over the joints in the rails.

These people had as much spirit as the dwarves I had met at Mount Elbrus. More so since they had fallen on such hard times. I supposed these mines were all they had left to live for.

The carts continued to pick up speed as they dipped down on the tracks which ran deep within the belly of Charnac. Light peeked out from all sides as the wind whipped at my hair. The light was pale pink and became redder as we descended deeper. I realized that was because the mines went as deep as Charnac was thick.

The cart leveled out as we reached the bottom, the speed slowed by the gradual leveling of the track. The sounds of pickaxes striking rock echoed on all sides, many sets of arms swinging them up slowly and letting them fall by their own weight. These fae weren't hardworking, they were weary and had no other choice. As the cart slowed to a stop the fae all poured out.

I turned to the rotund fae at my side. "How do we get up?"

"Fly of course." She clapped me on the back. "You do got wings, don't ya?" She laughed and continued into the mines.

My original plan looked bleak. I was hoping to hide in here long enough that I could blend in with those leaving. But that plan wasn't going to work.

Fae chipped away at the smaller deposits that surrounded the tracks. The light that I had seen was because the floor of the cavern was thin. Too thin. Through its crystalline surface I could see the trees and mountains far below. The fae of Charnac had exhausted their mines. It wouldn't be long until they needed to find other ways to sustain themselves.

I wasn't sure why the Fae Wars had started, but this was as good a reason as any for them to begin again.

A cry rang out, and one of the fae passed out at my side. The plump woman ran over and slung him over her shoulder, placing his body in the cart that stood on the track. She tapped the side of the cart and it pulled backwards and up towards the top. An idea formed in my mind.

I snaked around the workers, trying to look as if I was looking for a good spot to mine. They were so focused on not passing out that they barely noticed me.

As my plan formed I pressed absently at my mother's grimoire that dug into my side. This had to work. In my mind I could see Pryn shaking his head at me. If I had focused more on my magic skills perhaps I would have a better chance of getting out of here. Dooley had tried to teach me, but in my usual fashion I shunned any teachings of magic and seduced him into bed instead.

I wanted to take a deep breath, but the soot-filled air wouldn't allow me to. As much as I wanted to melt into my memories of Dooley, I had to remind myself that he had left me and there was no guarantee I would see him again.

The thin crystalline bottom of the cavern floor shed an eerie red iridescent light on all the workers. I imagined this probably looked a lot like the dominion of Ravanna, Acheron. But I had no sympathy for him. These people were fighting for their lives. He was a demon King fighting for his own immortality, and who knew what would happen if he ever got that.

I passed a fae who had several full baskets of silver rock behind him. I slowed as I passed him and bent to the ground, fumbling with the non-existent laces of my boots. Quickly I replaced one of his full baskets with my empty one and slung it over my shoulder as I rose to standing. If I was going to fake an injury, I needed to look like I had been working.

The fae didn't turn around, and I continued along the track until I got to the space where the track began to rise upwards. I ducked beneath the rise and planted myself under the track. A loud rattling sounded as another row of carts descended into the cavern. *How many more workers could they send down here?* In a few days' time there wouldn't be any more silver to mine. As I squatted into my hiding space I checked the ground beneath me for cracks. It felt solid enough beneath my feet, but as I knew all too well, looks could be deceiving.

I needed some time to pass before I faked an injury. As I searched through the basket for some silver I realized that beneath the upper layer of dirt and chunks of plain rock lay pure silver flakes. The fae I had stolen from must have been down here for weeks in order to collect this much, and he had several baskets full. I grew sick again. Hopefully he would find the basket here after I left.

The heat of the amulet against my chest returned. Just what I needed. I had hoped that the reason Aric fell ill was due to the break in our connection and all that would be needed would be for me to have it again for him to regain his strength. After that he would need to get out on his own. He was the one with wings. I needed another way out.

The heat of the amulet receded, but the sweat had started to break out on my brow. I wasn't sure how many hours had passed. My hands were clammy as I gripped the handle of the pickaxe. The light was dim underneath the rails and I had to brush away the debris that seemed to constantly float down from the tracks. Or perhaps it just constantly hung in the air.

If I was going to get out of here I needed to give it a few good swings. There wasn't any way I was going to be flying out. I stood up and lifted the axe above me, bringing it down on the solid rock at my feet. Vibrations ran down my arms and I almost lost my grip.

Suddenly another set of carts flew in from overhead. There were shouts from the end of the line where the cart came to a stop. I peeked out and saw the unmistakably red wings of Calliope as she gestured to the fae flanking her sides.

Valora, you are in grave danger. They are searching for you. I don't know what you were thinking. Aric's voice echoed in my ear.

I was thinking that oaf was about to have his way with me. Besides it wasn't my fault he was too blind to see my sword. I didn't mean to kill him. Was he terribly important?

I peeked out again. Calliope's face was strewn with tears.

But she wasn't saddened, she was angry. Fiercely angry.

You killed Calliope's son. The prince of Charnac.

❧❧

"You stole my silver!" The fae who had been working at the railroad tracks was now in my face shaking his fist at me. He pointed down to a swath of red that was painted across the side of the basket, something I had failed to see when I took it. "That's my blood on the side there. That's my silver."

Calliope and her men fanned out across the cavern floor. They were approaching each fae and ridding them of their coverings so they could check their wings. Because of course, I would be the only one whose wings would look different.

The angry fae collected his basket. There was nothing I could do to stop him that wouldn't cause a commotion. The fae didn't want a fight, he just wanted his silver back. He tottered off with the heavy load.

I was left with a grimoire which wouldn't do me any good, a pick axe I could barely wield, and my sword.

Aric, where are you?

There was no response to my call. A thin sheet of proustite crystal lay at my feet. Darkness had almost claimed the night. If I could escape outside the walls of the city I might stand a chance. Or I might end up like a splat on the plains.

"The thief is over there, hiding underneath the rails. She stole my silver." Calliope looked down at the fae who still held his overflowing basket of silver in his hands. Then she saw me.

I pulled my sword from my side and plunged it down into the floor at my feet. The initial thud was replaced by the

266

sounds of cracking. Small fissures shot out from the place where my sword was embedded into the crystal floor and grew rapidly.

Calliope stopped in her tracks and watched as ground threatened to open up beneath her. "What have you done? What have you done!"

My intention had been only to open up enough of the floor so that I could get through. Apparently the proustite was so thin that my actions had caused a cascade of destruction which was slowly ripping through the entire floor of the silver mines.

The walls began to shake as the integrity of the underside of Charnac disintegrated. From somewhere an alarm sounded, not unlike the alarms which sounded through the streets of Dell'Aria when a wave of the Blight hit. All the fae gathered what they could, ripping away their coverings and shooting up to the surface with their loot.

Calliope remained where she was. The two guards I had seen hovering over Henryk's body stood by her side. The tension in their muscles told me that they were just looking for the right time to strike. The chaos surrounding us was enough to cause her to rethink how she was going to get her hands on me.

Then the reins snapped, and she ran towards me screaming. I pulled the sword from the crystal floor, the linchpin to the entire structure. The floor beneath my feet crumbled.

For a moment the scene was surreal. The entire floor had given way at the same time and for a second Calliope was still only several feet away from me, along with her men and the abandoned baskets and carts from the silver mine. Then gravity took over, and each piece twisted its own way. Calliope and her men spread their wings, slowing their descent, but I continued to fall.

I closed my eyes and recalled the spell Pryn had taught me, the one I was hoping might stop me from falling to my death. However, since Calliope was likely tracking me, falling to my death might be preferable.

As I started the enchantment a voice rang out in my head. *Keep falling. Trust he will catch you.*

Dooley.

I didn't know how or why I was hearing his voice, but I was. Did he mean Aric?

I opened my eyes just in time to see Aric swooping down, faster than Calliope and her men. I also noticed I was almost to the ground.

Aric slammed into me and pulled me into his chest as he continued to race across the sky.

Calliope and her men won't stop pursuing us until I'm dead.
Soon they will have bigger things to worry about.

A screeching sound rang out across the sky. I looked back to see the swarm of dragons that Aric and I had escaped earlier, eager to avenge their slain brethren.

But those dragons are after us, aren't they?

Yes, but Calliope and her men don't know that. The only thing they know is that they're behind them.

Sure enough, Calliope and her men noticed the dragons and quickly shot back up to take cover on Charnac. The dragons didn't typically travel to the heights of Overworld, preferring instead to live somewhere in between.

How will we enter Dell'Aria without you being captured?

The shadows of the dragons drifted away. Aric had a long head start on them and the desire to go really fast.

The answer is, we let them capture me. That's the only way.

After I found out that his actions had caused my mother's death I wanted nothing more than for him to face justice at the hands of the fae of Dell'Aria. But at the moment I was anything but joyful.

But we need you in this war.

You'll just have to convince them of that before they put a sword to my neck and hope that they need to at least take time to sharpen that sword.

Are you sure they would give you the courtesy of a sharpened sword?

I'm not sure of anything other than you need to get to Dell'Aria and I need to be by your side.

The isle of Dell'Aria came into view, its craggy underbelly a stark contrast to the ruin I had just left in Charnac.

I destroyed the livelihood of Charnac. I will be responsible for their deaths. A sudden thought occurred to me. *What if we don't go to Dell'Aria? What if we return to Earth, get Dooley and find some other way to defeat Ravanna?*

We both know what running from our problems can do. You run from your battles, the battles come and find you, no matter what different setting you choose to surround yourself with.

I clutched at him tighter, pressing my head against his chest, hearing the rapid thrum of his heart and feeling his heat. I wasn't certain I could keep my father or any of the fae of Dell'Aria from killing Aric after what they had seen. They believed Aric had murdered the Queen when it really was Calliope.

And you don't need to worry about Charnac. Their people have needed to find another way to survive for many cycles. They have just been lazy. So lazy that they caused that disaster. You only lit the fuse, but it had been ready to blow for quite some time.

I nodded into his chest, even though I didn't really believe him entirely. I had done something awful, just as awful as the terrible mistake that Aric had made.

Dell'Aria got closer and closer. There was no swaying Aric from his course. He was aiming straight for the castle walls. No sneaking in this time. He was going to knock on the front door.

Before we could get any closer the Guardians descended from their places along the battlements. Aric made sure to position me where I could be seen.

"I have Valora, daughter of your King. You may want to put away those arrows so that you don't accidentally poke any holes in her."

CHAPTER NINETEEN

The Guardians were swift as they came down and pulled Aric in one direction and me in another. He offered them no resistance. I, on the other hand, fought to remain with Aric.

"You have to bring him with me. Straight to father." I tried to stand up straight and make my whole five and a half foot frame seem taller than the fae that towered above me. They weren't buying my show of power.

"Your father gave us his orders directly as soon as the two of you were spotted. You can take it up with him if you don't like it."

"Aric!" I freed myself from the Guardians momentarily and rushed towards him. I knew I could speak to him without needing to be near, but there was one last thing that I needed to do which could only be done in person. I flung my arms around his neck and pulled his mouth to mine for what might be the last time. He returned my embrace, but with a sadness instead of with passion.

As the Guardians pulled at me, time seemed to slow down. Wings of the fae around me fluttered at the edges of my vision as they tore me in the opposite direction. Aric mouthed to me, "I love you, sweet Valora."

He smiled and I did the same just as the iron fist of one of the fae made contact with his jaw. He dropped to his knees and looked up at me again, blood dripping from his mouth as he turned his gaze to the fae who had just hit him.

"Really, is that all you have for me? I did slaughter your brothers and sisters." Another kick to his gut, and I was pulled away kicking and screaming by the five fae surrounding me. They pushed me through the courtyard towards the King's keep.

Aric, are you okay?

I'm drawing up my shields. You don't want to feel my pain.

And then his voice was silent.

The fae continued to push me up the stairwell towards the door to the King's keep. The door swung open, and my father sat at the desk which was once occupied by Aric.

He saw me and stood abruptly, causing the fae who were bent over his shoulder to take a few steps back.

"Everyone clear out of here now. I need to talk to my daughter alone."

The man at my father's side was dressed in priest's robes and gave a few slight bows as he exited. The Guardians were the last to leave and shut the door behind them.

"Father, I need you to listen."

"No! You disobeyed me, Valora. And now we are on the brink of a war so fierce I don't know if any of us will survive." He paced behind his desk and I half wondered if it was the way of a king to pace. His thumb and forefinger cupped his chin.

"Calliope is massing an army of fae. Elemi is massing an army of selkie. And who knows what else will follow her out of that hell," he said.

"I think I know."

My father sank into the chair behind his desk, his eyes full of sadness. "I know you do. It's all written here actually. Pryn brought it to me this morning."

I examined the papers on the desk. "Are those scrolls from the temple?" He nodded as I approached the desk and ran my finger along the upside down lettering. The meaning of the test slowly sank in and explained the look on my father's face.

"No, this is all wrong. It can't be. It can't." I backed slowly away from the table and shook my head, as if it would all go away if only I could deny it. "I can't lose you, too."

"As fae we live long lives, but they all end at some point. This says a king's sacrifice will be required in order to stop the evil from rising against the Goddess. I have already ordered the Guardians to make sure the colony is prepared before I use the portal to travel to Mavrovo and hopefully end this all."

"You're putting your trust in some old scrolls? No, father. There is more to it than that. Much more."

He already knows about all that. The voice was so near that my eyes darted around the room to see if he was standing there next to me.

"Speaking of trust. I saw you with Aric in the courtyard. I am not sure what kind of magic he has woven around you, but you will need a visit with Pryn before you retire to your chambers to make certain you are not afflicted with anything."

"You have no idea what I have done." I stared at my feet which were planted to the floor. "Calliope and her son…"

"…have caused you no end of grief." Dooley stood in the doorway. His very presence made my knees go weak and I wasn't sure if I was hallucinating because I so badly needed him by my side.

"I was wondering when you were going to show up. Very good of you to come. I think my daughter needs an escort. She's been acting very strangely, and I want Pryn to have a talk with her."

"But what will happen to Aric?" I stood before my father.

He gave a heavy sigh. "Aric will get what is coming to him, in good time. At the moment I have preparations to make. I'll see you in the morning after you have had a chance to rest. We'll have a meal and hopefully a discussion which makes some sense."

At the mention of Aric, Dooley's stance became less relaxed, but I needed to know what would happen to him. Dooley reached his hand out to me, "Care to come with me to see Pryn?"

I slid my hand into his, and his touch was warm against my skin. His eyes were full of intense longing. I wasn't sure how that would change once he knew the extent of what I had done with Aric.

He gave a quick nod to my father and escorted me out the door which was flanked with two Guardians. They stared at him, and Dooley gave a quick wave. Dooley tucked his hair behind his ear. He looked in front of us and then down to his feet again. He was focused on something, but I couldn't tell what. If I searched his mind then I wouldn't get the benefit of his thoughts after some consideration, only raw emotion. I didn't think I could take any hatred from Dooley, even though I deserved it.

"What made you return?" We continued our slow pace through the castle gates and towards the temple where Pryn practiced his magic and prayed to the Goddess Varuna.

"Ravanna." He gave a quick glance at me before looking

back down the hall.

"I wasn't expecting that answer. You said you were staying away specifically because of him."

"He has a tight hold on me."

"But I thought you were able to control it."

"It's not me that I am worried about. He seems to be able to get through to you now because we are all connected by these amulets." Dooley patted his chest and I could see the chain of the amulet which disappeared beneath his white cotton shirt.

"I wonder if that's true anymore." I pulled the amulet from my bodice which still had the broken chain attached. "I had this ripped from my neck and it didn't affect me, but it made Aric terribly sick."

"And I."

I stopped and brought my hand to his shoulder forcing him to face me. "You fell ill as well?"

"Yes, it was also when I received the message from Ravanna." Dooley took in a sharp intake of breath. "He enjoys playing games. It seems for now, instead of you being reliant on Aric and me to keep you alive, we are reliant on you. If you remove that amulet we will be drained of our magic and die."

"But the both of you are only half-fae."

"Yes, half-fae who aren't quite fit to live in either world and who have the weaknesses of both, I am afraid. Being in the Realms puts me closer to Ravanna's influence, being on Earth drains me of magic and makes me no good to anyone. It's a double-edged sword."

"So why would you be concerned about me?"

"Because he could change his mind, Valora. You are the conduit. The force linking the magic of the Goddess and of Ravanna. I've had a long talk with Pryn who has knowledge of this demon. As long as you remain, he cannot defeat the Goddess. He knows that if Aric and I die you will be given the powers of both of us and become the ultimate warrior. He also knows that if he transfers the power to Aric and me to decide whether you live or die, then you will never die. We won't let it happen. So he plays with us. Tries to surprise us, make us weaker."

"What if only one of you were to die?" The question escaped my lips before I had time to process what it meant and what I would want the answer to be.

"Then you would be free of your role as a conduit, but you would take in the powers left behind by whoever of us dies. If I die, you take in Ravanna. If Aric dies, you take in the Goddess. Our life forces have become fused, and there really is no hope of separating them without severe consequences."

We walked again in silence. The dirt crunched beneath the feet of my boots as the road dipped down and the dome of the temple came into view. "What is it that Pryn is supposed to do?"

"Help us find a way to convince your father that Aric can't be put to death." He grit his teeth as he finished his comment.

"So you wish him dead as well?"

"I wish his influence over you would die. It's a wedge between us that shouldn't be there, Valora. One I had hoped would be squelched as soon as I had given you permission to be with him. But it seems to have gotten worse. I blame myself for that."

I stopped again as we got closer to the temple door. "Gave me permission? Since when do I need permission from you to do anything?" I crossed my arms over my chest, his words provoking my rebellious nature.

A slight growl seemed to come from Dooley's throat. A mixture of anger and passion. Both of our amulets glowed briefly, and Dooley gripped the sides of his head.

"Are you okay?"

He waved me off, speaking through a clenched jaw before standing up and looking at me once more. "First you need to meet with Pryn." His eyes smoldered again, and my heart sank down to my toes. Dooley had something in mind for me, that was for certain.

෨෴

We were swiftly escorted through the temple doors. It was as if I had never left and nothing had changed. My crimes against Charnac weighed heavy on my mind. Although Calliope had killed our Queen, she had done so to protect her people. Where was the line of right and wrong anymore? I guess it all depended on who you asked.

"I am not sure Pryn will be able to convince your father to keep Aric alive." Dooley took my elbow and guided me through the halls. Halls which I had grown up in. Other than the walls of the Court, the temple had been my only reprieve. My mother often came to temple to practice her healing arts and sometimes took me with her. The last thing I needed was for Dooley to guide me through the halls like someone who was out of their element. Dell'Aria was my home, my city. I wasn't sure about many other things, but of that I was certain.

I gently shrugged my elbow out of his hold. "Thanks for the assist, but I do know where I'm going."

"You're not going to make this easy, are you?" I looked over my shoulder at Dooley whose mouth was drawn in a tight line.

"Make what easy?"

277

I hadn't realized that we were already at the door to Pryn's inner chamber until it opened in front of me. "Valora!" Pryn wrapped his arms around me and gave me a loving embrace.

"I am so happy you made it safely back to us. You had us all worried for a bit. This one especially." Pryn tipped a finger towards Dooley who nervously ran his fingers through his hair.

"Really? I had him worried?" It was more a jest than a question, but then I realized he had every right to be worried and to be angry, and my normal playful personality tucked itself into submission.

"Yes, well, come along then. Your father wants me to check you for unwanted charms."

It didn't take long for Pryn to come to the conclusion that everything I had done and said had been of my own free will. I almost wished he had found something. Then I could blame someone else for what I had done.

"She is clear." Pryn said to Dooley and then turned to face me. "Your father will be glad to hear it."

"Will he?" I leaned forward, practically on top of the old priest. "Will he be glad to know that I bedded down with the man whose head he put a bounty on and that I, Guardian of Dell'Aria, have killed the crown prince of Charnac and caused an even greater rift between Dell'Aria and Charnac than ever existed before?" My voice squeaked out the last few words. I wasn't sure who I was asking, him or myself.

Looking into the priest's eyes was like looking at my mother. She had golden eyes just like Pryn. I, on the other hand, was not even meant to live. I studied my feet again, unable to look at him. I had soiled my mother's memory. The grimoire pushed into my gut as I hunched over trying to collect a full breath and not pass out. A stiff reminder of my failure. A constant reminder.

I pulled the grimoire out of my vest and thrust it at Pryn. "Take this. Put it to good use. It's no good to me. She would never have meant for me to have it if she knew."

I raced out of the room, ignoring the calls of Dooley. Pryn said nothing. He knew my shame. I made several turns and quickly found the passageway that I now knew lay between the temple and the castle and followed it until I had made it into the castle crypt.

It had been too long since I had visited my mother's grave and I needed another night upon it. To sleep on the hard earth and to be reminded that the road ahead was not going to be easy. This was only the beginning. I was in over my head and there was no one who was going to save me.

I was the Guardian. The one charged by my father to save Dell'Aria and the one charged with protecting the spawn of the Goddess and of Ravanna. The two who had to merge as one and become at peace with one another in order for this world and Earth to survive. The only problem was, they were both fighting over me.

At every turn the weight upon my shoulders increased as I got closer to the crypts that lie under the castle. How many bodies was I going to be responsible for on Charnac? How many mothers would have to bury their children because they didn't have the means to provide food for them anymore? How many of the fae of Dell'Aria would die in this coming war?

The tears continued to spill down my face. I was so immersed with my own thoughts that it took me a second to realize that the new sound I was hearing was Pika's small yelp as he bounded around my ankles.

I stopped and scooped him into my arms, burying my face into the fluffy orange fur of the pikaki. "What are you doing here, Pika? How did you find me?"

Dooley rounded the corner and stopped once he saw me. He bent over, resting his hands on his knees. "That would be because I told him to find you. He seems to be good at that." He took another deep breath and stood upright. "Pryn took a quick visit to Mount Elbrus after you and returned with the pikaki."

I kept Pika cradled to my chest. "Look, Dooley, I need this time alone right now. A lot has happened since we last saw one another. And I know you must know some of it." I pointed errantly to my head to acknowledge that he could likely have seen all he wanted to see by now. "But so much of it I haven't even figured out, and I need to do that. I promise you and I will have time to talk soon."

It was more than I could ask of him, I knew that. Humans generally expected monogamy, and I had never even experienced a true relationship until I met Dooley. Now in a short span I had somehow thrown it all out the window. I needed to sort it out.

"Look, I get it." Dooley touched my arm and a wave of warmth and calming pulsed through my body from his touch. However, at the same time his grip was rock solid. He wasn't going to let me go anywhere. "I get it."

This was a new kind of magic. One I had never felt from Dooley before.

"What is it that you get, Dooley?"

I was careful with my words. At this point I wasn't even sure that I was speaking to Dooley, but his eyes remained the same deep chocolate brown. There were no flashing red lights. Nothing to warn me off of him, and as he continued his grasp on my arm I realized that he was affecting me on another level entirely.

I placed Pika on the ground, freeing Dooley's hand from my wrist. As I did the calming effects of his touch wore off and it made me want more.

"How is it when you touch me, I feel calm?"

In one swift movement Dooley pulled my arms above my head and pushed me against the wall. His voice was ragged and I wasn't sure if he was himself anymore. As he spoke hot puffs of air danced across my neck. "Spending so much time alone gives you time to learn new things."

I took a sharp intake of breath as his grip on my wrists tightened. A second ago I could have easily broken his hold on me. Now I might cause him injury if I were to bring my knee up between his legs.

"You are not going to visit your mother's tomb this evening. You are not going to let the oncoming battle weigh heavy on your mind. Neither of those things will help prepare you for what is to come."

He moved his face so that he was looking straight into my eyes, our noses almost touching.

"And you know what I need to do in order to come?" The words were out of my mouth before I realized what I had said. His intense gaze and grip on my wrists caused a scorching heat low in my belly.

Dooley slid his free hand down the front of my pants. "Yes, I think I do know what you need, but first you have to earn it."

Something was wrong. I tried to get past the shields to see inside Dooley's thoughts, but I couldn't. Dooley gripped at the hair on the nape of my neck, his gaze holding me like a fae charm could hold a human. But he was the human, not I. My mind battled against the wishes of my body, but my mind was losing.

He threw me over his shoulder. "Unless you want to do this in a dank hallway I suggest you point me in the direction of the nearest bedroom."

Dooley somehow found Aric's old living quarters in the temple and tossed me onto the bed. Pika darted inside before he closed the door and hid underneath.

I took my time watching as Dooley pulled his shirt up over his head revealing the tan muscles of his stomach, pushing the red flags into the recesses of my brain. His strong shoulder muscles flexed as he balled up the shirt and tossed it into the corner. A shiver ran down my spine, a mixture of fear and lust.

His jeans hugged his muscular thighs. He didn't take his eyes off me as he pushed one boot off and then another, kicking them to the side.

"I'm going to make you forget about everything for a while, Valora Delos. Everything but me." A peaceful apathy wove its way around me. Yes, I wanted to forget. Everything.

Dooley walked towards me, and I leaned further against the bed as he hovered over me. He slid his hand underneath my backside and gave me a little shove towards the top of the bed, taking his other hand and pushing my wrists above my head.

Dooley pressed his lips against my mouth and pulled at the sides of my bodice, making quick work of the clasps. His smooth chest brushed against my own. He took the broken chain of the amulet and wrapped it around my wrist, pressing the stone into my hand as he had once before. As he did, it flared briefly.

My hands were useless. All I was able to do was focus on Dooley's powerful embrace. He brought his hand up and gently grazed the side of my breast leaving behind a tingling sensation. I tugged at his hand holding my wrists, longing to pull him onto me.

Still holding me firmly he pulled down the edge of my pants with one hand and then unbuckled his belt, pulling out his gorgeous erect length. My mouth went dry. I needed him inside of me. I was desperate to have Dooley's acceptance again.

He gripped my hip and plunged into me, pounding against me with a rawness that engulfed me at each thrust. The heat built up in my cheeks and I felt flush with the desire that welled up again inside me and suddenly burst forth, clenching down upon Dooley and causing him to do the same.

We both collapsed on the bed. I turned lazily towards Dooley. "I like the little bad in you, my love."

"So glad to hear you say that." An unmistakable red flash passed across Dooley's eyes. I touched my lips and looked at my fingers which were covered in cinnabar dust. And then it hit me all at once. Everything I had ignored because I so desperately wanted Dooley's approval. I had just had sex with Ravanna, the demon King.

CHAPTER TWENTY

Dooley fell asleep quickly. Pika poked out from under the bed and snuggled down between the two of us. The little furry hairball didn't seem to think anything was amiss.

I kept a watch on Dooley, noting the rise and fall of his chest as it became slower and deeper the more he slumbered.

"Looks like there is nothing more I can do tonight, Pika." I patted the orange fluff ball and laid my head on the pillow, keeping my eyes faced towards Dooley. If Ravanna showed up again I wouldn't miss it this time.

At some point I must have fallen asleep. It was difficult to tell when the morning came since there were no windows in Aric's inner sanctum. I awoke to Dooley sitting up in bed, staring down at me. He looked slightly confused.

"What are we doing here?" he asked. "The last thing I remember was chasing you down the hallway."

"Yes, and you took a nasty spill. You're lucky Pika was here to lead me to you and that he was there to heal your wounds. You had a knot on your head the size of Mount Elbrus." I was fairly proud of my quick recovery. There was no way in hell I was going to let Dooley think he had been bested by Ravanna. The last thing I needed was for him to abandon us again if he thought that he was a danger. I was fairly certain that Ravanna was only trying to poke at our defenses. It should have been obvious the moment I saw Dooley clutching his temples. Ravanna couldn't cause any real damage unless we let him. Unless I let him.

Dooley rubbed at his forehead. "Seems like I still have a headache."

I jumped out of bed and fetched him a glass of water before sliding under the covers.

"Don't tell me I missed all that as well last night. I would hate to think I didn't give you the attention you deserve." Dooley sipped the water and ran his fingers through his brown hair, pulling out the errant tangles.

I held the sheet up, covering my naked chest, a gesture he would certainly find suspect. If it were just he and I there would be no way I would be shy, but I had Ravanna to worry about.

"No, just got comfortable for sleeping. You passed right out after Pika healed the concussion you gave yourself." I pulled on my pants and bodice, slipping my shoes into my boots as I tossed Dooley his jeans. "You better get dressed. We'll need to report to Court first thing this morning if we're going to keep Aric alive. I really hope that Pryn thought of something to tell father."

This time I let Dooley lead the way to Pryn's quarters. I hadn't exactly endeared myself to the old priest by shouting in his face and running out on him last night. I also wanted to stay several steps behind Dooley so I could watch him. It didn't hurt that the view from behind wasn't bad at all. I shivered as I recalled what we had done the night before. *But that wasn't Dooley.*

Pryn opened his door and motioned for us to come

inside. "Quickly, we haven't much time."

He fetched a small chest on the table and shoved it into Dooley's arms. "Bring that and follow me. They already have him on trial and we need to hurry."

"What?" I raced after Pryn who moved with surprising deftness through the corridors between the temple and the royal court, leaving Dooley behind.

"Well, yes, I think he wanted his decision made before you knew." Pryn's voice bounced up and down in time with his footfalls on the stone path. "He would really rather not upset you."

"How about not removing Aric's head? That would be a start." Dooley followed closely behind, Pika bounding about his heals.

"Don't worry, I'm sure we'll make it."

"Have you heard from the Goddess Varuna yet, Valora?" asked Pryn as he rounded one last curve and came to a wooden door. He stopped and turned to look at me. "Well, have you?"

"No."

"Well, then we know he is still alive, now don't we?" He pushed open the door and it smacked against one of the Royal Guard who had been posted around the periphery of the room. "Official business, step aside please."

Pryn looked over my shoulder and leaned over to grip Dooley around the wrist. "Come now, you must follow behind me. Valora, don't get lost in this crowd."

The Guard seemed slightly perturbed, but he let us get by without trouble. The last time I had seen a crowd like this was when Aric was about to behead Dooley after he had proclaimed him a traitor. Now it was Aric whose life was on trial.

The crowd parted in front of us. They had all squeezed

into the courtyard to see what was to become of the fae that they believed murdered their Queen and stole the magic which killed their brethren. As we got closer the press of bodies closed in all around us as everyone strained to get a better look of Aric.

I knocked into someone fairly hard as I tried to keep up with Dooley, and a strong hand clamped down on my shoulder. I looked up into Mane's fierce eyes. "You don't want to see what is going on in there." With his height Mane could easily see past the tops of the fae who were still standing. There were also those who had taken a place in the air, hovering about to get a better view.

Kit popped out from behind Mane, her hand clinging to Mane's bicep. Her expression was pained, and she opened and closed her mouth a few times, unable to form any words. Whatever Mane had seen was bad.

"Glad you guys could make it, but I need to go help Aric."

Mane nodded, as if he knew that would be my answer. He had to have known I wasn't going to stay hidden in the crowd. I dropped my shields and reached out to Aric as I continued to push through to the center of the room, but I could tell as soon as I did that he was still locked tight. My mental plying bounced right back at me. He was using all the strength he had to shield himself. As I finally made it to the inner circle of the crowd and pushed past the fae who were standing shoulder to shoulder I found out why.

My boot slipped on the floor and I ran into Dooley who stood clutching the chest. I looked down and realized that what I had slipped on was blood. Aric's blood. A lot of it.

My stomach was nauseated again, and I swallowed hard. Dooley was frozen at the sight before him. I don't think even he expected that his brother would be punished in this way. My father was leaning in towards Orris, speaking to him in a hushed voice.

The crack of a whip brought my attention to the center of the room where Aric was on his knees, the upper portion of his body bent back as he stared at the sky. His hands had been tied behind him. His upper body was bare and covered in bloody lashes. They had obviously been torturing him for some time.

He parted his swollen eyelids and turned towards Dooley and me. I couldn't tell if he could see me or not.

Get her out of here, Dooley.

The shields were down, and with that he fell over onto his side.

"No, father, stop!" I ran towards Aric, but before I could get to him I had a Guardian on each of my arms, restraining me. I struggled against them and they clamped their arms down tighter.

Dooley, why won't the amulets help heal Aric? What's wrong?

He still holds the shields up between us. He won't allow us to be drained of power to save his life. Each of us has to reach out to the others in order for the amulets to work that way.

"Father, hear me now! You've never bothered to hear my words before, but you can't ignore me any longer."

The room fell silent. The fae weren't used to seeing bursts of emotion at court, and I hoped I had everyone's attention.

"You assigned the Guardians to protect the fae of Dell'Aria and now you use them as your torturers? How does that make us any better than you believe Aric to be?"

"Who says we need to be better? This traitor deserves punishment for killing the Queen. He deserves punishment for killing your mother."

If the room was silent before, it was even more so now.

I could hear the sound of my breath filling and exiting my lungs. Pryn approached my father's side. Dooley held the chest and looked to Pryn. Mane pushed to the front of the circle, arm gripped tight around Kit's waist as she reacted to the blood that stained the white marble floor.

I took another step towards my father. "My mother was a healer. She would never have asked for the sacrifice of one life in exchange for her own."

My father balled his fists at his side. I could tell that he had wanted to punish someone for my mother's death for a long time and I was taking away the satisfaction of his revenge.

"The fae of Dell'Aria demand retribution." A cheer rose from the crowd who seemed firmly in my father's court. Blood had already been shed, lots of it. What was one more fae? Especially one they believed was responsible for all of this.

"If you seek retribution you should all take a look in the mirror. Each and every one of you is responsible for where we stand today. In fact, if you don't stop seeking blood you will all fall. All of you, and not even your wings or the Goddess Varuna will be able to stop you from plummeting into the depths of the hell that will come knocking at our door." I pointed to Aric where he lay on the ground. I couldn't tell whether or not he was still breathing. "He is not responsible for the Queen's death."

"Valora, no." Dooley stepped forward.

"Listen to your betrothed. He knows what is right." My father's face reddened. He wouldn't be able to contain his anger for long.

You will make things worse if you tell them it was Calliope. We will need her help and that of all of her people. Dooley's usual even-keeled manner had returned.

I had the attention of the crowd, but now I wasn't sure what I was going to say. *You think she will help us even after I killed her son? That's madness, she'll want me dead.*

You were willing to give Aric another chance even though his actions caused the death of your mother. She will see that there is something more important than revenge, just like you have today. If we are going to save our Realms we will need to put these petty feelings aside.

Pryn lifted a finger as he spoke. "If you will, Sire, I offer you proof of Aric's innocence in the death of our Queen."

Pryn motioned to Dooley to bring the chest forward. He went to it and opened it slowly, looking first to me and then to my father before turning his attention to the chest and pulling out the one thing that would guarantee Aric's innocence and reprieve from a death sentence.

My mother's bloodstone.

Only Pryn and I knew how it truly worked. The secret was deep within the pages of my mother's grimoire. My father's eyes widened as he recognized the trinket of my mother's which hung on a length of cord which used to be tied around her neck.

"With this we shall learn the truth. You can ask him one question with a yes or no answer. I'm afraid that will be all he is good for in his current state."

Would my father ask the right question? If he asked Aric if he was on the side of the fae of Dell'Aria then I was afraid he wouldn't get the right answer. I knew deep down Aric still blamed his father for taking him from Earth and his mother whose mind had disappeared in the mire of the battle between the Goddess and Ravanna. A battle that we all soon would be entangled in.

Dooley stepped forward. "If I can be so bold, your highness, to ask to be the one to put the question to Aric?"

I took a sharp intake of breath. I wasn't sure if Ravanna had snuck into his mind so as to sabotage Aric or if it was indeed Dooley behind those eyes.

Don't worry. Dooley's voice echoed in my mind.

My father liked Dooley. Thank goodness he still didn't know about Ravanna's influence over him. He nodded, and Pryn placed the stone into Dooley's outstretched hand. The fae who had been coasting around the periphery took hold of the outcroppings of the battlements, craning their necks so they could watch as Dooley slowly walked towards Aric.

He dropped down to one knee beside him and placed a hand on his shoulder, rolling him onto his back. A cry escaped my lips and I clamped my hand down over my mouth. Both of Aric's eyes were swollen shut from the beating he had received, but somehow he managed a thin smile at Dooley's touch.

"Brother," his voice rasped. "You have come to send me off. How kind of you."

Dooley reached a hand behind Aric's neck and raised his head off the ground high enough to slip the silken cord around his neck. He laid the bloodstone alongside the amulet which connected us all and lay dormant. A shudder went through Aric's body as the stone contacted his skin. The fae all around me spoke in low whispers.

"Injustice."

"Treachery."

"It all has to be a lie."

"Silence!" My father's voice boomed through the inner ward. The crowd fell silent again. "Ask the question, Dooley."

Dooley looked to my father and nodded. "Aric, former King of the fae of Dell'Aria, are you in fact the spawn of the Goddess Varuna?"

Aric was compelled to answer even though it was the last thing he wanted. He never wanted the fae of Dell'Aria to be endeared to him. He snarled out his answer, Dooley handing him both a reprieve from execution and his worst nightmare.

"Yes."

CHAPTER TWENTY-ONE

Pryn had two of the Guardians help him escort Aric to the temple where he could work on healing him. Aric still refused to reach out to Dooley and me for help in his healing, and he shut down all the shields between us. Aric's new home would be in the temple. Now that the fae of Dell'Aria all believed he was descended from the Goddess they would likely come to worship him. It cleared all suspicion of his guilt, though the question still remained, if he didn't kill her, who did? Given the current state of affairs between the selkie and the fae, it was easy to point the finger at Elemi. After all, it was she who had tossed the head of the Queen at Aric's feet.

The inner ward cleared out, and my father made himself scarce. This was one development he wasn't prepared for, but he was still preparing himself to ride out into battle against the forces amassing in Mavrovo.

No one said a word to me. Dooley stayed by my side, and Mane and Kit appeared as the crowd thinned out.

Kit ran over towards me and flung her arms around my neck. "Valora, I am so happy to see you again. Oh goddess, I am glad you're okay."

She quickly explained that she and Mane had seen the dragons descend upon Aric and me as they were leaving, but it had been too late for them to turn around.

"And you left your satchel in the car." Kit handed me my bag and I draped it over my shoulder.

"It's worse than I thought in Mavrovo." Mane wasted no time in filling us in. "We were able to get Ralph to his apartment on Earth, but I don't know that he is much better off there."

Kit bowed her head. Tears dripped from below the rims of her red glasses onto her cheeks.

"Is your father okay?" I knew that Ralph meant everything to Kit and vice versa. I had always envied her relationship with her father. There was never a doubt of his feelings for Kit. When it came to my father I could never be sure what his feelings towards me were.

She nodded. "I had to glamour him and make him forget everything about the Realms." She took a deep gulp before continuing. "I had to make him think I was dead."

"Why did you have to do that?"

"Because we tried it the easy way," said Mane. "The man is so devoted to Kit that he was willing to die to fight by her side. But die is what he would have done. We couldn't make him believe anything else about Kit other than she was gone, because it was the only way he wouldn't chase after her."

Mane pulled Kit into his arms. "After this is over we can reverse everything."

"Not if we all die."

Mane rested his lips upon the blue mass of hair as Kit sobbed softly into his chest. "If we all die than there will be nothing to alter in your father's mind. He will have to live out his days and deal with the actual truth. But I have no intention of dying."

"Did you see Kali?" My friend's fate had been sealed when Ravanna had taken her but I still held out some hope.

Mane looked up at Dooley. "You haven't told her yet?"

"No," said Dooley. "I can't believe I forgot. I had a little accident last night. There is a blank spot in my mind." Dooley rubbed at his head. "I had meant to tell her."

Mane crinkled his brow and gently released his hold on Kit. He took two steps towards Dooley and reached out his hand. "Place your hand in mine."

Dooley held his arms tight to his body. "Why?"

"I think you know why." Mane gave him a look which was more a command than a question.

"I don't need your help."

Mane quickly reached out and grabbed Dooley's wrist. Both their eyes flared red. Dooley snatched his hand away.

"What the hell?"

Mane turned his glowing red eyes to me. "Did you know the demon had surfaced?"

"You don't need to worry, Mane. I am the conduit. I can keep it under control."

"Really? I just got a good picture of the control Ravanna had you under last night."

"What is he talking about, Valora? What happened last night?"

"Damn you, Mane. I did not need this right now," I shouted at him.

Kit reached up to touch Mane's face. "Mane, I don't think I can be in this room much longer. The hunger." Her words became stilted, and Mane turned to look at her. The red in his eyes faded instantly.

"You need to talk to him. You both need to figure this out. Because if he loses control all three of you will be in danger. Valora, if he doesn't know it's happening he can't control it."

"You can only attempt to control the demon if you accept it as part of you," said Kit.

"Yes, exactly." Mane wrapped his arm around Kit's waist and pulled her in tight. "I am going to take Kit out to hunt. We'll be back this evening for feast and to discuss where we go from here."

Mane brought out a dried piece of meat from his pocket and took a bite. As he did I noticed the cinnabar dust at his lips.

"Where did you get that?"

"From the fish I caught at Lake Mavrovo. It's my last piece. I've been savoring it."

"Did you let Dooley have some?"

"The last thing I remember eating was a lovely feast provided to me by Pryn as I awaited your arrival. Come to think of it, I am getting hungry," said Dooley.

"Dooley, you need to bring her to Kali."

"She's here in Dell'Aria?" I asked. But Kali couldn't be the first of my worries right now.

Mane nodded as he turned with Kit in his arms. She quickly scooted out of his embrace and ran over to Dooley, reminding me so much of when she was young. She took both of his hands in hers and looked up into his face. "You will be okay. Mane has taught me so much. So much of what you already know. Your demons are more powerful than mine, but you are also much stronger than I will ever be. You can do this, Dooley. I know you can."

Dooley squeezed her hands and gave her a smile. "Thank you."

She returned to Mane's side. At least there were two people in the Realms I didn't have to worry about. But it seemed like I was going to have to have a talk with Pryn.

৯৯

The door shut quietly behind Mane and Kit. Dooley and I were left in the spacious outer ward alone.

Dooley spoke first. "You should know that it was never my intention to keep the news of Kali from you. I awoke confused this morning. I intended to tell you last night, but apparently things got out of my control."

I stifled a laugh. "I actually thought you had complete control last night. I just didn't realize that you weren't in control of yourself."

"Are you laughing?"

Dooley crossed his arms over his chest and pinched at his chin with one hand.

"You know you look a lot like your brother when you do that."

Dooley dropped his arms to his side. "Are you trying to anger me? I certainly don't need you comparing me to him."

"No, you wouldn't want me to do that, would you? You just want me to fuck him while you watch and then make me choose you." A dam inside of me had been unleashed, but it was more than anger and hurt bringing these words to the surface. I had to attack Dooley and the only weapon I could use was my words. My sword, which hung by my side, was not an option.

A red flash passed over Dooley's eyes, and I knew I had him where I wanted him. He took a few steps towards me, dropping his gaze down my body and back up again. "You know you loved every minute of that."

"You're right, I did, but I would have liked it better if you hadn't been there."

That did it.

Dooley's face contorted in anger, the beast brought to the surface. Finally, something I could work with. I was used to fighting enemies I could see.

"You are playing with fire, little fae."

"Oh, these?" I spread my black wings to the side and took that moment to slip a hand into my bodice, closing my fingers around the vial inside. "They aren't small because I am young, they are small because I was born this way."

"I shall enjoy your soul more than the others I think. So much moxie in such a hot little package."

I tried to ignore the fact that the voice I was hearing was Dooley's, because I knew all too well that it wasn't Dooley I was talking to.

"Ravanna, hear this. Try all you want to break through the Realms and steal your immortality from the Goddess. Believe me when I say I will do everything in my power to stop you. But the first thing you are going to do, whether you like it or not, is to get out of Dooley's head because both of us have had quite enough of you."

I reached out, grabbed Dooley under the chin and pinched his jaw open, quickly pouring the contents of the vial of dragon's blood into his mouth. The last bit of blood taken from the dragon I had slain. And I think the Goddess would approve of its use.

"With the power of the beast of the Goddess, by the blood of the dragon, I banish you out of Dooley for good. You may still be able to speak to him and have dominion over his soul, but you will not control his thoughts or his actions any longer."

I released my hold on Dooley's face and took a few steps back. Ravanna looked at me through Dooley's eyes for the last time. "When I reach the Realms I will come for you first, Valora. I will let you watch as I destroy this world, take my immortality from your Goddess and rape her senseless before claiming the Earth Realm as my own. Then I will have my fun with you. I can make that last forever."

A drop of blood fell from the corner of Dooley's mouth which had formed into a crazed grin. His eyes rolled into his head and he dropped to the ground.

"Someone help!"

৯৩ৎ

My father assigned Orris to watch over me and so he had been just outside the door when I yelled for help. Dooley was too heavy for me to lift on my own, and he was going to need some help.

"Please bring him to Pryn." I placed my hand on Orris' arm. There was a time when Orris would rather spit in my face than listen to me, but no matter what he thought about me he had taken a shine to Dooley. "Promise me you'll watch over him. Trust no one. Tell Pryn I have banished the demon for now, and make sure he helps Dooley. Where are they keeping Kali?"

"She is in the prison cells. I believe your father was on his way to see her not too long ago."

"Father?" All he wanted was for someone to pay, and if he could take it out on Kali he probably would. I had no idea how she had appeared back in the Realms. The scene of her being pulled down into the ground still haunted me.

I ran through the keep and down the staircase into the tunnels below the castle. When I rounded the corner I froze at the sight. The prison cell that Kali was being kept in faced me. My father stood before it with a short blade clutched in his hand. Crouched in the corner of the cell was Kali. She was whimpering, and her wings were gone. The only things left in their place were the bony frames which she had lived with ever since the black magic had infected them. The majestic emerald green wings were gone. The prison cell door was closed.

"What have you done?" I yelled at my father from the other end of the hall as my feet began to move.

He slowly faced me, his complexion drained of color. The knife fell from his hand and clattered to the floor. "I never touched her. I did nothing. I learned everything from Pryn. I came down here to seek vengeance for the death of your mother but the demon was already inside."

I ran up to the cell door. "Do you have the key? I need you to open this door now."

My father reached a hand into his pocket and handed it to me. I quickly turned the key in the lock, ignoring the slight singe to my arm as I made contact with the iron bars when I pushed the gate open with my shoulder.

I dropped down to Kali's side and tried to pull her hands away from her face. "What happened here? What is Father talking about?"

"Ravanna." Kali forced the name out of her mouth in a low whisper. "I don't know why he sent me back, but he said he would leave you alone if I sacrificed the wings. He said he would leave Dooley alone. Please tell me that it worked. I never meant to hurt you, Valora." She grabbed at my hands with her own, her emerald eyes red with tears.

"Please tell me you didn't give Ravanna your wings."

"She did." My father stepped forward from the shadow. "I watched as the black hands rose from the ground and plucked every last feather from her, returning her to the way she was before. Then he just disappeared as quickly as he appeared."

"How is it possible that he was able to appear? That isn't possible," I said. It was one thing for him to appear on

Earth. Another for him to appear in Dell'Aria. His strength was growing, and it was all my fault.

Alarms sounded throughout the castle. "It's the Guardians. Something has happened." My father turned and ran up the stairwell.

"Come with me." I pulled Kali up to standing and dragged her behind me as I followed in my father's footsteps up the stairs. I continued to ascend towards the tops of the battlements to get the best view. As I exited the top I saw everyone leaning over the battlements, staring down into the Underworld.

Mane and Kit were amongst them. Mane turned and saw Kali and me. "That explains it."

I walked up behind Mane, Kali following close behind me, and pressed between Mane and Kit to peer down below. Lake Mavrovo, once crystal blue, was bubbling and red.

The crowd below gave a gasp, and a fae woman yelled out, "Look!" In the distance the top of Mount Elbrus was visible as it spewed forth steam and ash into the sky.

"What is causing this?" I asked Mane.

"The cinnabar is causing the lake to turn red. The doorway between Acheron and the Realms has opened. And I am guessing that Kali gave Ravanna the key."

"No, no…" Kali took a few steps backwards. "It was supposed to fix everything, make everyone safe. No."

"You've unleashed a demon, Kali. None of us is safe anymore." Mane's words were short and harsh. All eyes focused on Kali who turned and fled down the castle steps.

I started to go after her, but a hand clamped down on my wrist. "Let her go. You have more important things to focus on now. That one has already caused enough damage."

"But she didn't mean to, Mane." I wrenched my wrist from his grip.

"You need to take your blinders off, Valora. This war will be won or lost on your judgment."

"And it is my opinion that, had I talked to her in the first place, maybe she would never have given up her wings to Ravanna to try and save me when I didn't need saving. In the future, I need to make time."

Mane grunted and backed towards the edge. Kit stayed by his side.

I raced down the steps and out the castle into the streets. Kali had gotten a lead on me and I had no idea which way she had gone. I rounded the corner to go down towards the docks when I almost ran into Pryn.

"What are you doing here? Aren't you supposed to be taking care of Dooley and Aric?"

Pryn took my hands in his own. "I came to find you. They need your help. But they won't listen to me."

I followed Pryn to the temple and into the bed chambers where Dooley and Aric lay in beds side by side. They both looked weak. Both still had their amulets around their necks. And I knew both of them knew I was in the room.

"Listen to me, both of you. You've had your time to feel sorry for yourselves, but now that's over. Kali was the key. She has given Ravanna the power to enter the Realms, and we need to stop him. I don't know how, but I know I will need you both."

Dooley turned his head and looked over to Aric. "She doesn't have your powers of great speech, I have to say that."

Aric turned to Dooley. "No, but she has a cute ass. I wouldn't mind saving it. Hold on, sweetheart."

The shields between us all dropped, and the amulet at my throat glowed as did theirs. My knees weakened, but I stood my ground. I could feel both of them healing and somehow, even though they were draining me of my magic, I felt stronger inside.

A clap of thunder roared through the sky as rain started to pound down. The light of the amulet faded, and I regained control of my stance.

Dooley sat up in bed and motioned me towards his side. As I neared him he pulled me down into a deep embrace. My knees weakened again.

"Aren't you tired? You need your rest." I pushed playfully against his chest as he held me tight.

"I feel like I have been sleeping for days. You need to know that all those things that have happened. I didn't want...it wasn't all me."

"I know that now. I'm sorry I didn't realize it before."

"I'm not sorry," said Aric.

"Do we really need him to make this thing work?" asked Dooley.

"Unfortunately you do." Pryn stepped forward and I reached into my satchel to finger the folded bit of paper I had retrieved from the book in Mane's apartment. Someone had more answers than they were letting on.

"Right. Well, let's slay this demon because I want to get you back to Winter Haven as soon as I can."

Dooley pulled me down into the bed with him and slung his leg over my thigh. I nestled into the warmth of his chest knowing it was but a brief reprieve. The skies wept with ash, the red sea boiled, and Ravanna had awakened.

Thank you for reading *Fae Guardian*.

If you enjoyed *Fae Guardian*, please consider helping others to enjoy this book as well.

- **Recommend it.** Please help other readers find this book by recommending it to friends, readers groups, and discussion boards.

- **Review it.** Please tell other readers why you liked this book by reviewing it at one of the following websites: Amazon, Barnes and Noble, or Goodreads.

ALSO AVAILABLE FROM NICOLETTE REED:

FAE HUNTER (*The Soulstealer Trilogy, Book #1*)

Valora Delos is a Hunter, charged with tracking the treacherous Soulstealers and bringing them to justice. Unlike the other fae of her kind, Valora was born with stunted wings that render her flightless, driving her to prove herself in the eyes of King Aric, with whom she has been infatuated since she first set eyes on him as a young prince.

She descends to Earth and finds herself trapped in suburban Seattle after the portal to her world closes. With the help of a sexy half-fae named Dooley, Valora must find her way back to save Dell'Aria. Dooley uses his own brand of magic to help Valora discover memories buried deep within her, which produce more questions than answers-questions about her growing attraction to Dooley and her devotion to her King. Uncovering who the Soulstealers are and who is behind the destruction of Dell'Aria brings Valora a truth she may not be able to handle.

MANE ATTRACTION
(A Soulstealer Novella, Book #1.5)

Being a demon trapped in an elf's body seemed a prison at first, but Mane has gotten used to his new home in the Riparian forest amongst the elves. When the waters of Lake Mavrovo start to run red it seems a sure sign that the demon king that cast him out may rise again. In order to investigate he will need to navigate the dominion of the selkie, and they aren't known for playing nice.

Going from an apartment in the suburbs of Seattle to living in a castle at the bottom of a lake in the Realms was one change that Kit had to get used to, being half-selkie was another. Now she has to get used to the changes she undergoes after the selkie sleep, one that involves bloodlust and lust of a whole different kind. A problem she is hoping Mane will help her with.

ABOUT THE AUTHOR

Photo by Phil Holden

Nicolette is a mother, wife, paralegal, writer, knitter, traveler, violinist and anything else she can get her hands on. She turned to writing stories at an early age, when filling out Mad Libs just wasn't enough.

She enjoys watching dark comedies, warped fairytales, and cheesy 80s comedies. Her interest in music spans from George Winston to Thrill Kill Cult to Bel Canto and U2. She loves to travel, and plans to do more as her son grows older. In her younger days she loved to go out dancing, and you may still, on occasion find her shaking her booty during 80s or goth rock nights at the few clubs they still exist at. She is constantly picking up new hobbies and interests. She knits socks, grows mini cucumbers in her garden, and played the violin for 5 years. She has a pug dog with a nervous temperament and speaks a little Spanish. She's eclectic.

Please come visit Nicolette Reed at: www.nicolettereed.com